SHELLY
AND THE COWBOY
Cowboys of Wildcat Creek, Book Two

BARBARA MCMAHON

1

"Hey, Tuck, any chance you are heading to Jenny's place next?" Carrie Sue called over to the cowboy at the counter.

Rosie's Café wasn't crowded this late in the morning—breakfast was over and the lunch crowd hadn't begun to arrive. Carrie Sue had stopped by the table to talk to the woman and teenager finishing their meal. After asking them if they wanted anything else, she'd asked what brought them to Wildcat Creek. Learning they'd inherited Mitch Lancaster's ranch, she'd called to Tuck.

The tall cowboy swiveled on the stool at the counter and nodded. "As it happens, yeah. Why? Do you need me to take something to her?"

"No, but these folks are looking for Mitch's ranch. You know it, right? I thought you could lead them out there. It's not far beyond Walt's place."

Tucker Mason looked at the young woman sitting at the table. She looked hopeful. He glanced to the teenager next to her. "I reckon I can get them to Mitch's place. I'll be ready to go in about five minutes."

Shelly Palmer smiled at the cowboy. "Thank you. We'd appreciate it. As you can tell, we aren't from around here," she said.

He nodded once.

"I'll be ready in just a few minutes," he said and turned back to his coffee.

"Tuck will take you right out there. His fiancee, Jenny Schofield, lives about sixteen miles out of town on a small cabin on Walt's ranch. As I recall Mitch's ranch is not too far beyond Walt's, but it's been neglected in recent years so the drive into the place might be hard to spot."

"I appreciate the help. The attorney gave me directions, but they aren't very specific and I don't know my way around here at all. I was only nine when I was last here," Shelly said. She was glad the waitress had been so friendly.

"Hey, it's what neighbors do. And since you inherited Mitch's ranch, that makes you one of us."

Shelly smiled and glanced at her brother. He was finishing up the last of the stack of pancakes, swirling the bites in the ocean of syrup he'd poured. He had a sweet tooth for sure.

"I'll pay now," Shelly said, fishing her wallet from her purse. "That way we'll be ready to go as soon as Mr. Mason is."

"Call him Tuck, sugar. Everyone does."

When Tuck Mason finished his coffee, he put some money on the counter and headed for the table.

"I'm Tucker Mason."

He held his hat in his hand as he introduced himself to Shelly.

"How do you do, I'm Shelly Palmer. And this is my brother Carter."

The teenager looked up and gave a polite smile.

Tuck put his cowboy hat firmly on his head.

"If y'all are ready, we can head out. I'll signal when you should turn as the driveway's overgrown and there's no wide place to turn around close to the highway. At least it was pretty bad the last time the Cattleman's Association held a meeting there months ago. I can only imagine it's gotten worse over the winter."

In no time they left the town of Wildcat Creek behind and headed out on one of the main roads. Shelly followed the big black pickup truck as it turned onto the highway. She tried to pay strict attention to scenery and landmarks as they drove along so she'd recognize the way when she was on her own.

It was a good thirty minutes later when Tuck slowed down and put on his right turn signal. She slowed and searched for the driveway. Thankful for his help when she noticed the drive, Shelly knew she'd never have found it on her own. It looked like an unused dirt road with parallel tracks where tires had worn down with weeds growing up between the tracks.

Tuck made a U-turn in the highway and waved as he headed back.

Shelly turned onto the drive, noting the distance they'd traveled since leaving Wildcat Creek—almost twenty-five miles. If that town was the closest place to shop, she was in cultural shock. Wyoming was a far cry from San Francisco where there were stores and shops on almost every block.

She'd stocked up on essentials that morning on advice of the attorney. Stopping for a late breakfast at Rosie's Café before leaving the town she hoped she'd bought enough supplies to keep her from having to go back into town too soon.

As she wound her way along the narrow drive, she

carefully watched as they lurched from rut to pothole. When they finally saw buildings, she began to relax and eagerly look around. The driveway curved along an embankment, then straightened out as the land sloped down slightly. Green grass grew as far as she could see, rippling in the breeze. In the distant horizon the purple silhouette of the mountains rose against the blue sky, a couple of peaks tipped in snow.

The setting was beautiful. For a moment she wanted to stop the car and savor the view. It was entirely different from the San Francisco Bay Area, where space was at a premium and houses and buildings stood side by side crowded in on each other. Here there was nothing between her car and the mountains but open range.

She glanced at her brother. Carter leaned forward, his eyes scanning every inch of land. He'd never been here before.

"Almost there," she signed.

He grinned and nodded.

The lawyer in Wildcat Creek had been handling her great-uncle Mitchell's estate until she and Carter arrived. He'd reviewed things briefly with her and asked her to come back next week for the rest. He was unexpectedly due in court and had to cut their appointment short.

Shelly had been nine the only time she'd visited her uncle Mitchell's ranch and was much more interested in horses and cows than the route her mother had taken to get here. She remembered thinking she was the luckiest girl in the world that summer.

Looking back, she realized their visit had been right before her mother had become pregnant with Carter, a little over sixteen years ago.

She'd pushed to complete the trip from San Francisco in the shortest time possible after she picked her brother up at the end of the school term. They'd been on the road for two days and she was tired, stiff and sick of driving. Only another few moments and they'd reach their final destination.

Her ranch.

It still seemed surreal. Who would expect an army brat to inherit a ranch in Wyoming? Shelly had never had an inkling she was her great-uncle's heir.

According to the attorney, Mitchell owned fifty-five hundred acres, more or less—now all belonging to her. His family had been in Wyoming since the homestead days. Originally a large family who'd made a place for themselves on the open range, the Lancasters seemed to have fewer children with each generation. Mitchell himself had never married. Her mother, Maureen, was the only niece of Mitchell Lancaster. She in turn had had two children—Shelly and Carter. They were the last of the family.

She couldn't keep the place, of course.

Once Shelly sold the property, she'd be able to better provide for herself and Carter.

It seemed sad to relinquish property that had been in their family for more than one hundred years. Yet what choice did she have? She knew nothing about ranching and Carter was only sixteen. They'd traveled the world with their father and had settled in the San Francisco Bay Area when her father retired from the Army. Wyoming was not home.

Tomorrow a real estate agent was meeting them at ten. He'd check things out and give her an estimate of how much to list the property for and how long before she should expect a sale.

Wire fences stretched along both sides of the drive. The one parallel on the right looked in need of repair. There were broken strands; some of the posts were leaning. She glanced around.

To the left, in the distance, she spotted several head of cattle.

Was that a man on a horse? She squinted to see better, but couldn't tell. According to the lawyer, there was one cowboy still on the ranch—Adam Wilson. He'd agreed to stay until the new owner arrived.

Shelly hoped he'd stay a little longer—until they could sell the place.

When they reached the old house, Shelly came to a stop. The house looked as if it had been built a century ago—two stories tall, weathered wood, sash windows. Beyond stood an old barn. It wasn't nearly as large as she'd remembered. Corrals surrounded the barn, six horizontal wooden rails affixed to upright poles. This fence looked sturdy at least. Two horses ambled over, watching them.

Carter was out of the car heading for the corral before Shelly could open her door.

"Be careful," she called, then shook her head.

He couldn't hear her. And he wasn't looking in her direction so signing was out. She hoped the horses wouldn't bite.

Picking her way across the uneven ground, she wished she'd worn more suitable shoes. The high heels and tailored skirt and blouse had served her well for her meeting that morning with the attorney, but were totally inappropriate for a ranch.

Carter first stroked one horse, then the other, his face beaming.

Shelly smiled at his delight. Since their father's death a year ago, financial concerns had been a constant in their lives. She hoped this gift from out of the blue was going to solve their problems.

In the meantime, it was good to see her brother behaving like a teenager again. She hated to have him worry about the future. He deserved a carefree childhood. Life was going to prove enough of a challenge to him when he went out on his own.

"Want to see the house?" she signed.

He shrugged. *"Sure. Then can we ride?"*

There was so much to do, riding was low on her list. But Carter had been talking about horses ever since they'd left California.

As she turned toward the house again, Shelly's heart sank. The place needed major renovations. The clapboard siding had lost whatever paint had once adorned it; the weathered boards were warped in some spots. Was the inside as bad? What would it take to paint the entire place? It was huge, with a wraparound porch and gables jutting from the roof— obviously built when families needed lots of bedrooms. It looked as if her uncle Mitchell hadn't been able to keep it up over the years.

Carter caught up with her, studying the house.

"It's bigger than I expected," he signed.

"Older, too," she returned. *"It would take a lot of work to make it a showplace. I hope someone will want to buy the ranch as a fixer upper."*

When she opened the door using the key the attorney had given her, Shelly was assailed by a musty smell. The place must have been closed up since her great-uncle had died in March. Stepping inside, she looked around.

She recognized the sofa in the living room. It was a little shabbier than before, but still looked comfortable and masculine with its dark brown nubby material. The room was spacious, with windows on two walls. The front ones overlooked the porch and then the rolling hills to the west, with the rugged line of mountains in the far distance. The side window gave a view of the corral.

Dust coated everything. But since the place was going to be home until they sold it, or until September when Carter would return to the California School for the Deaf, she'd give it a good cleaning first thing. She hoped the ranch sold before the end of the summer.

Carter had gone upstairs. Shelly heard his footsteps on the wooden floors.

For a moment she tried to feel some connection to the place. The Triple L ranch had been in her mother's family for generations. Shouldn't she have some sense of connection?

There was nothing.

She turned to check out the rest of the house. There was no point in trying to rake up sentiment for the homestead. She wasn't staying. She wasn't a rancher.

Despite her practical outlook, she tried to imagine what it would be like to live in a place steeped in family history. To trace the steps of grandparents and great-grandparents. Not that she'd known any of them except her great-uncle Mitchell. And that had only been for one summer. Her mother had died a few years later and her father hadn't kept in touch.

The dining room held a large rectangular table with ten chairs. For a moment Shelly remembered some of the stories Uncle Mitchell had told and could picture a bunch of noisy children—and the chaos at mealtime. Where had they gone to school? Had any stayed to work the property? How sad that a large family had dwindled to only two members.

Shelly continued to the kitchen. It was large and well equipped with no dust evident. While the appliances were old, they looked serviceable. She gazed out the window. No neighbors near enough to see. She felt alone at the end of the world.

Shrugging away the thought, she completed her tour and found a pantry—stocked with canned goods and packaged goods and containing a large freezer against the far wall. Peeking inside, she saw it was equally full. Her uncle had probably shopped for months at a time to keep trips to a minimum.

She heard Carter clattering down the stairs and went back through the dining room.

"*Five bedrooms, one bath on the second floor. Two more bedrooms and a big junk room in the attic,*" he signed. "*I want the bedroom at the front.*"

"*All furnished?*" she asked.

He nodded. "*What's here?*"

"*Check it out, I'm going upstairs. Then we need to bring in the groceries and our things.*"

Shelly headed up the stairs, anxious to see the rest of the house. Surely someone would want the ranch even if the house was old. Couldn't a developer tear down this place and build dozens of new homes?

But would people want to move out here? she asked herself as she peered into the different bedrooms. There was no industry, no recreational sports, no town close by. Who'd want a twenty-five mile commute?

Not that she thought Wildcat Creek had much going for it either.

This country was so different from where she'd lived for the past six years. And unlike any of the Army bases she'd grown up on.

But at least here no one knew her past. She wouldn't be subject to whispers and covert glances. Wouldn't be hurt over and over by people she'd once thought of as friends.

For as long as it took to sell the ranch, she'd be content to have a place to stay rent free.

2

Adam rode along the perimeter fence. He'd seen the car turn into the driveway and knew it had to be the new owner. Nathan Salsbury said she'd be arriving today. Adam knew his time on the ranch was growing short.

Blast Mitch for dying. Not that he could help it. But they'd had the perfect setup. It had been two years and counting since he'd arrived at the Triple L. The longest he'd stayed in one spot since he'd gotten out of the service. But nothing lasted forever. Time for him to be moving on. It wouldn't take long to pack. He'd update the owner and be ready to head out in the morning.

Keeping one eye on the fence, he took stock of the cattle. Looking good. The grass was thick. There had been a large number of calves this year. Summer feeding would make them prime for sale in the fall.

Adam turned at the double fence, the one that separated the hay field from the grazing land. The crop was almost ready for the first cut. More men were needed, but that wasn't his worry anymore. The level ground made cutting relatively easy despite Mitch's antiquated mower. The man should have bought a new one years ago, but his old one worked—most of the time. No sense wasting money, Mitch had often said.

Adam missed the old man.

Each summer Mitch had hired four ranch hands. He'd always respected the men who worked with him. He shared meals with his crew, spent time after dinner working on tack with them or whittling away on the steps of the bunkhouse. Winters he reduced the staff to two cowboys. Adam considered himself lucky to have been one of them the last couple of years.

Now he was the only one left. And soon even he'd be gone.

He'd learned so much from Mitch Lancaster. Enough to get a good job at another ranch. He'd come a long way for a boy who grew up in the Bedford-Stuyvesant neighborhood of Brooklyn. Who would expect a kid raised dodging bullets from rival gangs to end up punching cows?

Man, he missed that old man.

Completing his circuit, Adam headed back toward the homestead. Once Mitch had become seriously ill, Adam had known the life he'd enjoyed for the past couple of years was doomed. Now he'd have to find another spread to work, starting over with all the grunt chores and establishing his place in the hierarchy of cowboys.

At least this time he had experience going in. Mitch had taken him on as a greenhorn. A Wyoming ranch was a far cry from his childhood neighborhood or even the battle hills of Afghanistan. But out here he was definitely safer all the way around.

The car was parked in front of the house. He didn't see any sign of the woman. He knew from Nathan that the new owner was Mitch's grandniece—granddaughter of Mitch's favorite sister. According to the attorney, the new owner was planning to sell.

Not that it was any of his business, but Adam couldn't help but notice during the months he'd worked with Mitch that no letters or calls had come from the woman. Seemed to him anyone set to inherit a spread like the Triple L should have at least kept in touch.

Mitch had rarely spoken about his heir around Adam. Even at the end when the pneumonia had been so bad he could scarcely breathe, he'd only asked Adam to keep an eye on the ranch for him. Had the old rancher known this heir would sell the place for as much as she could get?

Some legacy for the almost ninety-some years Mitch had worked on the land. Still, the old man had this niece, said she'd visited once. And who else would he have left it to? She was the last of Mitch's family.

Adam unsaddled the horse and slung the heavy saddle across a stand. Slipping off the bridle, he fastened a halter and began brushing down the gelding's damp back. He'd turn him loose in the corral when he was finished, toss in a flake of hay and head for his room. Maybe he could even pack up this afternoon and head out.

He looked up from his task. Standing in the doorway to the barn, back lit by the sun, was a teenager dressed in jeans and wearing a ball cap. Adam looked at him for a moment, unable to make out his features clearly. He hadn't expected a kid. He turned back to the horse.

"You one of the new owners?" he asked.

The kid didn't answer. Adam shook his head at the rudeness. Was this the owner's son? If so, she needed to teach him some manners.

He continued brushing while mentally running through the things he had to do to get on the road.

The boy walked into the barn and came over to Adam. Tentatively he reached out to touch the horse's flank.

"Come away from the back," Adam told him. "If he decides to kick, you're right in his path."

The teen was almost as tall as Adam, but lanky. His cap hid most of his hair, but Adam saw some dark strands. His brown eyes watched Adam's every move.

"Don't say I didn't warn you," Adam said.

"Warn him about what?" a female voice asked from the doorway.

The young woman who came into the barn had to be the new owner. Adam turned to watch as she hurried over and touched the boy, moving her hands.

"To stand clear of the back of the horse," Adam said.

She looked to be in her mid twenties. No way was she his mother. Siblings?

Brown hair skimmed her shoulders, silky and soft looking in the subdued light in the barn. Her blue eyes were the color of the sky. The skirt and blouse and makeup she wore were totally out of place here. Mitch must be rolling in his grave. High heels in a barn?

"Will he kick?" she asked.

"Never can tell. Roddy isn't in the habit, but if something spooks him or startles him, he could lash out in reflex."

"Carter is deaf. He didn't hear you. I told him to move away."

Sign language. Adam had heard of it, but he'd never seen it. So Mitch's heirs were a city girl and a deaf kid.

Mitch had never mentioned the boy.

"I'm Shelly Palmer. This is my brother, Carter. Mitch Lancaster was our great uncle. I've inherited the ranch."

"Adam Wilson."

Adam was growing uncomfortable. It happened every time he got near young women or children—flashback to women with their heads blown partway off or dead children with no chance at a future. The pleading in their eyes, the helplessness he'd felt time and again at being unable to stop the machine of war. The horrors never left.

He worked hard to keep the images at bay, but he felt himself tensing. He needed to get away. Ground himself in the reality of Wyoming and not memories of the bloody hills of Afghanistan.

"The attorney in Wildcat Creek said there was a cowboy running things. I appreciate your staying on after my uncle died," she said primly.

Adam nodded.

Finished with the horse, he unhooked the lead line and led him to the corral and released him, slapping his rump. He turned, almost bumping into Shelly. He took a breath, confused by the light fragrance that competed with the smell of horse, cattle, sweat and hay.

It'd been a long time since he'd been this close to a woman. He gritted his teeth and stepped around her.

He went to the section of the barn where the hay was stacked. Grabbing a couple of flakes, he turned around. This time it was the boy he almost ran down.

"Look, either you two help or stand aside," he growled. "There are hungry horses to feed."

The boy reached out for one of the flakes of hay. Adam relinquished it and walked through the barn to the corral, the teenager dogging his footsteps. Adam tossed the hay over the rail, then watched as the boy did the same. The horses ambled over and began eating.

"Sorry. We'll get out of your way," the woman said.

Fingers and hands flashed. The boy shook his head and moved his own hands in rapid motion. Adam didn't have a clue what they were saying, but it was definitely an argument.

Walking around them, he returned to the bench where he'd dumped his reins and began to clean the leather. Then he'd head over to the bunkhouse to pack. The deal when he signed on had been no women and no kids.

"Mr. Wilson?" Shelly called after him.

He turned. "What?"

"Can you teach Carter about the horses? Maybe this afternoon he can ride."

"Does he know how?"

"Not yet. But he learns fast."

"Look, the deal was I stayed until the new owner showed up. I'll be pulling out. If he wants to ride, he better find someone else to show him how. What about you?"

"You're leaving now?"

Was that panic he heard in her voice?

"I stayed on to keep the stock fed and watered. You're here now. You take over."

"I don't know anything about taking care of horses or cows," she said. "It'll take a little time to learn."

"Cattle."

She reminded Adam of himself when he'd first come back

from Afghanistan, and was determined to make a living as a cowboy. He'd wanted something as different from his past as he could get. He hadn't had a clue about ranching when he'd started. But he'd picked it up fast.

"The term is cattle. Your uncle runs about four hundred head. There are only three horses because he sold off a few last fall. There's enough feed to last several weeks. Hay's ready for the first cut."

The uncertain look in her eyes let him know she hadn't a clue. His gut tightened. Sweat broke out. He didn't need this. He'd signed on for wide open spaces and no one dependent on him. He was used up. He absolutely couldn't deal with other people's problems anymore. Call him selfish, but he had to look out for himself if he was to make it.

Forget the saddle for now, he wanted solitude. Heading for the bunkhouse, he fought his curiosity. He would not turn around to see what they were doing. It was their ranch now, let them deal with it.

Temptation proved too much. As he swung the door open he glanced over his shoulder. Shelly stood in the barn doorway staring after him. The boy hung on the rail, watching the horses.

Not his problem. He'd had his fill of trying to save the world. Let someone else be the hero in this scenario.

Shelly watched Adam Wilson go into the low building beyond the barn. He closed the door and she was alone with Carter and three horses she hadn't a clue how to take care of. She swallowed hard. Surely Adam would stay a few more days. Just until she could hire someone else. This was his home, wasn't it? Where would he go? Did he not expect to be asked to stay?

Taking a deep breath, she tried to organize her thoughts. What was she going to do? If the only person who knew how to run the ranch left, she'd be in big trouble. She didn't even know how much hay to feed the horses. How soon could she hire another cowboy?

She made her way over to the corral. Carter was mesmerized by the horses. They ignored the humans, munching contentedly on the hay. The water trough was full, with a device on the side that looked like a paddle. Was it some kind of automatic device that kept water in the tank?

She remembered riding with her uncle and hanging around the horses and playing with the dog. How long had she and her mother stayed on the ranch? She couldn't remember. It had seemed like forever. That stage of her childhood had been carefree and happy.

When she got Carter's attention, she signed, *"I'm tired, let's unload the car and fix lunch. The horses will still be here in the afternoon."*

Everything she owned was in the used car she'd bought a few months back. Twenty-six- years-old and she had very little to call her own.

Of course she'd had to sell everything to pay some of her ex-husband Thomas's debt. And even then she'd come up short. But the judge had waived the balance given the circumstances.

Six months ago, she'd started life as a single woman again without any debt.

But without any assets either.

They had to make a quick sale.

By the time their things had been unloaded and carried up to the bedrooms, Shelly was exhausted. She quickly changed into clothes more appropriate for a ranch. Glancing around, she vowed tomorrow she'd begin cleaning the house so it'd be habitable for the few weeks they planned to stay.

She was pleased Carter liked what he saw so far. Part of the reason she'd decided to come to Wyoming rather than handle the sale long distance, was to give him some time on a ranch. She thought the experience would be good for him and they'd have time to spend together.

Maybe she'd better reevaluate her summer plans.

If Adam left, she'd have to scramble to hire another cowboy. How long did it take someone to get up to speed on a ranch? Surely an experienced cowboy would be able to step in and take over until the property sold.

Once they had money from the sale, Shelly would have to decide what to do with her life. Carter had two more years of high school. Would he want to go to college? He'd never talked about a particular career.

It would take more than two years of college to finish her own degree. She'd been working toward a major in French literature, but there weren't many jobs in that field other than teaching. She'd had so much fun when she'd first started college. Then she'd met Thomas and the world had become a magical place.

She'd quit college to marry him, despite her father's arguments. If only she could have seen the future, she'd have done so many things differently. How many other people had said that over the years? She couldn't change the past, only try for a better future.

When the phone rang, the sound startled her. No one knew where they were. She hadn't told anyone of her plans, not even their stepmother.

Marjorie had been horrible after Shelly's father died. She'd been cordial to her husband's children while he was alive. Once he was gone, her true colors showed. She wanted nothing further to do with them. Bob Palmer had left his estate to his wife and a small stipend for Carter until he turned eighteen. She didn't have an obligation to make sure his children were provided for and surely would never attempt to track them down here.

"Hello?" Shelly answered.

"Ms. Palmer?" an unfamiliar voice asked.

"Yes."

She'd taken back her maiden name when the divorce became final. No sense in advertising that she'd made a monumental mistake in marrying Thomas Farmington. Enough people knew in Palo Alto, but she was in Wyoming now. Maybe that part of her past could stay hidden. She had done nothing wrong—except marry Thomas.

"Geoff Bradshaw, from Wildcat Creek Realty? Just confirming our appointment in the morning."

"Yes, at ten," she replied.

"Are we going to be able to see over the property?" he asked.

"See over it?"

"Ride the boundaries, take photographs of the lay of the land. I need to know about rivers or streams or other water rights. Any mineral rights? Things like that."

"I don't know the answers to those questions," she said.

Did she need to contact the lawyer again?

"I'll have one of my assistants look up the legal description," he said. "And Adam can show me around."

3

She should have expected something like this. When she'd sold the house in Palo Alto, the real estate agent had examined every inch. But somehow a house and a ranch didn't compute as the same thing in her mind. Wasn't it enough to know how many acres the ranch had?

"Fine. See you in the morning."

Shelly looked for Carter. He had his head in the freezer. She went over and pulled out some meat—steaks. Figured, they were on a cattle ranch. Well, why not. Might as well use the food that was there.

She pointed to the microwave and handed him the frozen strips to thaw. Signing quickly, she told him she had to check on something with Adam and would be right back.

Knocking on the bunkhouse door a moment later, she waited. It seemed like a long time before Adam opened it.

"You don't need to knock on this door. It opens into the communal living room. My bedroom is one of the ones in the back."

"I'll remember that next time. I need to ask you a favor. I don't know yet what my uncle paid you, but I'd be happy to pay you the same if you could stay a little longer. I'm putting the ranch up for sale. A Realtor is coming tomorrow morning and wants to see around the place. I haven't ridden a horse in forever. Plus, I haven't a clue about where the boundaries are or what special features the ranch might have. Do you know where the water supply is?"

He nodded slowly.

"There's more than one. A portion of the Wildcat Creek runs through part of the property and there are some wells that produce a steady supply using windmills."

"Could you show the man around?"

If he refused, she'd have to hope Geoff Bradshaw would be satisfied with riding out to the nearest hill and taking pictures from there.

Adam narrowed his eyes, his gaze never leaving hers. Shelly felt awkward. She wished now that she'd handled the entire matter from California. But she'd jumped at the chance to stay at the ranch for a few weeks until it sold.

Carter had the summer off. Marjorie had made it clear they were no longer welcome at the home their father had provided for her. Spending time at the ranch had seemed like a good idea. Now she wasn't so sure. Nothing was turning out the way she'd expected.

Shelly was still hurt and angry at her father for leaving everything to Marjorie. Surely he could have left something to his only daughter. Granted, he'd thought she was well taken care of by Thomas. The Will had been written when Thomas was flying high. At least her father could have left her a picture or a watch.

And he should have provided more for Carter.

She knew why he hadn't. And that hurt, too. She just hoped Carter never learned the reason.

But right now she had more immediate things to think about. Was Adam going to help her out or not?

"I'll show him around," he said at last.

She felt the relief like a tangible weight being lifted.

Letting out a breath she didn't realize she was holding, she said"Thank you, I appreciate that. He'll be here around ten."

"I can leave in the afternoon as well as the morning."

"Please reconsider. It'll only be for a little while—until the ranch sells. I really need help. If you leave, how would I go about hiring someone else?"

"Run an ad, I guess."

"Are there a lot of unemployed cowboys?"

"Not that I know of around here. Most get hired on early for the summer months."

"Oh. Still, there may be one or two looking for work. Will you stay until I find someone? And if you'll stay for a few weeks until the ranch sells, you can leave with a hefty bonus in your pocket."

She'd gladly pay a substantial sum to keep him here.

He shook his head slowly. "I wouldn't count on this place selling fast."

"Why not?" She looked around. "It's not in the best shape, but I'd sell as is. Cut a deal because of it. Someone could make a real killing on it."

"Do you know how much this place is worth?"

"No. I expect once the real estate agent sees it, he'll give me an estimate."

"I can give you an estimate right now. Probably more than five million dollars. Do you think buyers with that much money are a dime a dozen? It could take months or years to sell a spread this size."

She stared at him, dumbfounded.

"Five MILLION dollars?" she repeated.

She had no idea the ranch would be worth that much. Or even a fraction of that much. She'd been hoping for a few hundred thousand, enough to enable her to return to college and provide an education fund for Carter. The amount staggered her.

Could Adam be right? She glanced around at the log barn, the weathered house. The gravel driveway.

"If it's worth so much, why does it look like it's about to fall down around our ears?" she asked, reality taking hold.

How would a cowboy know what a ranch was worth?

"Land rich, cash poor. The plight of many ranchers."

He leaned against the door frame, crossing his arms over his chest.

"Your uncle ran a good spread. The cattle are healthy and prolific. The hay supplies feed for winter months with some left over to sell. Cattle sales in the spring and fall provided enough income for him to live the way he wanted. But it's an iffy way to make a living, subject to beef price fluctuations and weather."

"I thought maybe I could sell to a developer," she said.

"Do you see tract homes going up all around here? Who would live in them? There's not a lot of industry around Wildcat Creek, much less out this far. And the winters can be pretty bad—we get snowbound occasionally for a couple of weeks at a time. Not ideal commuter weather."

She glared at him.

"Someone will want this place. Besides, if it's worth all that, maybe I can get a loan until it sells."

Not that she needed to run her ideas by him. Especially since he was set on leaving.

"And pay it back how? If you don't have the income to service a loan, you wouldn't qualify. And if selling is your way of repaying, the bank won't lend you money unless it knows you have a buyer lined up."

"Any more good news?" she snapped.

It was wrong to get angry with him. It wasn't Adam's fault that she was at the end of her rope.

He shrugged.

"Sell some cattle if you need some ready cash. And be prepared to ride out the sale of the ranch. It's fine property. Someone or some conglomerate will want it eventually."

She turned and gazed out over the rolling hills.

"Mr. Bradshaw will be here around ten," she said.

"I'll be ready and have a horse saddled for him. You coming with us?"

She debated. It had been an eon since she'd ridden. But surely they wouldn't be out for too long. The purpose was to look over the land, not have some endurance competition. Chances were Mr. Bradshaw wasn't any more used to being on a horse than she was.

"I'd like to."

It'd give her a chance to see the entire ranch. And she could hear firsthand what the agent had to say.

"We don't have enough horses to include the boy," he said.

"His name's Carter. And he needs to learn to ride around the homestead before taking off cross country. He'll be fine here on his own. He's sixteen."

She glanced back at the man. He continued to lean against the doorjamb as if he had all the time in the world. But there was a tension around his eyes that belied his stance. He wanted her gone.

He was tall—taller than most men she knew. His muscular physique attested to the constant physical activity of ranching. She thought he was probably in his mid thirties. He had an elemental maleness that was not something she liked. It challenged her and made her conscious of being a woman. She'd had it up to her eyebrows with men of any type.

Her father had been authoritarian, Army through and through. Thomas had been refined, sophisticated, elitist—and a crook.

She plain wasn't interested in forging a new relationship. In the future, she wanted to be totally independent.

If she sold this ranch for even half what Adam said it was worth, she could be independent for life.

Shelly turned toward the house.

"See you in the morning," was all she said.

Adam said nothing.

Head held high, she walked confidently away until she rounded the corner of the house and was out of his sight. Shoulders sagging slightly, she wondered what she would do if Adam was right and the sale took years.

4

Worry kept Shelly from falling asleep as soon as she went to bed. Carter had regaled her with stories most of the evening, fascinated by everything he'd seen that day. He asked if Adam would teach him to ride and rope cattle. Asked if there were any neighbors nearby or was the town the closest place to visit.

His enthusiasm was wearing—not invigorating. She knew she'd been as carefree when she was sixteen, but now worry about the future threw a pall over everything. She wanted to get some sleep and have the real estate agent show up and tell her he had a buyer in his back pocket.

It was great to be with her brother again, though. Carter attended the deaf school as a resident student, staying with her only on holidays and during the summer break. Their mother would be so proud of her son. She'd grieved that he'd been born deaf, but he was so adorable she forgot his difference and focused on his delightful personality.

Not that Carter was perfect by any means. He could sulk and be as annoying as any teenager, Shelly thought. But their mother would have been happy at how well he did in school and how successfully he lived in a hearing world.

Shelly wished again that her mom had survived that drunk

driver. The unfairness of his walking away unscathed still rankled though the accident had happened ten years ago.

She turned onto her side, her thoughts moving to Adam. Could she come up with a way to persuade him to stay? If not, how long would it take to find someone to replace him? And what was she going to do in the meantime? Would Adam give her a crash course in the feed and care of horses and cattle before he left?

She was beginning to think coming here had been a huge mistake. It sounded as if Adam might have stayed had she not shown up.

But she couldn't leave. Not with Carter loving the place so much. She wanted this to be a summer they'd always remember.

Maybe Adam was wrong. Maybe there was a neighboring rancher who'd been longing to buy this property and would jump at the chance.

Five million dollars. Unbelievable. Could Uncle Mitch's spread really be worth that much?

With thoughts of spring vacations in Paris and winter ski trips to Gstaad, she finally drifted off to sleep.

Carter had a dozen questions at breakfast, all to do with great-uncle Mitchell and the ranch property. Shelly was sorry she didn't know more about the family history. She knew Mitchell was the older brother of their grandmother—their mother's mother. As the oldest boy, Mitch had been the one to inherit the property when his father died.

"*You've been here before, right?*" Carter asked his hands moving fast.

"Yes, as I told you—when I was nine. Uncle Mitch had lots of horses and several cowboys and a cattle dog then. I remember riding a horse and feeling scared and excited and so proud. Then eating with him and Mama. Remember, Dad didn't like kids at the table until they were older, so I felt all grown up that summer."

She smiled at the memory. Uncle Mitchell had frightened her at first. He'd been a large man and rather gruff, not unlike Adam. But he'd been kind to a little girl who had been so enchanted with his ranch. As enchanted as Carter was today.

"How long can we stay?" Carter asked.

"Until the property sells. Or school starts, whichever comes first."

She hoped she could stick with that. She decided not to raise his hopes about the amount of money Adam thought the property would bring. She'd believe it when she had the cash in hand, not before.

"Tell me more about when you were here," he signed.

It was hard to sign a conversation and eat at the same time. She told him about her riding efforts, the little calf that had to be bottle-fed, and of course playing with the dog.

Carter laughed at some of her comments.

"Can we get a dog?" he asked.

"We won't be here that long."

"We could take it with us when we leave. I've always wanted a dog. I can't keep it at school, but it would be company for you. I graduate in another two years. Then I could look after it."

"Not if you're going to college," she returned. *"I don't think they allow dogs in dorms."*

He shrugged. *"I don't know what I want to do when I graduate from high school. Not sure about college."*

"College," she signed with emphasis.

He stared down at his plate and didn't respond. Shelly tapped his arm to get his attention.

He looked at her, frowning.

"*College*," she repeated.

"*Maybe*."

He glanced away, essentially ending the conversation.

Shelly studied him for a long moment. They'd never really discussed college, but she'd always thought of him attending Gallaudet University in Washington, D.C. Maybe they needed to make some plans. Or at least get him thinking in that direction. What else would he do?

It was hard to think of her little brother growing up. But he was right. In two years he'd be graduating from high school and he had to decide whether to continue his education or get a job.

She had never thought beyond college for him. What kind of work did Carter want to do?

She heard a car on the gravel and glanced at the kitchen clock. It was almost ten. Jumping up, she carried her plate to the sink and quickly ran water on it.

"*The Realtor is here*," she signed and headed for the front of the house.

Today she wore jeans and a long-sleeved shirt. Cross-trainers were the best she could do for shoes. If she planned to ride a lot, she'd have to get boots. She was sure there'd be a place in town to buy them.

The dusty dinged-up pickup truck that pulled to a stop near the barn didn't look like the vehicle a prosperous Realtor would drive.

Or was she letting Thomas's prejudices influence her? She needed to get past those.

"Ms. Palmer?"

The tall, lanky man who stepped down from the truck seemed to be in his mid fifties. He wore a cowboy hat, faded jeans and well-worn boots.

"Yes. Mr. Bradshaw?"

"Call me Geoff. Sorry about Mitch's passing. He was a good man."

"Thank you. Please, call me Shelly. Did you want to see around the house first or any of these buildings? I've asked my uncle's cowboy to show us the rest of the ranch. I haven't seen it all myself."

"Adam? Another good man. He worked well, according to Mitch, which is high praise. Your uncle was a stickler, that's for sure."

Before Geoff finished his sentence, Adam came from the barn, leading three saddled horses.

"Hey, Adam, we were just talking about you," Geoff said, walking over to greet the man.

Adam handed him the reins to one of the horses and shook hands. He glanced at Shelly.

She smiled politely, feeling awkward again at the fact they'd been talking about him, though the comments had been positive.

"I can't believe this place is going up for sale," Geoff said, turning back to Shelly.

"Why? Is there something wrong with it?" she asked.

"Not a thing. It's been in your family for more than a hundred years—since the area was first settled back in the 1870s. Seems odd it's being sold off."

"I'm not a rancher," Shelly reminded him.

"You could get a manager in," Geoff said. Then he smiled and shook his head. "What am I doing, trying to talk myself out of a sale? Let's get riding."

He mounted his horse easily.

With another look at the dusty truck, Shelly turned back to Adam and eyed the two horses standing docilely.

"I've given you Bonny Boy. He's the gentlest we've got. But he shies if things blow by him. You shouldn't have any problem today, but if the wind kicks up, beware. Even a little leaf will cause him to sidestep out from under you."

She patted the brown gelding's neck and then prepared to mount. He was tall and the stirrup was higher than she could reach. Before she could even ask about a mounting block, Adam's hands encircled her waist and lifted her up and into the saddle. She clutched the horn and glared at him.

"I could have managed."

She felt breathless. How strong was the man? She was no lightweight.

"I doubt it. Anyway, we need to get going. There's lots to see. You need a hat."

"I'll be okay. I put on sun screen earlier."

He didn't respond but went back into the barn. A moment later he returned, carrying an old felt cowboy hat. He handed it to her. Shelly considered refusing, but she still didn't have an answer about whether or not he'd stay. She couldn't imagine managing the ranch without someone who knew what to do. Taking the hat gingerly, she grimaced as she set it on her head. It was large and came to rest on her ears.

Adam swung up easily into his own saddle. Geoffrey Bradshaw was already walking beyond the barn.

Shelly settled herself, gathered the reins and looked at the real estate agent.

"Is he really good?" she asked softly, leaning closer to Adam.

"One of the best around as I hear," Adam said, urging his mount forward. "You think differently?"

"No, but his truck is sort of old and run down. Doesn't seem very prosperous."

Adam looked at her for a moment, then glanced behind him at the truck.

"You think he should drive a Mercedes out here? Fording creeks sometimes, spinning up dirt and rocks?"

Put that way, no, she didn't think an expensive car would be a good choice. Once again she felt Adam's disdain.

Once again she realized the summer was not shaping up the way she'd hoped.

By the time they'd ridden to the far boundary of the ranch, Shelly was saddle sore. Her legs ached and her butt was numb. Yet she was having a fabulous time. She loved the freedom of riding across empty acres of range land with only cattle and wild grass.

Adam was a good guide, pointing out watering holes, the area where the river meandered through a corner of the ranch, the fields of hay ready for harvest and the fencing that needed constant monitoring.

She listened attentively, contributing little. There was so much she didn't know, but the men did. Sometimes it sounded as if they spoke in code with their discussion of cattle and how many head the land could support. They talked about the possibility of sporting activities for a resort, but there were no large stands of trees for game and only a small portion of a river for fishing.

Carter would love to come fishing. She'd have to ask Adam later if Uncle Mitchell had any poles.

On the ride back, Shelly couldn't wait to get off the horse and sit in a soft chair all afternoon. But she kept her back straight, ignored the pain and kept up. She'd learned how to provide a false front to the world this past year. She wasn't a quitter and she wasn't letting anyone get the better of her again.

"There're a good number of calves this year," Geoff said as they moved through a portion of the herd.

"Mitch used Boroff's bull, so they should provide a lot of beef, too."

"Thought he had a bull of his own," Geoff said.

"Yeah, he did. One mean son of a gun we keep in his own field over by Tally's place, double fenced. But Mitch wanted some fresh blood in the herd. And I think this is the largest percentage of calves he's had for a long time. I wish he was still here to see them."

As he rode, Adam's gaze constantly swept the land.

Both men spoke well of her great-uncle. Shelly wished she'd made more of an effort to correspond with him. Once her mother died, her father had shown no interest in keeping in touch with his wife's only family.

But Shelly had lived on her own for a number of years. She should have made contact herself. She could have invited Mitchell to San Francisco or visited him. Why hadn't she?

It was something she'd always regret.

Adam listened as Geoff talked about some of the bulls he'd heard about in his travels. As one of the major real estate agents for the county, Geoff knew everyone and could find out anything about a ranch with a few minutes research.

Adam wondered how he felt about finding a buyer for the Triple L.

They were approaching the rocky area of the ranch. Though he'd worked for Mitch for two years, Adam still grew tense when he approached one of the rocky outcrops. They were perfect hiding places for snipers. The rest of the land was open, unable to offer concealment.

He shook his head, consciously forcing himself to relax. He wasn't in Afghanistan. He didn't have to witness the death and destruction that had once been a daily part of his life. No more women raped and mutilated. No more children blown up by a car bomb or shot by marauding insurgents. No more soldiers groaning in pain or bleeding to death on the dusty desert a million miles away.

He couldn't lose his best friend in Wyoming. That had happened outside Kandahar. The danger of being shot on the Triple L was nil.

And he didn't make friends anymore.

Adam focused on the herd as they rode through. Mitch would have been happy with this year's numbers. He'd have culled the older heifers, kept the most promising of the young ones, and sold off the rest of the calves after a summer of fattening.

Mitch hadn't been any better at making friends than Adam, but the two men had hit it off. Despite the age difference and their unrelated backgrounds they'd formed a working relationship that had benefited them both.

Mitch talked a lot about the past toward the end, those last two weeks when he knew his time was coming to a close. He'd hoped the girl would take on the ranch, but didn't really think she would. His niece and nephew were city people. A person needed to be raised on the land to really know it. Still, the ties of family went deep in this Wyoming soil.

If the ranch belonged to him, Adam would fight tooth and nail to keep it.

He wondered what Shelly Palmer planned to do with the money when the place sold. Buy a fancy condo in some major city probably. Indulge herself with expensive clothes and jewelry and fancy cars. She'd never have to work. Never have to find ways to pinch pennies to buy food the way his mother had.

"Adam!"

He looked over at Geoff.

"Hey, man, you already planning the next roundup or something? I asked about the well over there near that clump of rocks."

Adam looked at the high windmill turning steadily in the light breeze. "It produces several gallons a minute, keeps the troughs full. Hasn't run dry once since I've been here. We rotate the sections where the cattle graze. There's either a seep or a well in each one. Water's never been a problem."

"What has been a problem?" Geoff asked. He reined in his horse and leaned over to rest his arm against the saddle horn.

"Getting enough men hired to handle everything. No one wants to live so far from town if they even want to live in Wildcat Creek. We are not exactly the hotbed of activities."

He glanced at Shelly. She frowned at his comment, but she might as well learn now that it wasn't going to be easy to get men to work the ranch.

"Distance also plays a part in shipping the beef. The cattle have to be driven to the homestead and trucked out from there. Mitch erects—erected—a holding pen to contain them until loaded. There's only one area big enough to let the cattle trucks turn around. Winter can be a bitch, too."

"That's true all over Wyoming. Don't see anything to stop a sale. This is good land," Geoff said.

"I have no idea what property values are around here," Shelly said. "Adam gave me an estimate yesterday, but I'd like your valuation of the ranch."

"I have to see the house and buildings, but I'd say the land alone is worth about $1,200 an acre—so that'd be about six million or more. Won't be a fast sale, however. Not a lot of call for start-up ranches in this area."

Shelly frowned.

"Start-up? Isn't it a working ranch? Someone could move right in and be all set. We could leave with hardly any notice."

"Sure it's a working ranch and makes a profit most years, I expect. By start-up, I meant someone coming in to start up in ranching. It would take a lot to buy the place. Someone needs to come in with expansion ideas, not start-ups."

"Any neighboring ranches interested in more land?" she asked.

"Well now, I asked around after you first called to list the property," Geoff said. "No one can take on the expense right now."

5

Adam knew Geoff had probably been hoping one of the neighboring ranches wanted to double in size. A quick sale meant faster commission for him. The amount of money needed, however, was hard to come by these days.

They headed back to the homestead. Adam had already finished the crucial chores, but there were more to be done. The ranch usually had three to four men working in the summer months. He was barely keeping up with the basic day-to-day running of the place.

Now that Ms. Palmer and her brother were here, he could dump the entire problem in her lap. It was her ranch now.

Yet for some reason, he was loath to do that. Maybe he felt an obligation to Mitch for giving him a chance when he'd been so green. It wouldn't hurt to stay another day or two to give her an overview of what needed doing. He had no place to go; he'd be hunting work himself when he left. Maybe he'd give it a chance.

When they reached the barn, Geoff easily dismounted and tossed the reins over the top rail of the corral fence. Adam slid off his horse and looked around for Shelly. She had ridden to the corral and sat looking at the fence as if planning to use it as a ladder to get off Bonny Boy. He'd like to see that. But she'd probably fall flat on her face.

He studied the glossy sheen of her hair now that she'd discarded the hat, and wished the Triple L was a men-only ranch as it had been with Mitch.

Reluctantly, he tied his horse and went to assist his new boss.

"Need help?" he asked.

"Please," she said, looking uncomfortable.

He lifted her down and set her on her feet. She hardly weighed anything. She was tall enough, but thin. He could feel her ribs through her shirt.

She took a step and almost fell. He caught her and held her upright. The fragrance of her scent filled him. He took a deep breath. The warmth of her body wasn't unpleasant.

Instantly Adam stepped back, releasing her slowly.

"It'll take a minute to get your bearing if you're not used to riding," he said gruffly.

She was warm and feminine and it'd been a long time since he'd been around a woman. But he wasn't going down that road. No involvement—with anyone. He'd set his path a few years back and nothing had changed.

Geoff ambled over. "Shaky legs?"

"Yes." Shelly grimaced. "I'll be fine in about ten years, I'm sure."

He chuckled and swept one hand around.

"I'll check over the outbuildings, then we can look over the house," he said, ambling away.

Adam wasn't needed. Soon she'd have her land legs again. He'd see to the horses and then start a list of everything to cover before he left.

"I'll take care of the horses," he said, taking her reins from the rail.

Carter ran out of the house and headed for them.

Shelly looked up at Adam.

"Could you please give him some pointers? No matter how long the sale takes, we'll be here a couple of months. It may be the only chance he has of being on a ranch and I'd love for him to learn as much as he can."

"I'm not a babysitter," Adam said.

She gave a small sound of annoyance.

"No one is asking you to babysit him. He just needs to learn. I can't teach him. I don't remember that much from when I was here before. Consider it on-the-job training so you can have someone else helping out."

She'd hit probably the only reason he'd agree. He'd been as green as grass when he'd started out. Who was he to deny passing on what he'd learned to a relative of Mitch's?

"I don't know sign language."

The last thing he wanted was some kid around. Yet he had a feeling he was going to end up being a kind of temporary teacher until the boy got up to speed.

"He can read lips a bit. And follow any directions if you show him instead of tell him. Please?"

Carter reached his sister and grinned, signing.

Adam watched the hands and fingers move. Did the boy's entire family and circle of friends sign?

"Tell him to follow what I do," Adam said, remembering back when he'd been a kid in the neighborhood and Tony Bartotelli had given him instructions on tearing apart a car engine and building it back. He'd hero-worshiped Tony for years.

Adam looked at Carter. There was no way he planned to

be a hero to the kid. Maybe a few honest pointers on how hard it was to work a ranch would have Carter backing away. Ms. Palmer had made it perfectly clear they weren't staying long. Maybe he could hasten their departure.

He handed the kid Bonny Boy's reins and took the reins of the other two horses, leading them into the barn. Carter followed with the gelding.

Adam showed the teen how to put on the halter, cross-tie the horse, take off the saddle and begin grooming. The kid had the most delighted expression on his face. For a moment Adam felt the sense of accomplishment Carter experienced.

When he'd first come back from Afghanistan, Adam had decided city life wasn't for him. His first job on a ranch in Texas was really the pits, the dregs of ranch chores—but he'd relished every new skill he'd mastered. Anything was worth the freedom of the range and the peace he felt away from crowds of people.

He took care of the other two horses in the time it took Carter to finish grooming Bonny Boy. For a moment, Adam could almost imagine he was working side by side with Mitch. Neither had been much on talking. The silence was not awkward, definitely more companionable.

Shelly appeared in the opening to the barn.

"Touch Carter on the shoulder and point to me," she called.

When the boy turned, she signed and spoke. "*I'm going inside with the agent. You can stay with Adam if you don't bother him or come with me. I'll fix lunch after we discuss the sale. I'll ask Mr. Bradshaw to join us. And Adam.*"

She looked at him. "Can you?"

His first inclination was to refuse. But he was interested in what Geoff had to say about the ranch. He nodded.

He was even more interested in what Shelly planned to do until the ranch sold. Would she and her brother really stay for the entire summer or would the reality of a working ranch have them returning to California within a few days?

Shelly felt herself growing stiff as she and Geoff walked through the house. As soon as he was gone, she planned a long hot bath. In the meantime, she wished she'd been able to thoroughly clean the entire dwelling. It looked shabby and run-down.

"Good solid home," Geoff said as he knocked on walls. "They built them well back then. And the modern improvements, while not completely up to date, will make it easier to sell. But the big advantage to your property is the land—most of it usable. Your ancestors chose well."

Every time Geoff commented on the place being in the family for so long, Shelly felt another twinge of guilt. As if she were essentially selling her birthright.

After Thomas' defection, she'd sold the house they'd bought together. No loss there. It cost a fortune in upkeep, the mortgage was astronomical, and it had been a constant reminder that the happiness she'd expected had vanished.

But this was something else. If their background had been in ranching, maybe she and Carter could have lived here and made the Triple L their home. There was no mortgage on this property. Renewable assets roamed the range.

That was fanciful thinking and she had to be practical. An

experienced rancher would buy the place and love it. And with six million dollars, she could do anything she wanted.

She just wished she had some goal in mind.

Geoff accepted Shelly's invitation to lunch. After the house tour, they ended up in the kitchen. While she was making sandwiches from leftover steaks, the bread she'd brought from town and a salad from the cans of fruit in the pantry, Geoff sat at the kitchen table, discussing strategies.

"I'll talk some more with the ranchers in the area to see if anyone might consider expanding. If no one wanted the entire ranch, would you be willing to sell some acres to adjacent neighbors?"

"Is that a good idea, breaking it up?" she asked.

"Might get you some ready cash. I don't know if there's any interest of course. I'll list the property with a national brokerage service, on the Internet and with cattleman's associations. Then I'll target resort venture capitalists. You never know—this could be the next place for a destination resort. Unlikely to be another Disneyland since the winters are so harsh. You don't have enough height in your hills to encourage a ski resort. Still, a resort sale is worth a try. I won't kid you, this sale is likely to take a long time."

"But you do think it will sell eventually?" she asked.

"Sure to. But it's not like houses in a residential market where sales are expected in days or weeks."

Shelly bit her lip in discouragement. She'd thought she'd swoop in, list the property and have it close escrow before Carter returned to school in September. Could she stick it out here until it sold?

What choice did she have? At least she'd have a roof over her head and plenty of food to eat.

When Carter and Adam joined them for lunch, Shelly put on a brave front, unwilling to let Geoff or Adam know how desperate she was for money. It had taken all she had and then some to settle the legitimate debts Thomas had left, not counting the thefts. His case was in the hands of the police. She'd obtained a divorce and wanted nothing more to do with the man she'd once loved.

Her foray into working for herself had proved a bust, though she was wiser now. She drew in a deep breath, meeting Adam's eyes. Looking away, she forced the anger aside. She wouldn't dwell on the past. Nothing could be changed. She'd learned a hard lesson. Now it was time to move on.

Carter signed his excitement at working with the horses. He asked if Adam could teach him how to be a cowboy.

Shelly looked at Adam, not sure which way she wanted him to answer. He had a scowl on his face. So far he hadn't exactly welcomed them with open arms. She hadn't forgotten he'd said he'd be leaving soon. She should make certain Carter knew.

"He sure can make those hands fly," Geoff said, watching.

"It's American Sign Language. My mother had us learn when he was just a baby and we found out he was profoundly deaf. He attends a school for the deaf, but does fine in the hearing world. He can read lips a bit, too."

While she was talking, she also signed so Carter could be part of the conversation.

"*Ask Adam if he'll learn enough sign so he can teach me about being a cowboy,*" Carter persisted. "*Or use you as interpreter. I can watch him and pick up a lot.*"

"What was that?" Geoff asked.

"He wants to know if Adam will teach him how to be a cowboy," Shelly said, watching the man in question from the corner of her eye.

"I won't be here long enough," Adam said without looking up.

"You're leaving?" Geoff asked, surprised.

Adam nodded. "I signed on with Mitch. After his death, I agreed to stay until the new owner showed up. Time to move on."

"Where you heading?"

"I don't know yet. Wherever the truck winds up, I guess."

"If you don't have another job lined up, please consider staying here until we sell the ranch," Shelly said, signing for each speaker so Carter was included.

"*He can't leave. We need him!*" Carter looked shocked.

"*I know that, but I can't make him stay if he doesn't want to,*" she replied silently.

Geoff rubbed his chin. "I don't know of many ranch hands hunting work right now. Could be dicey finding a good worker on short notice. Most signed on in the spring when work started up again. The good ones, that is."

"So she can post an ad and I'll stay until she finds someone," Adam said, taking another bite of his sandwich.

Shelly didn't know why he was so anxious to move on.

"It seems to me this is a good setup. With me knowing so little about ranching, you really get to run things. I'll make you manager and throw in a bonus for staying, and for teaching Carter and me what you can until the place sells."

Once she had the money from the sale, she could afford to be generous. Would it make that much difference to the man if he stayed a bit longer?

Adam thought it over for so long she was afraid he'd say no. But finally he nodded.

"You post a job opening in town. I'll stay until someone comes along that's suitable or you sell, whichever comes first," he said. "I figure I owe it to Mitch."

"Thank you."

She wanted to throw her arms around him in gratitude. For a long moment she'd faced the fear that he'd leave and she and Carter would make a complete mess of trying to keep animals fed, watered and cared for.

"*Can we get a dog?*" Carter signed.

"*One thing at a time*," Shelly said, signing back at him.

"What's that?" Geoff asked.

"He wants a dog."

"A good cattle dog would be an asset," Adam said. "Mitch had one that died last fall. I think the old man was too tired to train a new one. But that dog sure was a help."

"Sam Hardman has a couple he's letting go. He might sell one," Geoff said.

Adam looked skeptical. "I saw one of his dogs in action at the branding last spring. Highly trained. Why would he sell any?"

"He's cutting back on his herd, going into buffalo, can you believe it? Anyway, wouldn't hurt to ask."

Shelly looked at Adam. "Could you?"

Adam met her gaze then glanced away. She was asking him as if he were the one to make the decision. He didn't want to be manager of the ranch. Too much responsibility. Too much like putting down roots, becoming involved.

But it wouldn't hurt to call Sam and talk about the dogs.

No denying that old dog of Mitch's had been a big help on the range. Some of those dogs were scary smart they were so savvy about cattle.

"Yeah, I can give him a call after lunch," he said.

Was he doing this for Mitch or to help Shelly Palmer? He wasn't sure which. He glanced at the boy.

Carter could hardly sit still. He ate his lunch, smiling all the while at Adam.

The kid was fast becoming a pain. Adam didn't want hero worship. He knew firsthand how fast circumstances could change. In the blink of an eye, lives were altered forever. One kick in the wrong place by a horse and the kid would be injured or killed. An unexpected rattler could wreak havoc or an angry bull.

And he didn't even want to think of that pretty woman out on the range fending for herself.

He wasn't a blasted babysitter. He had work to do.

6

After he'd finished his meal, he said goodbye to Geoff and headed back outside. Within seconds, Carter was on his heels.

"I have work to do," Adam said gruffly.

The boy watched his mouth, then nodded. "I wan' to help."

Adam stopped and looked at him. "You can talk?"

His voice sounded rusty from lack of use, and he spoke in monotone, yet Adam understood every word.

"Yes. Part of teaching so hearing people can understand me. Not everybody learns sign."

"Does your sister know?"

"Yes. But she can sign. That easier."

"How much can you understand me?"

Carter frowned, watching Adam's lips. "Slow, please."

Adam repeated the question slower.

Carter smiled and flicked his index finger up and down near his forehead. Pointing to his chest he said, "I understand."

Adam mimicked his hand movements. "I understand."

Son of a gun, he'd learned his first bit of sign language.

Not that he wanted any part of it. He turned and strode

to the barn. Blast it all–he was not putting himself on the line again. He knew he was burned out.

He'd get the kid started on cleaning tack and then go call Sam about the dog. And Geoff Bradshaw better get that job opening posted today!

Once Geoff left, Shelly quickly cleaned the kitchen, getting food from the freezer for dinner. The supplies were plentiful. The only things she didn't have a lot of were bread, eggs and milk. Anything that could be canned, packaged or frozen seemed available.

Deciding to take a quick hot bath, she headed upstairs to the only bathroom. Her legs were so stiff she used the railing on the stairs to pull herself up. She loved the large claw-foot freestanding tub in the big bathroom. An oval rod hung from the ceiling with shower curtains. But today she wanted to soak in hot water and get her muscles loosened.

She gathered clean underwear and her silk robe. Stepping into the hot water a few moments later, she gave a sigh of pure bliss. It felt heavenly. Stress eased away as she leaned her head back and closed her eyes. She felt the warmth soaking in, felt some of the strain of the last few weeks melting away.

Events had been put into motion. There was nothing further she could do. The sale of the ranch rested in Geoff's hands.

She'd have to ask the attorney about money to carry the place until it sold. He'd mentioned an account at the local bank, but had said there wasn't much in it. He was working to get her as a signatory on the account.

How much money was there? she wondered. Enough to pay Adam? How had her uncle managed? There must have been some regular income she didn't know about. Hadn't Adam said she could sell some cattle? Maybe she should sell the entire herd if they weren't going to stay on the ranch. Would the next owner up the buying price to cover the value of cattle? Not likely if he wasn't a rancher.

She wished she'd asked Geoff about that.

Shelly felt much better by the time the water began to cool. She dried off and slipped on her silky dressing gown— one of the few items she'd kept when trying to salvage the mess Thomas had left. It made her feel glamorous. She brushed her wet hair, fluffing it up a bit with her fingers, and went to change into fresh clothes when she heard a knock on the front door.

Had Carter locked himself out?

As she ran down the stairs, she was pleased to feel her muscles respond with hardly a whimper of protest.

Opening the door, she stopped in surprise. It was Adam.

He looked at her. Shelly was immediately conscious of her damp hair, her flushed skin, and the fact she wore hardly anything beneath the slinky material.

"Is Carter hurt?" she asked.

Why else would Adam have come back? He'd gone out of his way to make it clear he didn't want anything to do with her.

"He's fine. I called Sam about the cattle dog. He's willing to sell you one or two of the dogs he's letting go. No other buyers yet but he has had another call about them. If you want first choice, you'll have to head over there in the morning."

"Oh."

The message could have waited.

"I didn't know you'd be lounging around in a bathtub all afternoon," he said. "I thought I could go over some things about the ranch with you."

"Hardly lounging. I took a hot bath to loosen up my muscles. I'm not used to riding. I'll be changed in a minute. Come in."

"I'll wait out here," he said, turning and going to sit on one of the old wooden rocking chairs on the wide porch.

Adam heard the door close. He took a deep breath. He did not need to see his new boss rosy from a warm bath and wearing some feminine thing that made her look alluring and sexy.

He drew in another deep breath. Shelly was strictly off-limits. Even if he wanted to become involved with someone she wouldn't be what he was looking for.

For a moment the thought stunned him.

When he'd come back from overseas, the pain of losing Brian, of futilely trying to save lives had been too fresh. He'd sought a different life from what he'd known. And he'd sworn not to let himself become involved with anyone. It hurt too much when things went wrong.

He'd found a certain peace working with Mitch. The old man had never pushed, never tried to change him. Maybe that was the ticket, finding acceptance where he could. He hadn't been able to save people when death had summoned. But working cattle and dealing with horses made it possible to find peace in his portion of the earth.

It was selfish, but he liked the way things had been since settling in here. Mitch's death had been sad, but the man had been in his nineties. He'd lived a good life, one Adam wouldn't mind looking back on. Mitch had been a good neighbor, had the trust and respect of all who knew him. He hadn't changed the world, but he hadn't contributed to its problems, either.

Adam frowned. He was becoming philosophical. Brian would have laughed at him. They'd been two boys from a poor section in Bedford-Stuyvesant, bound and determined to make the army their jumping-off point for great things. Instead, Brian died, and Adam was more messed up inside than when he'd joined.

Shelly came out onto the porch. Her hair was still damp and she wore no makeup. Not that she needed it in his opinion. He stood. The sooner they finished their business, the better.

"Tell me about the cattle dog. Is one really necessary?" she asked as she walked over to stand near him.

"Maybe not if you're planning to hire more help. But I can't move the entire herd myself when it's time to rotate fields. I don't think you and your brother are going to be much help. Especially if you only plan to stay until September."

She leaned against the railing, looking out over the rolling land.

"Even if we stayed forever, we wouldn't be much help. I know nothing about cattle. Our lives are in California."

"You could hire a manager, have him run the place. Probably what you'll have to do until the ranch sells."

Adam stayed back by the chairs, watching her gaze out to the horizon. Did she miss the city? Find the empty land desolate?

"That's why I want you to manage it. I'd like to know that the man running things knew Mitch and would do his best because of that."

Adam didn't say anything. He didn't want to be a manager. But he wouldn't mind her leaving soon. The solitude of the ranch these last few months had suited him to a T.

"It's really pretty here, isn't it?" she said. "I almost forget how crowded the Bay Area is until I look out over all this open land. Traffic isn't much either around here."

She smiled wryly and turned to face him. "Not that lack of traffic makes Wildcat Creek any closer. Long way to go for groceries."

"It's not the largest town in the county. Coleville is. And it's not too far from Wildcat Creek. The turn off for Coleville is on the way to Hardman's ranch, we'll pass it tomorrow. Need something? What you can't get in Wildcat you can probably get in Coleville."

"I'll make a list. So how much does a good cattle dog cost?"

Was that the real issue—lack of money? Adam found it hard to believe with the clothes she wore. Yet the car was an old heap of junk and she kept alluding to the cost of things.

"I have no idea. Want me to call before we go?"

If she couldn't afford a dog, how would she hire a new hand?

"It's bound to be cheaper than hiring another cowboy, wouldn't you think?" she asked, almost reading his mind.

"Yes."

"Carter's always wanted a dog. We didn't have one when we lived with my father, he couldn't stand dogs. Carter's been in a boarding school for the last decade, so no pets there."

"These aren't pets. They're working dogs. They'll be friendly and loyal, but their focus is their work. Queensland

Heelers are bred for cattle. Don't expect a cuddly puppy to share his bed."

She nodded. "Maybe that will make it easier to leave it here on the ranch when we return to California. What time tomorrow should we be ready to go?"

"Before ten—after chores, and time enough to get home in time for chores."

She motioned to the rockers and went to sit in one. "So, give me a crash course in all I need to know about ranching for the time I'm here."

Adam sat and thought a moment before he began. She didn't have to know much. They would only maintain things until a buyer was found. No repairs beyond the basic necessities. No painting the house or installing new lights in the barn. But if Geoff was right and it took months or years to sell, they'd have more work to do.

Maybe she should sell the herd, take the money and live on that until the land sold. That would eliminate the most pressing work.

Adam began to tell her what he'd learned over the last few years.

Shelly listened trying not to panic. The place was way too big for one cowboy to run and she knew she and Carter were next to useless. She tried to remain confident, but nothing in her past had prepared her for a challenge like this.

And her most recent experiences had shattered whatever confidence she used to have. She was feeling overwhelmed. There was no one to turn to. Worse, Carter depended upon her.

Her brother wouldn't be so complacent if he knew the full

extent of her screw-up with her marriage and her attempt to go into business for herself.

She glanced at the man beside her. Adam wouldn't either.

She drew a deep breath, concentrating on what he was saying. She had to succeed at this, to hold on until the place sold. It was her only hope for the future.

Carter came around the house and saw them. He looked tired. Shelly hoped he wasn't pushing himself too hard in his desire to learn all he could about working on a ranch. Yet he also seemed happier than she'd seen him in a while.

"*Finished,*" he signed, looking at Adam as if for approval.

"Whatever he was doing, he's finished," she said.

"*Tomorrow we'll go see about a cattle dog to help with the cattle,*" she said as she signed to Carter. "*Adam knows someone who has a couple of dogs to sell. But they are working dogs, not pets. If they're suitable, we'll get one.*"

"Carter can be in charge of it," Adam said. "The dogs work better following directions from one person. And he can feed and play with it when they aren't working. They're high energy dogs."

Shelly told Carter and his grin grew broader. Nodding, he said he was going in to wash up before dinner.

Shelly glanced at her watch, it was almost five. Even though she felt they'd just finished lunch, it was time to get started cooking dinner.

"Do you want to eat with us?" she asked. "You could tell me more over dinner."

Adam rose and shook his head. "I've got chores to do before I can eat. Tomorrow you and Carter can step in and help. I'll fix my own dinner. We'll leave in the morning around ten."

She watched him amble toward the barn, struck by the difference between this man and Thomas. Adam was even better looking than her ex-husband—and he certainly was more masculine, with broad shoulders and muscular physique. But he seemed totally unaware of it. He was completely focused on the work to be done rather than on himself.

She thought back to her time with Thomas. She'd been so crazy about him when they'd started dating. He'd already done well in the dot-com arena and had pots of money to show her a good time. After the rather austere life-style her father had espoused, it'd been a heady experience. When they married, the sky had been the limit. Fancy home, expensive cars, trips to Hawaii and the Caribbean. And constant parties. She could throw a dinner party for thirty at a moment's notice.

She looked at the ranch land. Nothing in her past had prepared her for this.

She thought of selling the place and having a lot of money again. What would it be like to never have to worry about money?

But the sale wasn't a reality yet. And tomorrow she was expanding her holdings by acquiring a cattle dog or two. She hoped Wildcat Creek had a store that sold boots. If she was going to do any riding this summer, she needed proper attire.

A hat that fit was also on her list.

And another visit to the attorney, one to the bank. The tasks seemed to multiply.

Sighing at all she had to figure out, Shelly rose and headed in to start dinner. At least she could cook.

Carter claimed the small office after they ate, e-mailing his friends in California. Mitch had a dated computer with dial-up capabilities. Carter's ease in using the computer gave her hope he might pursue a career in that field. But he'd need to go to college. And if the ranch sold, he could go to any school he wanted.

7

When Shelly awoke the next morning, she could hardly move. Her legs screamed in protest at the slightest attempt. Even her shoulders ached. Slowly she eased herself out of bed, limping to the bathroom. Standing beneath a hot shower didn't help as much as she wished. Still, as her muscles loosened, she could walk with only an occasional twinge. She dressed slowly and headed downstairs.

Entering the kitchen, she saw the note Carter had propped up—Gone to help Adam. I ate.

She shook her head. She bet the teenager had scarfed down last night's leftovers. Checking the refrigerator, she saw she was right. What else was there? He wasn't one to fix an omelet or even fry a couple of eggs. She should get some cereal for him. She hunted for a pen and paper to start a list. She wanted to stock up when they reached Wildcat Creek.

The phone rang. Shelly answered, slowly stretching her leg muscles, hoping to have them loosen up even more before she saw Adam again. She didn't want to be limping around him!

"Ms. Palmer, Nathan Salsbury here. I'm calling about the bank account. The bank will mail new checks with your name once you come in to sign so they have your signature on file. I've already put the account in your name. In the meantime,

I'll arrange for some money to go into your current checking account in San Francisco. I'll continue to pay Adam from the ranch account until you get the new checks and I'll see to some of the other current bills. If you can come to town in the next few days, we can transfer the utilities into your name, like the electricity and phone."

"That would be fine. What day?"

She was relieved to have the attorney handle these things for her, but how much would it cost? Was she running up a huge bill?

"Thursday is best for me. How about eleven?"

"That works. How much will you transfer?" she asked, jotting a note on the calendar hanging by the phone.

"I told you the account doesn't have a huge sum. Mitch didn't have any medical insurance so the hospital took up a lot of his cash. You'll have to think about selling some cattle or something before things get critical. I can transfer about five thousand now, but you'll need more before long. That should help until you have all the accounts transferred into your name."

She blinked.

"You'll transfer five thousand dollars?" she repeated.

She thought he'd said there wasn't much in the account. Not much was the four hundred dollars in her own account. Five thousand sounded like a fortune.

"Only around fifteen thousand remaining after the transfer. Not a lot when running a working cattle ranch. But you've got time to get some cash before you run short. Mitch often sold off some cattle in the spring, but the big sale is in the fall."

If fifteen thousand wasn't a lot in his mind, she wondered what was.

Yet she had no clue about the expenses of a ranch. Adam's salary probably ate up a lot. Did they have to buy food for the horses or did the field of hay she saw cover that?

"That'll be fine. I'll discuss it with Adam. He'd be able to tell me what we need to do, wouldn't he?"

"He would. I'll see you next Thursday. I'll wire the funds now."

"Thank you," she said, feeling safe for the first time in months. She could stretch that money a long way.

She grabbed some canned peaches and ate them for breakfast, then got ready. As she headed out to her car, she didn't see Adam or Carter. Turning toward the barn, she met Adam as he walked out.

He looked at her, glanced at his watch. "Time to go?"

"It's ten."

"I'll get my wallet and keys."

"We can go in my car," she said.

"I don't think so. Where would you put a dog and all your supplies?"

"Dog in back seat, supplies in the trunk."

"You need more than that car of yours will hold, and you don't know where that dog's been. Told you they aren't pets. They don't go into the house. We'll fix him up a place in the barn. Good for guarding the ranch at night as well as working cattle. We'll take the pickup."

"Fine."

She walked over to the truck. It was a big one, dented and dusty. Opening the passenger door, she peered in. The cab was larger than she'd expected—and higher. Stepping up put a strain on achy muscles. She kept quiet though, not wanting to give Adam any cause for more disparaging remarks.

Carter joined her in the cab and slammed the door shut. He quickly told her about his work that morning, how he'd learned how to tack up the horses, groom them and pick their hooves. Adam said he was a quick learner and that maybe he could be a rancher when he got out of school and—

Shelly interrupted him. *"You have to go to college first. And we won't own a ranch by then. This one is up for sale, remember?"*

"It's been in the family for generations, maybe we shouldn't sell."

"We are not ranchers."

"Our family has been. We can learn. Anyway the agent said it could take years to sell. We could learn all we can, and if we like it, stay."

Shelly was dumbfounded. Her brother thought they could stay and raise cattle? They'd been here two days. She didn't know one bit more about the job than she had when she'd arrived.

She had no intentions of staying in this out-of-the-way place. She wanted a big city like San Francisco or Dallas or Miami. She wasn't going to live twenty some miles from the nearest town, which didn't even have a movie theater much less the ballet or symphony.

Yet she could see his enthusiasm.

Give him time, she thought. Once he had to do chores in the rain, or was bone tired and still had to do chores before dinner, he'd be excited about something else. She wouldn't argue with him, that would only strengthen his defense.

Adam joined them a moment later. The cab, which had seemed so spacious, now seemed crowded. With Carter on one side and Adam on the other, Shelly felt hemmed in.

Settling back for the ride, she tried to ignore the man beside her, which wasn't easy. He took up a lot of space. She studied his hands for a moment, capable and large. She noted a couple of scars. How had he gotten them?

She could smell the scent of hay and horses and man. Swallowing, she glanced at her brother. He was all arms and legs. Slender, he'd shot up over the last couple of years and now was several inches taller than her own five feet six inches. But he didn't reach Adam's height, and it'd be a few years before Carter filled out.

She wondered what he'd look like as a man if he worked on a ranch. Muscular and fit, she was sure if Adam was anything to go by.

But she had envisioned Carter working with computers or something, not such a dangerous, physical job as ranching.

For a moment she let her imagination run with the idea of staying on the ranch and learning how to manage it. She could see herself wearing jeans and boots and a Stetson, striding around the property. She'd meet her neighbors and be the belle of local dances, having cowboys hanging on her every word.

No one would know she'd foolishly married a man who'd stolen from investors. No one would know how her second client, Brittany, had stiffed her for the money she owed Shelly for that lavish big party. Unable to pay her bills on time, Shelly had lost her chance to continue in events planning.

As a successful rancher, she'd be respected.

The truck hit a pothole and Shelly was thrown against Adam, Carter slamming against her right side.

"Umph," she said, straightening. That ended her daydreaming.

"I thought we'd go to Sam's first, get the dog, then stop for supplies on the way back. That way if you get cold things they won't spoil while we look at the dogs," Adam said. "Plus we can pick up anything we need for the dog that Hardman doesn't throw in."

"Fine."

She should have thought of that. In fact she needed to begin thinking like the owner of a ranch and not someone on vacation. The surroundings might be foreign, but the realities weren't going to change. She was the sole person responsible for her brother and herself. And the ranch was their one hope. Daydreaming didn't get things done. She needed to make concrete plans and follow them.

8

They drove through Wildcat Creek on the way to the Hardman Ranch. Shelly gazed out the window taking in more than when she was driving. The main street hosted the café they'd eaten in just two days ago, the post office, several shops and the two story professional building where the attorney's office was located. On the other side of the street were more shops and an impressive building that was the bank.

There were side streets and glancing down them as they passed she saw more businesses, a feed barn, a grocery store and a gas station. On another side street she spotted a bar. Cowboys probably kept it in business. How many other ranchers found this the closest place to shop? There were several pickup trucks parked along the road, only one car.

"*I need a hat and boots*," Carter signed as they came to the edge of town.

"*Me, too*," she returned.

As well as at least one other pair of jeans. Should she get leather gloves as well?

Geoffrey had worn them. Adam's hands were hard and calloused. The skin was tanned, and nicks and scars dotted the backs of them. A man's hands.

Thomas had had his nails done.

She almost shuddered when she remembered how much she'd loved the man—or the man she'd thought he was. And how blinded she'd been to his actual character by the lavish things he'd provided.

In retrospect, he now seemed ostentatious, shallow and not worthy of another second's thought. Yet, she couldn't let go. She'd been married to him for almost six years. How could she not have suspected something was wrong during those years? Had she been so shallow herself that the parties, the fancy clothes and trips to exotic locales had blinded her to honesty and the truth?

"What's he saying?" Adam asked.

"He wants boots and a cowboy hat. I need them, too."

He glanced at her, his straw hat curled and shaped to shadow his face without interfering with seeing. Sometimes he wore it low on his forehead, other times pushed back.

"They'll probably have a small selection here," he warned. "You could wait to get into Coleville. The feed store there has a lot of clothes, boots and hats."

"Too long, we want them today."

He didn't say anything and Shelly wondered if she'd sounded impatient, as if she was dismissing his suggestion?

"Unless the quality isn't good here. We'll need you to help us make selections," she said in appeasement.

He clenched his jaw. "You're on your own."

No matter what she did, she missed the mark with the man. Why should she care? If she found another cowboy to hire, she could let Adam go on his merry way. Not that merry was exactly the word to describe Adam Wilson.

A short time later they arrived at the Hardman ranch. Dogs came running to the truck, barking and prancing around. Adam got out without a worry. He said something to the dogs and they wagged their stubby tails like crazy.

Carter jumped out almost as fast and went around the truck to the dogs. They immediately turned their attention to him. He leaned over and began to rub their necks, laughing when they jumped on him.

Shelly wasn't as brave. She didn't know these dogs or they her. Adam said they weren't friendly house dogs. What if they bit Carter? After a minute she slid across the passenger side and got out. Her muscles protested and she walked around trying to loosen up.

Thankfully a man was coming from the house. If that was Sam Hardman, he could control his dogs.

"Hey, Sam," Adam said, coming around the truck.

"Thought that was you. How're you doing, Adam?"

Sam and Adam shook hands.

Then Adam introduced Shelly and Carter. The teenager reached right out to shake Sam's hand and smiled. He then turned his attention back to the dogs.

Shelly also shook hands, feeling the toughness of the old rancher's palms.

"I knew your mother a long time ago," he said. "She came to visit Mitch one summer."

"I came with her. The only time I've been on the ranch."

"And now it's yours. Nice spread. Seems odd to have Mitch gone. He was ranching before I was born. My dad always spoke highly of him. So you want a dog to help Adam here?"

Sam Hardman looked to be in his late fifties. He carried a bit more weight than Shelly would expect of a busy rancher. His place looked in tip-top shape, though. She wished her own place looked better. Would the run-down condition hinder sales?

"Maybe," she said. The dogs swarmed around the truck and spotted her. They came over, tails wagging.

"Get away," Sam said, and they backed away a little distance, sitting, almost vibrating with excitement, their entire attention focused on the man.

"That blue merle is for sale and the spotted one next to him. The merle is the better dog, canny like you wouldn't believe. I can let you have one or both."

"Queensland Healers make great cattle dogs. Can we see them work?" Adam asked.

"Sure."

Sam turned and headed around the house.

"I've got some cattle in one of the fields nearby. Saves getting the horses out. Come along."

A five-minute walk led them to a fenced section where several steers were grazing. Sam gave a command and all the dogs laid down. He pointed to the blue merle and whistled. The dog ran into the field, circling the cattle, watching them, glancing back at Sam once in a while.

Another series of whistles and the dog began moving the steers toward them. Shelly watched, fascinated. The cattle were huge in comparison to the little dog. But the Heeler knew his business and darted here and there, keeping the steers bunched and moving steadily toward the fence.

She glanced at Carter. He was entranced. A quick look at

Adam and she was surprised to find him watching her.

"Amazing," she said in a low voice.

He nodded. "Sam, will the dog work to hand signals?"

"Some. He'd need some conditioning to get used to that. You can't whistle?"

"I was thinking Carter might like to work with him," Adam said.

"Don't even suggest that," Shelly said. "He can't ride yet. How do you think he'd manage out on the range where anything could happen? We're only here a short time."

"You're not staying?" Sam asked in surprise.

"No. I've listed the ranch for sale."

Sam looked as if he was going to say something, then closed his mouth. Glancing at Adam, he raised an eyebrow.

"She's hunting another ranch hand. Once she finds one, I'm moving on."

"Sorry to hear that," Sam said. "She won't be wanting a dog if she's only staying a little while. What will happen to him next?"

Shelly didn't like the two men talking as if she wasn't there.

"Actually the Realtor said it could take a long time to sell. We only have two and a half months before Carter has to get back to school in September, but we'll be here until then. Whoever runs the place will need help until it sells. How much for the dog?"

Sam rubbed his chin, then shrugged. "Six hundred."

Shelly paused. It seemed like a lot of money for a dog. Yet the attorney had transferred funds to her account. A dog was cheaper than hiring another cowboy.

"I can write you a check."

"Be fine with me. You taking him today?" Sam asked easily.

"Yes. What's his name?"

"Hank. I have some papers for him. And I can show Adam the hand signals so he can get started with the dog."

Shelly signed the information for her brother. His eyes lit up. He insisted on staying with Adam and Sam to learn the hand signals as well. Shelly argued to no avail.

The men climbed through the barbed-wire fence and headed for the cattle and the dog. She watched anxiously, hoping the large steers didn't charge Carter. But the bovines drifted away as the men approached. They were talking and watching the dog. Knowing Adam and Sam were comfortable gave her some reassurance Carter would be okay. She returned to the truck to get her checkbook from her purse.

She wrote out the check, then continued to sit in the cab of the truck. She leaned her head back, feeling as if things were spinning out of control. She'd soon own a blue merle Queensland Healer dog in addition to several hundred head of cattle and thousands of acres of Wyoming. A far cry from a woman who had loved to party and had briefly wished for a career as an event planner.

Now she'd need to become proficient in riding. Learn about raising cattle. Show Adam that she could run a ranch however temporarily.

What was she thinking? She wasn't here to impress Adam Wilson. Running a ranch was hard work. She wanted Carter to have a fabulous summer, but she couldn't let him think they'd be staying—no matter how much he thought he wanted that right now. The novelty would wear off soon.

She wasn't sure how long she sat in the truck, but when she saw the men heading back, dogs dashing around them, she knew her quiet time was over. Reality always had a way of intruding.

By the time they reached the Triple L later that afternoon, Shelly was stiffening up again. Despite his comments earlier, Adam had stopped at the feed store in Wildcat Creek and Shelly and Carter had bought boots, hats and jeans. She'd also stocked up on as many items from the grocery store as she thought they'd need for the next few days.

Hank rode in the back of the truck without a problem. Shelly hated to admit it but the purchases would never have fit in the trunk of her car. If she were staying, she'd have to get a pickup truck to haul things around.

"Did my uncle have a truck?" she asked. From what she'd seen, every man in Wyoming owned a truck.

"Yes. It's parked in the shed behind the barn. I've been using mine for supplies and things, but that one's yours."

Thursday she'd drive it into Wildcat Creek.

After dinner, Carter headed back outside to practice commands with Hank while Shelly went into the small room that served as Mitch's office. It was as dusty as the rest of the house had been. Only the computer that Carter had been using was clean.

She quickly ran a cloth over the desk and bookshelves then sat down. Turning on the computer, she looked at the programs listed. Her uncle had been an orderly man. There were only two programs—an accounting program and a database. She clicked on one and was confronted with financial records going back several years. She skimmed through them quickly, not understanding all the ins and outs, but recognizing he'd made a solid income from the ranch, though in spurts.

He'd sold hay to help his cash flow. A few months later he'd sold some cattle. That had brought in a larger amount. And Mitch had invested money in fairly conservative funds, which paid quarterly. There were expenditures to a medical facility through March—then nothing after he'd died. She was too tired to study this right now, but maybe in the morning she'd get a better handle on things. Maybe she could liquidate some of the remaining investments.

Carter would be in before long, wanting to e-mail his friends. She could imagine the stories he had to share with them. She knew he was having the time of his life.

Feeling a little lonely, she wished she had someone special to e-mail. Her friend Beth was away on a cruise with her husband. There was no one else that Shelly wanted to talk to.

She heard the dog barking so she went to the window and raised it. Leaning out, she saw Carter throwing a stick. Hank raced after it, barking the entire way, then picked it up and raced back to drop it at her brother's feet. The two of them looked as if they were having a great time. She smiled. This was a summer Carter would always remember.

Besides the barking dog, she could hear the breeze rustling through the old trees near the house and in the distance the lowing of cattle. She rested against the window frame to absorb the evening. There were clouds gathering over the distant peaks. The sunset would be spectacular. It was peaceful and beautiful. No wonder her uncle had loved it.

And her mother. She'd spoken fondly of their summer visit. And of Wyoming.

Shelly should have come to visit again after she was grown. Vague guilt rose when she thought of how mindless her life had been. She was twenty-six and had nothing to show for her years. What did she want to do in the future?

9

Adam sat in the shade on the bunkhouse steps and watched the woman gazing at the horizon. She annoyed him to no end and it wasn't even her fault. He couldn't expect her to know how to help around the place. When she asked to be shown how to do something, he resented the time to teach her.

Yet if not him, who would show her?

He didn't like the way she had him feeling emotions that had long been dormant—ones he didn't want to feel. As if he'd been asleep for a long time and was now awakening.

Which was stupid. He had his life exactly as he wanted it. He had no family except his grandmother. And she was back in Brooklyn. He called her every Sunday. He could pick up and move whenever the mood struck. And if things didn't go the way he liked, he could always pack up again.

Yet he sat in the shadows of the bunkhouse porch watching Shelly. What was she thinking—how she'd spend all those millions when the ranch sold?

She hadn't been feigning surprise when she'd learned how much the land would bring. It had flat out astonished her. But it wouldn't take long before she got used to the idea. Once she had all that cash in the bank, she'd be gone so fast he'd probably only get a glimpse of the dust.

Or was the magic of the place getting to her? He'd felt it soon after he'd arrived. The timelessness, the feeling that the land had been here at the beginning of time and would be long after he was dust in the ground. The breeze carried secrets from long ago, and the peace invaded a person like a slow caress.

He took a deep breath, breathing in the scents that defined this part of the world. He could smell the green grass, with a hint of the hay that was ready to cut. The stink of cattle and the mud flats by the river. The small pond in the center of the trees near the house.

He had needed this healing place when he'd shown up.

Maybe Shelly Palmer needed some healing herself. Her eyes looked sad and fearful. As if the weight of the world rested on her shoulders. What could a woman like that have to mourn? A broken marriage?

He needed to pull back, do his job and not get involved. He did not want friends—and especially didn't want involvement with a woman needing to be rescued. She was on her own.

The kid was working out better than he'd initially thought. The boy learned fast. If he stayed long enough, he could conceivably become a competent cowboy. He had an endless thirst for information and a willingness to try anything.

Sometimes Carter taught him the sign for an object or action. The boy was cut off from the world through no fault of his own.

Adam had cut himself off from the world. But he could join back in if he ever wanted.

He rose and headed for the barn. There were endless tasks

to be done. Working kept thoughts at bay. He'd spent his entire life not knowing the Palmers. This short acquaintance didn't fundamentally change anything.

By the time Adam turned off his bedside lamp later that night, the wind was blowing hard. He hoped it wasn't going to storm. He hated storms. Running through the list of chores he needed to see to in the morning, he soon drifted to sleep.

Thunder rumbled. The wind blew. Rain began to fall softly at first, then with a drumming beat on the roof. The temperature dropped drastically. Adam tossed and turned.

A sudden crack had him sitting upright with a yell that shattered the night.

For a long moment he sat in the darkness, breathing hard. The images wouldn't go away. Another crack of thunder—or was it gunfire? Lightning lit up the night—or was it explosions in the distance?

He could smell the gunpowder, hear the screams, see the unrelenting landscape that offered little hiding space and no protection from the rockets that rained down.

"Medic!"

The cry echoed over and over.

He gritted his teeth and dashed across the room and out into the pouring rain.

The cold air hit him instantly and snapped him out of the flashback. For a long moment he stared out, seeing nothing, becoming soaked in seconds. He shivered. This summer rain was nothing like the arid climate of Afghanistan. Lightning illuminated the horses standing beneath the lean-to along the wall of the barn. He felt the cold nose of the new dog brush his naked thigh.

"Hey, Hank. It's okay, fellow."

Adam reached out to pet the wet dog. The scent was nothing like the blood and dust of a war zone. It grounded him in the present.

"Sorry to disturb your first night in your new home," Adam said, stepping back on the porch out of the downpour. He shivered with cold, but wasn't ready to go back inside.

Thankfully these nightmares didn't happen often. A jagged lightning bolt lit up the sky. Seconds later a large crack of thunder reverberated. Adam was prepared for it.

He took a breath, holding on to Hank. Sinking down on the wooden porch he ignored the cold and talked to the dog. His neighbor Jenny had a service dog to help with PTSD. He was glad for Hank's company tonight. He'd never told anyone about his flashbacks. No one would hire a cowboy who couldn't handle the work.

He took a deep breath of the cold night air. He was in Wyoming. He was alive and no longer responsible for trying to patch up the wounded.

He no longer had to identify the dead.

The storm gradually moved east, the rain settling into a gentle downfall, soaking the ground.

The storm meant a delay in cutting the hay. The crop needed to be dry. A few days of hot sunshine and it'd be ready.

After a long time, he was too cold to remain sitting outside. With a final rub on the dog's neck, he rose and headed inside. A hot shower, something to drink, and he'd see if he could get any more sleep without the nightmares of the past catching up.

Shelly lay in bed listening to the rain on the roof. Her window was open a crack and she could feel the coolness of the wind as it blew into the room. Water might be getting in, but she was too cozy beneath her covers to get up to see. Once again thunder rolled. She smiled, remembering other storms through the years.

The Bay Area rarely had thunderstorms, but when her father had been stationed in Texas, they'd been almost daily occurrences during the summer. She'd always loved the freshness of the rain, the fury of the thunder and the power the storm represented.

How was Hank doing? she wondered. Carter would sleep through the entire storm, but she worried about the dog—new to the ranch, alone in the barn. Should she go check on him?

Reluctantly she rose and went to the window. Despite the heat of the afternoon, the air now stirring was cold. Her bare feet felt the rain on the floor. She pushed the window closed and went to the bathroom for a towel. She blotted the floor until it was dry, her muscles still protesting.

Dressing quickly, she tried on her new boots. Seemed a shame to get them wet and muddy, but they'd do better for her than her cross trainers, which would be soaked in no time. Boots weren't for show.

Pulling on a light jacket, she went downstairs and out to the front porch. It was pitch-black outside. She could hardly make out the silhouette of the barn against the dark sky. The rain had slowed and was now more of a sprinkle. But it was so dark she wasn't sure she could make it to the barn without running into something.

A light caught her attention. She walked to the edge of the porch and looked at the bunkhouse. Lights were on. Was something wrong or had the storm wakened Adam, too? Had he thought about Hank? Probably not. Hadn't he said the dog wasn't a family pet? She didn't feel the cattle needed to come in out of the rain, but she did worry about the dog.

She stepped off the porch and carefully headed for the bunkhouse, using the light from the windows as a beacon. A moment later she knocked on the door. Then opened it. Adam had said not to knock.

"Adam?" she called.

He stepped out into the hall, wearing only jeans, with a towel slung around his neck.

"What are you doing here?" he asked, walking into the communal room.

"I got up to see to Hank. I thought the storm might scare him or something."

"He's fine."

"Are you sure?"

"I was out on the porch for a while. He came and sat with me."

"Oh."

Shelly didn't know what to say next. She glanced around the room. Comfortable sofas and chairs were scattered around. A large-screen television sat in one corner. A card table in another.

"I'm not used to storms like this," she explained. "I wondered if the dog would run or something and not come back since this is his first night here."

She hoped she didn't sound too foolish.

"First night, but I think he knows this is home."

He just stood there watching her. Shelly grew nervous. She'd found out what she wanted. Might as well return to the house.

"I was going to make something hot to drink. Want to join me?" he asked just as she was about to turn.

She blinked in surprise. It was the first friendly gesture Adam had made.

"Sure. Do you have hot chocolate?"

He nodded.

"I'll finish getting dressed and be in the kitchen in a minute. It's through that door if you want to wait there."

Shelly went to the large kitchen. When Adam joined her a few moments later, he'd donned a shirt and socks, but no boots. His hair was still damp.

"Did Uncle Mitchell eat here?" she asked.

"Most of the time."

"The appliances are newer than the ones in the house kitchen," she said.

He nodded and quickly took down the cocoa, got some milk from the industrial-size refrigerator and a pan from the cupboard near the stove.

"In summer we had three others working, so we all ate here."

Shelly sat on one of the chairs circling the table, which was large enough for a dozen people.

She watched Adam get cups while keeping an eye on the heating milk. Just as he was pouring the hot beverage into the mugs, a loud crack of thunder sounded and the lights went out.

"Blast it!" he said.

The pan clattered on the stove.

"What?"

"The last bit missed the cup and hit my hand," he said.

"Run cold water on it."

"The well won't pump without electricity. I don't want to deplete the holding tank for this. I'll get ice."

She heard the sound of a drawer, then a flashlight clicked on. Shelly was grateful for the glow as Adam got ice for his hand, then set the two mugs on the table. He took a chair near her and positioned the flashlight in the center of the table so that it shone up to the ceiling. It didn't give much light, but enough that she could see him.

She took a sip of hot chocolate. It almost burned her tongue. But it tasted heavenly.

"Does the power go out often?" she asked.

"Often enough. There's a generator. When we need electricity, I'll fire it up. We shouldn't need it tonight and the power may be back on come morning."

They sat in silence. Shelly couldn't think of a single thing to say. She waited a moment, then took another sip of her drink. Still hot, but manageable. The sooner she finished, the sooner she could return home.

"Now that you've talked to Geoff Bradshaw, how long do you think you'll stay?" Adam asked.

She met his gaze. He looked dark and dangerous in the faint illumination.

"For the summer at least."

"You don't have a job you need to get back to?"

She shook her head. She knew she could get work. She'd been a great waitress.

It was not the life she had envisioned when she'd been younger, however. But without a degree or any special skills it was hard to get a decent job.

"Carter has to return to school in September so we'll be gone by then."

If the ranch hadn't sold by the time they left, she'd have to find another cheap apartment, start a new job, try to get on her feet.

How hard would that be with the tantalizing thought of six million dollars' worth of land sitting in Wyoming?

She still couldn't wrap her mind around the idea of never having to worry about money again. How amazing that would be.

"We don't want to be a burden while we're here," she said. "Show us what we need to learn so we can help out."

"Carter's coming along with horse care."

"I want to learn, too."

"I'm not a teacher," he grumbled.

"Hey, until we hire someone else, you're all we've got."

He didn't say anything.

Shelly took another swallow. She could feel the warmth spread. Finishing quickly, she put the cup down and rose just as Adam stood.

So close together, they bumped into each other. Before she could step back, he leaned over and kissed her. His arms wrapped around her and pulled her closer. For a stunned second, Shelly could do nothing. She had not expected anything like this. The man didn't even like her.

His lips were warm on hers, moving persuasively. She wanted to savor the touch, the feelings that built. It had been more than a year since she'd been kissed, held in a man's arms.

She encircled his waist and held on as the kiss deepened. She felt warm and safe. Forgetting all the problems she faced, she let herself go.

When he ended the kiss and pulled back, she frowned, not wanting the contact to end. Then she realized what had happened.

"I'm going back to bed," she said needlessly, moving away from the table. She stopped as she realized it was black as pitch away from the flashlight.

"Take it," he said, scooping up the light and handing it to her.

Shelly turned and quickly left, her heart still pounding. She knew better than to get caught up with some handsome cowboy.

However her heart rate didn't slow while she was trying to be practical.

She relished the cold air when she stepped outside. Using the flashlight to illuminate the way, she hurried through the mud to the silent house. This was so not the situation she wanted to be in. How would she deal with things in the morning?

The kiss had been totally unexpected. Should she be outraged? Chalk it up to a midnight aberration? It meant nothing—it couldn't they hardly knew each other.

Yet she didn't feel Adam was the type to run around kissing every woman he met.

So—why had he kissed her?

10

Adam heard Shelly leave. He remained standing in the darkness, calling himself every name in the book. What had possessed him to kiss her? Granted, it had been a long time since he'd felt any interest in women, but that didn't make it a smart move to kiss this one. If he was ready to start dating again, there were plenty of women in town who had flirted with him. Any one of them would be better for him.

But when she'd bumped into him, he'd given in to instinct. The fragrance she wore drove him crazy. It reminded him of some sweet flower, pretty and innocent. Too far removed from his life.

For a moment the kiss had driven out all other thoughts. She'd been sweet and feminine. He could have lost himself in her kiss. Adam turned and bumped into a chair. Swearing, he made his way to the counter.

There were candles and matches in the drawer the flashlight had been in. He didn't like the dark. Finding a candle, he lit it and made his way back to the community room. He wouldn't get any more sleep tonight. Maybe he could read until dawn.

Adam was in a bad mood by the time 6:00 am. arrived. He'd already eaten breakfast and had two cups of coffee. Hay had been tossed into the corral for the horses and he was ready to work. If Shelly Palmer wanted him to teach her and Carter about cowboying, he'd start now.

He walked over to the house, his annoyance building. There was no reason to be mad at anyone but himself, but he felt as if he could take on the world.

If she made any mention of last night, he'd quit then and there.

After knocking on the back door, he waited a moment. To his surprise, Carter opened the door, dressed and holding a piece of toast in one hand.

"Shelly up?" Adam asked.

"Yes."

She came to stand beside her brother. "We're almost finished eating breakfast. Are we late?" she asked, studying him warily.

"There are a thousand things needing doing. Normally in summer we get an early start." Some of his anger faded as she stared at him. He waited a moment, but she just nodded. At least there wasn't going to be some big scene after one kiss.

Maybe she hadn't even liked it.

Adam frowned. The thought did nothing to improve his mood.

"I'll remember that tomorrow. What time should we be ready, five?"

There was an edge to her tone.

"Six is fine. I'll be in the barn."

Without another word, he turned and left.

Ten minutes later both Shelly and Carter showed up.

Adam nodded toward Carter.

"Have him saddle up two horses. You and I need to check on the hay. He can clean out the stalls while we're gone. They aren't too bad since the horses have been in the corral most of the time."

"I can saddle my own horse, if you show me how," she said.

"Fine. Catch Bonny Boy and I'll show you where the saddles are."

If he'd been in a better mood, Adam might have enjoyed watching a novice catch and saddle the horse.

Maybe a few days of hard work would scare her back to California, leaving him in peace.

More than thirty minutes passed before they were ready to leave. Carter cheerfully attacked cleaning the stalls as they rode out into the crisp, clear morning. The only traces of last night's storm were the puddles everywhere and the cool early morning air.

The mountains looked so sharp one could almost reach out to touch them.

Pulling his hat down low on his face, Adam whistled for the dog and then set a fast pace to the field. He wanted to swing by and check the main herd.

Shelly remained silent. He glanced at her a couple of times, but she was staring straight ahead. She'd saddled the horse, though Adam had tightened the cinch a bit more. Took forever, but so what? There was plenty of work to do, but it wasn't going anywhere.

When they reached the fenced area and looked over the hay, he almost groaned. The rain had practically flattened the entire field. He didn't know if the ground would dry soon enough to harvest. The hay was just right for cutting. Left much longer, the seeds would begin to bloom and a lot of the nutrition would be lost.

Shelly stopped beside him.

"Will we be able to cut this? It's all in the mud."

"Once the sun dries things up, I hope it bounces back. Can't cut what's lying down. It's still green enough to have some vitality. Once we cut it, we let it lie in the sun until it dries. It's more of a problem if we have a heavy rain then," he said. "Still, everything would have been easier if the storm hadn't been so strong."

"How do we cut it?" she asked.

"Mitch had a mower. It's as old as the hills, but he could always coax it into working. If I can't get it going, you'll have to call one of the other ranchers to see if they have a machine you can use."

"Won't they be cutting their own hay about now?"

"Yep."

"So chances aren't great for borrowing one any time soon."

"Don't court trouble before it shows up," he warned. "The old machine has a bit more life in it, I'm betting."

"I'm not much of a betting person. And the way my luck has run the last couple of years, I wouldn't bet on anything to go my way."

"Your luck can't be all bad. You inherited this place," Adam said.

She looked at him.

"Maybe it's changing or maybe not. You knew before Geoff told me that it could take years to sell this place. So now it's merely another problem to deal with. Maybe at the end of the tunnel there's a bright light, but this tunnel could be years long."

"You've got your health and a way to make a living until then," he countered.

She glared at him.

"This ranch is not my idea of a perfect solution. I've had a man run out on me and take millions of dollars that didn't belong to him, leaving me holding the bag. A client stiffed me for more money, and my father died without leaving a penny for me and hardly any for my brother. I don't have any work skills and don't much like you or this ranch. So where is the blasted silver lining?"

Adam stared at her. She was as angry as he had been earlier.

Yet the comments intrigued him. What was she talking about?

"Start with the man who ran out," Adam said. "Who was he?"

She pulled her horse around and walked along the fence.

"None of that is any business of yours," she said as she slowly rode away, studying the hay.

He stared after her for a long moment.

"Truer words were never spoken, but that doesn't satisfy my curiosity," he mumbled, turning his own horse and riding after her. Maybe there was more to this woman than he'd initially thought.

"So that's all we have to do, mow it down?" she asked, glaring at the field.

"What?"

"You said we have a mower."

"After the hay is cut, then we rake it into windrows, or long rows let it dry on the ground until it's just right, then bale it up and store it."

"How do we know when it's just right?"

"Rub a few stalks in your hands, know what you're looking for, and you can tell."

She was as green as he'd been a couple years back. The only difference? She wasn't staying.

Shelly kicked her horse into going faster when she heard Adam approaching. She felt the weight of the world on her shoulders with this ranch. But until it was sold, she had to keep things going for Carter's sake.

Adam thought she was lucky because she'd inherited Mitch's ranch. And she was, no denying that. Lots of people would love to receive a bequest like this. She just hadn't thought it would create so many problems.

Yet, as she felt the wind in her face and smelled the clean scent of grass, she felt freer than she had in a long time. She remembered riding with her mother and uncle, and sometimes just her mother. Those memories were some of the happiest of her life.

"I want to check the herd," Adam said, riding up alongside her. "If you want to come, fine, if not, I'll see you back at the barn. We'll check if the mower fires up when I get back."

"I'll go with you."

Hank had stayed near Adam, swinging wide a time or two

to explore some intriguing smells, but quickly resuming his place near Adam's horse.

Shelly envied the dog. He knew what he was doing and supposed to do. She'd learn to run this ranch for the interim or die trying.

By the time they headed back toward the homestead, Shelly's head was swimming with facts and figures. Adam hadn't displayed one iota of personal interest in her. He had been totally businesslike. If she hadn't been there last night, she'd never have known he'd kissed her.

But he had, and she could almost feel his hard body pressed against hers again. Without any effort she could remember how she'd responded, the wild feelings that he sparked. She refused to look at him unless absolutely necessary lest he guess how much that kiss had impacted her.

There would be no more. She'd be forever grateful the power had not come on until sometime before dawn. At least she'd got back to the house in the dark and had gone to bed— no one to see, no one to know.

She knew she wouldn't remember everything Adam had told her this morning, and if she had to ask again, well, so be it. She wondered if she could get some kind of book on ranching from the library when she went to town Thursday.

When they reached the barn, Carter was eager to take care of the horses. Hank danced around, but stayed away from the hooves.

"We should get Carter up to speed on riding. Much as he helped out this morning cleaning the barn, there's a lot more work and riding is imperative. Guess I'll get him on a horse this afternoon," Adam said.

"Fine."

Shelly was not going to argue about it, though she planned to be nearby to make sure Carter didn't get hurt. But if she and her brother were to pull their own weight on the ranch, they both needed to ride.

"We'll start at one. You need to be here to interpret."

Adam walked away.

Shelly stared after him. "Bossy."

Carter came over to her and she told him what Adam had said about learning to ride.

Carter could hardly wait.

Promptly at one they arrived at the barn. Adam was already saddling his horse.

"You and Carter get your mounts and saddle up," he said.

"Me? I know how to ride," Shelly objected.

"So you can show Carter how. With both of us working, he'll learn that much faster. Plus you can use the practice. We'll get Bonny Boy to shy and you can practice staying on."

She rolled her eyes and went to get the horse. She was stiff from the morning ride and her muscles were still recovering from a couple of days ago. She'd like nothing more than to soak in a hot tub again, but who knew what scathing remarks that would engender.

Carter needed no help in getting up on his horse. Shelly led hers near the fence and used the bottom rail for a step. She wished she had longer legs.

Adam hadn't said a word, but mounted with no effort and led the trio outside.

"Shouldn't we be in the corral?" she asked, seeing him heading to the open field behind the house. The old trees near the pond offered little shade.

"Why? The horses aren't going anywhere. This is home to them. Besides, it'll be cleaner if either of you fall."

She wanted to ask about his falling, but knew he probably never did.

She was proud of her accomplishments over the past few days. It had been years since she'd ridden and she'd done well. Of course a lot of credit was due to the horse.

Did he really shy so readily?

Adam had them practice mounting and dismounting. It was easier for Carter with his longer legs. Shelly persevered, however, and even when her legs were shaking with fatigue, she mastered mounting from the ground.

Then it was walking, with Adam issuing corrections like a drill sergeant. She gritted her teeth and refrained from yelling back when he barked out some order at her.

"He's helping, he's helping," was her mantra. But more than once she wanted to ride the horse back to the barn and quit.

Carter, on the other hand, seemed to love every moment. He couldn't hear the yelled orders, so when Adam directed them at Carter, Shelly had to interpret. Instead of taking offense, Carter would grin and correct what was wrong.

When Adam called it quits, Shelly wondered if she could manage to get off the horse and crawl to the house, up the stairs and into the tub before collapsing in exhaustion.

But Adam had other ideas. The horses had to be groomed and fed. The dog had to be fed and the tack put away after a quick cleaning.

On the way to the house finally, Shelly decided tuna sandwiches were all she could prepare for dinner. She hoped she could stand long enough to fix them. She didn't dare sit or she'd never get up until morning. Every inch of her ached with exhaustion.

When she finally headed up to bed, way earlier than normal, but late enough in her opinion, she swung by the office to pick up something to read. One of the books on the dusty shelf looked very old. Shelly lifted it down. It was a journal. Opening it, she read the elegant script. It belonged to Mitch's mother. Her great grandmother.

Shelly opened the first page and read *January, 1929. A new year and I'm pregnant again.*

Hugging the book to her chest, she hurried upstairs. She couldn't wait to begin reading.

The next day was more of the same. Shelly began to regret telling Adam they wanted to learn about ranching. She hated it. It was hard work. It was hot. It smelled. It was never ending.

And she hated the fact Adam seemed to be watching her every moment as if waiting for her to call it quits. He reminded her of her father, never satisfied, always looking for that little bit more.

11

Day by day, she and Carter improved their riding skills and increased their knowledge of ranch life. Shelly was so tired each night, she could scarcely stay awake much beyond dinner. The lure of the journal called, but after a page or two of deciphering old handwriting, she was too tired to keep her eyes open.

By six each morning, she and Carter showed up at the barn, ready to work, her brother as excited as if it were a rare treat.

Thursday morning Shelly rose elated. Today she had to go to town, meet with the lawyer and buy some more supplies. A free day from the grueling schedule they'd followed all week.

Carter had reluctantly agreed to go with her since he needed some more jeans and socks and she wanted to make sure they fit.

It was mid morning when they arrived in Wildcat Creek. Her appointment with the attorney was for eleven, so she had some time to get Carter started on his shopping. She parked near the lawyer's office and they began to explore the town.

"*I'll wait for you to finish at the lawyer's before shopping*," he signed. "*Be easier if you're dealing with the salespeople.*"

She nodded. The stores in Fremont, California, were used

to a large deaf community, but she couldn't expect the same in Wildcat Creek. They walked up one side and down the other, window gazing and taking in the limited sights of the old western town.

"Miss Palmer, do come in."

Nathan Salsbury rose to greet her when his secretary ushered Shelly into his office promptly at eleven.

"So glad you could take the time to come into town."

"This is a treat," Shelly said. "My brother came, too, but he's waiting outside. We've been working flat out at the ranch, so today is like a free day for us."

She smiled and sat in the client's chair feeling a bit stiff, but with none of the pain in her muscles she'd had earlier that week.

There was a folder on the desk in front of the lawyer.

"Learning everything now that the property is yours?" he asked.

"As much as we can, anyway. My brother loves it. I think I'll reserve judgment."

Nathan nodded.

"Big task, more suited to those born to it, I've always thought."

"We're lucky to have Adam Wilson working there. He knows what he's doing."

"Good. I know Mitch thought highly of the man. Not too many can come up to speed in such a short time. He was a natural, Mitch said."

"Short time?" she asked, surprised by the comment. "Hasn't he always been a cowboy?"

"Oh no. In fact, I remember when he first hired on with

Mitch. Your uncle told me he took a chance because Adam didn't have much experience, but your uncle wanted to do something for an ex-soldier. Mitch liked the fact the man had served in the armed forces. Your uncle always said that a man from the service knew discipline."

"Adam was a soldier?"

That was the first Shelly knew of it. No wonder he was so exacting.

"Yes he served in the army as a medic, I think."

Shelly could feel the antipathy rise. She'd thought he was bossy. A military stint would explain that. He was exactly like her father, giving orders, expecting people to obey. Never satisfied.

"So my uncle hired him. Was he a rancher's son before enlisting?"

"Grew up in New York City as I heard it. You might check with him about it. He showed up one day from Texas, where he'd been working. He told Mitch he wanted a change of scenery. I remember Mitch saying he didn't think Adam would stay long, that he didn't have that much experience. But he sure took to ranching. Never thought he'd outlast Mitch. I sure do miss your uncle."

"I only knew him when I was nine," Shelly said.

She'd told Nathan that when they'd first met last week.

"He kept up with you through your mother's letters, until she died. That was hard. She was so young."

"Hard on all of us," she murmured, remembering how things had changed once her mother was gone.

"We could reminisce all day, but you're here to get the rest of the estate sorted out."

With that, Nathan launched into an explanation of the accounts he'd changed into her name and gave her a recap of the financial situation.

"I've listed the property for sale," she said once she had all the information.

"I heard that. Mitch would have been saddened to see it go out of the family. But it's yours to do with as you see fit."

She nodded, once again feeling slightly guilty that she wasn't staying to try to step into her great-uncle's footsteps.

After taking all the documents he had for her, she said goodbye and headed outside. Carter sat on one of the wooden benches that were placed at intervals along the sidewalk of the town. Friendly place, she thought, sitting beside him.

"*All done?*" he asked.

She nodded. "*I am here. I need to stop by the bank, then we can shop.*"

An unexpected feeling of regret seeped in. Looking around the town, she wondered what it would be like to live in such a place one's entire life. Her family had moved five or six times—whenever her father had been posted at a new base. She'd moved out on her own after starting college. Still, the San Francisco Bay Area wasn't really her home. She'd been born in Fort Dix, New Jersey, but moved when she was eighteen months. She'd never visited the place. Would she feel some kind of tie to her birthplace if she went there?

"*After we get my clothes, can we have hamburgers and a milkshake?*" Carter asked, standing impatiently. "*Then head back to the ranch?*"

"*I have a list of other things we need to buy before we start back. I want to go over some of the paperwork while we have lunch, to make sure*

I don't have any more questions before leaving Wildcat Creek. A hamburger and milkshake sound perfect."

Shelly didn't share Carter's love for all things to do with ranching. She wanted to browse stores, have a meal someone else fixed, and maybe find a book or two at the library to read at night. At her current rate, she'd be finished reading through the journal in another couple of weeks. After that she would love to delve into a good escapist novel.

They entered the bank a few minutes later. The marble floor and high ceiling attested to the fact it had been built decades ago. The ornate wood counter at the teller's window was a throwback to old-time architecture, nothing like the sleek banks she was used to.

"Can I help you?" A woman rose from a desk at the side and smiled at Shelly.

"I'm Shelly Palmer. Nathan Salsbury said I needed to stop in and sign some papers? I just inherited the Triple L ranch. This is Carter, my brother."

"I knew Mitch. I'm sorry for your loss. I'm Patrice Canfield. Have a seat here and I'll get the paperwork," Patrice said with a smile to both of them.

Shelly and Carter sat in the chairs in front of her desk. In only a moment, Patrice returned with a folder in hand.

"Nathan's already set up the account and will transfer the funds from the ranch account when you're ready. We just need your signature on a couple of signature cards."

The transaction didn't take long and Shelly was appreciative with how friendly Patrice was. She handled everything efficiently, explaining how the account would be funded, banking hours, and gave her a card in case she had any questions later.

When they left the bank, Carter insisted they shop at the feed store, obviously considering anything non-cowboy not worth buying. Once there he picked out jeans, shirts, socks and another cowboy hat.

They discussed the advantages of another pair of boots, but Shelly didn't think it was necessary for the time they'd be there.

As she went to pay for the clothes, Shelly signed to Carter that they'd eat after they put everything in the trunk so they didn't have to carry it around.

"Deaf?" the woman behind the counter asked as she took the clothes.

Shelly nodded, defenses rising.

"Paul Simmons's daughter is deaf. I see them moving their hands all the time. Sure would like to learn that myself."

The woman began to ring up the items.

"How old is the girl?" Shelly asked.

"About fourteen or fifteen, I think. Land's sake, you'd think I'd know, she's lived here all her life. Goes off to school during the year, but she's home this summer. Call them up, I bet those two would love to hang out together."

Shelly smiled politely, but didn't agree to call. Even if they wanted to hang out, who had time to drive back and forth for a few hours of visiting with all the work they were doing on the ranch?

Once she and Carter placed their purchases in the trunk, they headed for Rosie's Café. It was crowded with people eating lunch. The aroma when they entered made Shelly's mouth water. She hoped they could find a table.

She spotted a vacant one near the back and they threaded

their way there. The same waitress that had introduced them to Tuck Mason soon took their order with a friendly smile.

"Look at all the cowboys," Carter signed. *"Do you suppose they think I'm one?"*

Shelly almost laughed at the question, then looked around. How astonishing. Her brother did fit in.

"I bet they do," she replied.

As they were finishing the last of the milkshakes they'd ordered with their burgers, a tall man and teenager entered the restaurant. Two people pointed out Shelly and the newcomers headed directly to their table.

"I'm Paul Simmons," the man signed. *"This is my daughter Suzie. I heard you are new in town. Welcome."*

He smiled right at Carter.

Carter rose and reached out to shake the man's hand. He quickly signed his name and Shelly's, then turned to Suzie, asking her if she lived in town.

Shelly felt the sting of tears. His manners were impeccable. Their mother would have been so delighted with this son she loved so much.

In no time Suzie and Carter were conversing. Paul looked on, smiling broadly. Glancing around, Shelly noticed delighted smiles on many of the other diners.

"Would you care to join us?" she asked.

He nodded and pulled out a chair for Suzie. She sat, practically not noticing anything but Carter. She was a pretty girl, almost as tall as Shelly with dark hair and dark eyes.

Paul went around the table and sat opposite his daughter.

"Sorry to barge in like this, but it's so rare other deaf people find their way to Wildcat Creek. During the year Suzie attends a school for the deaf, but she's lonely in the summer."

"News travels fast," Shelly said.

He laughed, his eyes watching his daughter. Shelly could see the love shining through.

"It does. Wildcat Creek's a small town. Neighbors look out for each other. Bettie from the feed store called my wife. Then one of the men here called me. 'Gotta get right over,' he said. 'Here's a friend for Suzie.'"

Shelly relaxed. She wasn't used to neighbors watching out for each other, but she liked it. And she could tell the two teenagers were pleased to meet each other.

The break for lunch extended a lot longer than Shelly had anticipated. Paul was interested in learning about her inheritance. He said he knew about the ranch and of Mitch Lancaster's passing.

She told him a little about their visit, making it sound like an adventure. As she spoke, she realized it was a great adventure. She'd been looking at it as a problem, but it was a tremendous opportunity.

And her brother was loving every moment. She'd longed to spend a lot of time with him the last few summers, but other obligations had always interfered. Now it was just the two of them against the world.

As the diner gradually emptied, Shelly glanced at her watch, surprised to find it was almost three o'clock. They'd been talking with the Simmons for two hours.

"I've got to go," she said. "I have lots of shopping to do still and need to get back. It's not fair to leave everything to Adam."

"We've kept you. I can't say I'm sorry, however. This has

been so nice. Next time you're in town, call us. My wife would love to meet you and Carter. Maybe you can come to dinner or something."

"Love to," she said without making a firm commitment.

Who knew when they'd next be in town?

He took a card from his wallet and jotted a phone number on the back before handing it to Shelly.

"Home and office numbers. And Suzie's e-mail address. Maybe Carter can instant-messenger her or email or something."

Shelly took the card and saw that Paul was in the insurance business.

"Now that he's met her, he'll probably want the computer whenever he's not on a horse. He loves riding, but there are limits."

She tucked the card into her pocket.

"Suzie likes to ride as well."

"Then she should come visit us one day. Adam's great with horses and could watch them."

She could just imagine Adam's reaction to her volunteering his services. She almost smiled at the mental image.

During the ride home Shelly considered what she'd learned from Nathan Salsbury. She'd thought Adam had been a cowboy from way back when. His tour of duty in the military explained the way he ordered them about when training them to ride. She hadn't liked taking orders from her father and she sure didn't like it with Adam.

Yet she had to admit that she was a better rider after only a week of his instructions. And Carter was amazing. Of course, he couldn't hear Adam's scathing tone, and when she translated, she didn't tell him how bossy Adam could be.

Carter had taken to riding like a duck to water. He'd probably be on the horse all day long if there weren't other chores to do. Adam had taken him out on the range a couple of times, working Hank and getting Carter used to longer rides. Her brother loved every moment.

Didn't Adam miss New York? She missed San Francisco and had been gone only a couple of weeks. She glanced around at the rolling land. The road and fencing were the only signs that humans had passed this way. No tall buildings, no theaters, shops, coffeehouses, restaurants—all the things she loved. Just empty land stretching as far as the eye could see. And clouds building over the mountains again. She wasn't used to rain in the summer.

Shelly wished she'd gotten a chance to speak to Geoff Bradshaw when she stopped in at the real estate office just before they left town.

The girl at the first desk had said there was no interest in the ranch. Shelly knew Geoff would call if someone wanted to see the place, but would he let her know if there was even an expression of interest? She'd have to check again and find out.

"*I'm going to the barn,*" Carter signed when she stopped at the house.

"*Not until you help me unload,*" she signed right back.

Carter could work fast when he had something he wanted to do, and in very little time, groceries had been put away and the other supplies they'd bought carried to their bedrooms. He waved and headed out to see the horses. Shelly figured he'd sleep with them if she'd let him.

He wasn't going to return to California easily, she thought, disturbed by the idea.

By the time Shelly reached the barn, Carter had saddled Tumbleweed, his horse. There was no sign of Hank. Had he gone with Adam?

"*Where's Adam?*" she asked. There was no sign of him.

Carter shrugged. He double-checked the cinch, then unsnapped the ties and swung into the saddle as easily as if he'd been doing it for years.

"*I'm going to ride out to see if I can find him,*" he signed.

"*Wait.*"

But he was already riding out of the barn.

12

Shelly glared after him. He knew she wouldn't want him going out alone.

As quickly as she could, she saddled Bonny Boy and followed. The ranch was huge, but the cattle were in one area so she figured that was where Adam would be. And Carter.

She tried to enjoy the ride, but she was concerned about her brother. He didn't have that much experience. What if something happened to him? Teenagers thought they knew everything, and Carter was a city kid, not some ranch-savvy teen.

Reaching a knoll, she pulled the horse to a stop and looked around. She thought she saw him ahead of her, a bit to the right, near the rocks that thrust up from the earth. They looked as if a giant had stuck them into the ground for some bizarre game. Had Adam gone that way? Maybe he'd spotted some cattle that had wandered in the area and he wanted them out before they got hurt.

She urged Bonny Boy forward. The breeze picked up. Dark clouds were building in the west. She didn't see any lightning, but she sure didn't want to be out in this open space if a thunderstorm blew up.

Shelly continued riding but a bit unsure exactly where she

was. She could hardly get lost. If she came to a fence, she'd just follow it until she found a better landmark. And as long as she could see the rocks, she had an idea of where she was in relation to the house.

As she passed the rocks, a gust of wind blew a small whirl-wind of dust. Bonny shied. Thanks to Adam's training, she kept her seat, though the movement startled her.

"Easy, boy," she said, patting his neck. She reached up to pull her hat down lower and kept a wary eye out as they continued.

Finally she spotted both Adam and Carter some distance ahead. She reined in her horse, debating whether to join them. Carter liked the freedom he had. He'd commented last night how different things were on the ranch.

They were for her as well, but she wasn't sure she liked the differences. She felt like a fish out of water. She could throw a dinner party for thirty with sixty minutes' notice, arrange a night at the opera for a party of sixteen, and knew the best deals for food for a buffet in the Bay Area. Here she hardly knew what to buy and where. The stores were so different from the state-of-the-art supermarkets and specialty shops she was used to.

She sat and looked around. When her ancestors had first arrived, there'd been no stores. There'd been only the land and the burning desire they'd had to make something of it. They'd brought stock, raised their own food, and made do with what they'd had.

She was spoiled with all the modern conveniences. She never would have made a pioneer. The thought of selling the ranch for a lot of money was tantalizing. Yet once sold, it would be forever lost to the family.

Should she consider only selling a portion and keeping the rest for Carter?

Surely once he was back at school, he'd forget about becoming a cowboy. He'd have memories and stories to tell his friends, but his destiny lay elsewhere.

Shelly turned Bonny Boy back and headed for the homestead. Adam would watch out for Carter. She needed to check in with Geoff. Maybe he'd have other ideas for making a quick sale.

As she drew near the rocky outcropping, Shelly thought she heard a calf bawling. Bonny Boy looked in the direction of the rocks as if he, too, heard the cry.

"Do you suppose some calf is caught?" she asked the horse. Without much thought, she turned to to toward the sound.

The wind blew in gusts and the dark clouds seemed closer than before. She'd take a quick look and then head for home. She didn't want to be caught in the rain. But if she could help an injured animal, she would.

Slowly the horse picked his way through the rough ground, ears pricked forward. Shelly strained to see the animal, the plaintive cries sounding fainter than before. She rose up in her stirrups, scanning the area.

A dozen head of cattle could be hidden among the rocks. There was no way to spot one without riding through the entire rocky formation.

When another gust of wind rattled some dead limbs from a scrub, Bonny Boy shied, snorting and half rearing, enough to throw Shelly off balance. She tried to hold on, but was too far over on one side. Putting out her hand to stop her fall, she crashed onto the rocky ground, her head bouncing on smooth stone. Everything went black.

Adam kept an eye on the clouds building in the west. They were in for more rain. It had been a wet spring and it looked as if thundershowers would be the norm for the next few days. He could handle them—if they came with enough notice.

The cattle ignored the weather, contentedly grazing on the lush green grass. Hank trotted around the perimeter of the herd, attentive, watching. Suddenly he paused and looked back at Adam.

No, behind him. Adam glanced back. Carter was riding directly toward the herd. When had they returned? Adam had left a list of chores for the Palmers to do. Instead, Carter was riding as if a posse was after him. If he rode through the herd, he'd scatter them all over the place, just when Hank was working to tighten the perimeter.

As if the boy read his mind, he pulled rein and slowed his horse to a walk. A few moments later he pulled up beside Adam.

"What doing?" he asked in his monotone voice.

Adam sighed in frustration. He wished he and the kid could communicate better. He pointed to Hank, who had resumed his patrol.

"Training?" Carter asked.

Adam nodded. He watched the dog, suddenly wondering why he didn't mind Carter's company as much as he'd thought he would. When he'd first mustered out of the army, he'd sworn not to get close to anyone. To keep the vow, he kept to himself. He did his job, spent his off hours riding, learning some new skill or reading. Not playing cards like a lot of cowboys did or going into town to hit the bars.

Not getting close to anyone was his protective mechanism. Friends could be killed. Family members died. Nothing lasted. The only way to escape the pain was to keep to himself.

The last thing he wanted was involvement with the Palmers. They were as green as grass and only in Wyoming for a short visit. Yet this kid was as enthusiastic about the ranch as he and Brian had been when they'd joined up.

How long before something happened to Carter to knock some of that cockeyed optimism to bits?

Adam had to give the boy some credit—he learned fast. And he remained steadfast in his enthusiasm, no matter how hard or unpleasant the task he'd been given.

Adam looked back around and then toward the homestead. Where was Shelly? He was surprised she hadn't ridden out with her brother. He checked the western sky. Those clouds looked even closer. And the breeze was definitely stronger than before.

"Let's head back," he said. Dumb move, the kid couldn't hear him.

He waved his hand and when Carter looked at him, he jerked a thumb in the direction of home.

Carter nodded, then gave a hand signal. Hank came bounding over and sat beside the teen's horse.

Adam knew they'd been practicing. He was glad to see the dog respond. Maybe he and Carter would make a team.

Tonight he'd go over some of the duties of a cattle dog and make sure Carter could tell when each activity was needed.

They slowly rode away from the herd. Adam mentally ran over some of the tasks they could do if it rained the next day. There'd be no cutting hay any time soon. If the bad weather continued for too many more days, the crop wouldn't be worth much.

Everything was more or less on hold pending the sale of the ranch, only the critical tasks being handled. He was as anxious as Shelly for the place to be sold.

Habit kept him swinging wide around the rocky formation. He knew there were no snipers, but old lessons died hard.

Suddenly Hank gave a bark and stopped, facing the rocks. The hairs on the back of Adam's neck rose. He stopped and looked at the imposing boulders. No rifle barrels. No scent of gun powder. No camouflaged soldiers lying in wait. Nevertheless, tension rose. He could feel the flash of adrenaline.

"What is it, boy?" he asked the dog.

Carter had stopped and was looking at the dog and then the outcropping.

"Whazit?" he asked peering in the direction of the rocks.

Adam shook his head. He urged his horse toward home, calling to Hank.

The dog trotted beside Adam for a few steps, then turned back to the rocks and barked.

"I don't want to go over there," Adam said, calling the dog again.

But this time Hank didn't return. He took a few more

steps in the direction of the rocks, barking again.

Carter started his horse after the dog. Once Hank saw he was being followed, he took off toward the rocks at a run.

Adam sighed, pulled his mount around and followed the other two. He had been in the jumble of stones before. He didn't like it, but it wouldn't hurt him. He hoped the fool dog knew what he was doing.

As he reached the edge of the rocks, Adam thought he heard the bleating of a calf. Was one injured or stuck? The dog had good instincts. Maybe he'd misjudged him.

He followed Carter and in only a moment was startled to see Bonny Boy standing docilely by a large rock. Crumpled near him on the ground was Shelly. Carter had seen her first, when Hank had run to sit beside the body, nudging her with his nose.

Carter flew off his horse and ran to his sister, Adam right behind him.

There was blood all over her face. For a moment he wondered if she'd been shot. When he turned her over would he find half her head blown away? He couldn't move for a second—scenes of other women lying on the ground overrode the present. He could hear guns in the distance. Or was it the rumble of thunder? He could see the innocent girls and old ladies, eyes wide, staring into eternity.

He swallowed hard and stepped around Carter to Shelly's other side. Her brother was shaking her. Adam reached out and pulled his hands away.

"We need to assess the damage first," he said, moving his hands knowingly along her legs, up to her torso, then her arms. He checked for any neck injury. Lastly he looked at her face. The blood was seeping from a scrape near her hairline Head wounds bled freely, which was good. It minimized dir in the wound.

He brushed back her hair. There was a knot on the lef side of her head the size of a ping pong ball. Other than tha and the scrape, he found no further injury. He shrugged ou of his shirt and pulled his cotton undershirt over his head Folding it to make a pad, he placed it against her forehead Carter reached out to hold it in place. Before putting his shir back on, Adam tore off a strip to hold the pad in place. He could ride to the ranch for help and get paramedics from town, but that'd take hours. The rain wouldn't hold off tha long.

Or he could risk injuries he hadn't discovered, pick her up and carry her back to the ranch.

If it had been a battle situation, he wouldn't have hesitated a second. But this was not a war zone. Which would be the better choice for Shelly? How long had she been unconscious? Was she injured anywhere besides her head? And what was she doing in the rocks anyway?

The bleating sounded again. She must have heard it and gone to investigate. With the wind gusting the way it was, he could picture Bonny Boy shying and dumping her.

The moments ticked by. Adam glanced at the darkening sky. He was running out of time. A decision needed to be made.

13

Adam motioned Carter to stay where he was. Giving Hank a seek command, Adam followed the dog as he trotted away from the humans. In only a few moments he located the calf, caught in a small crevasse, unharmed but unable to get out on his own.

Adam went back to the horses. He mounted his and used a rope to pull the calf free. It took off running in the direction of the herd. He wondered momentarily where the mama cow was but the situation with Shelly was more critical.

He'd have to take the chance and get her home as fast as they could safely move. He couldn't leave her. Even if Carter stayed with her, it'd be dark before help arrived. And the rain would beat the dark.

With minimum fuss, he pantomimed and spoke slowly to Carter that he was to lead Bonny Boy home, while Adam would carry Shelly. Lifting her, he was gratified to hear her groan softly. Maybe she was coming to. Adam mounted his horse and with Carter's help was able to pull Shelly into his arms. She moaned, but didn't regain consciousness. Slowly they headed for the house. Hank trotted alongside Carter's horse and Bonny Boy walked on the other side, not giving Carter any trouble.

Blood had dried on Shelly's face. Her eyes remained closed. Adam tried to keep her still, but it wasn't easy with the motion of the horse. He hoped she had no neck or back injuries if so, picking her up and riding like this wouldn't help at all.

He was grateful when the house came into view.

"I take horses," Carter said, dismounting and reaching for Adam's reins. "Help her."

Adam nodded and with Carter reaching up to help getting Shelly down, Adam quickly dismounted then took her in his arms and headed to the house, hoping they hadn't locked the door. Who knew how city folks behaved?

If the situation hadn't been so serious he would have smiled. Until a few years ago he'd been as city as they came. He'd changed, so why did he persist in believing Carter couldn't also learn ranching?

The door was unlocked. He entered and walked up the stairs. Shelly wasn't a big woman, but a heavier weight than he was used to carrying for such a distance. He glanced into a bedroom and recognized the signs of a woman's presence. Laying her on the bed, he stood up. Next step, assess the damage and fix her up. If she needed a doctor, he'd have to drive her to town. That was the nearest clinic. Maybe he could call Jenny Schofield. The nurse was much closer. She'd know what to do.

Before Adam finished washing her face, Shelly blinked at him, then glanced around the room with puzzlement.

"How do you feel?" he asked, holding the washcloth away from her face.

"I have the world's worst headache. What am I doing here?"

"Apparently you fell from Bonny Boy. Carter and I found you and brought you home. I was worried you had a neck injury or something worse."

She closed her eyes just as Carter thundered up the stairs and then burst into her room.

Opening her eyes, she looked at Adam and smiled wanly.

"Don't tell him," she said softly, "but I feel awful."

Carter signed something and she nodded slowly, moving her hands.

"Ow," she said, clutching her left wrist with her right hand. "I did more than bump my head."

She looked down at the swollen wrist.

"Man, that hurts!" she said, her eyes filling with tears.

"Let me see."

Adam tossed the washcloth into the bowl of warm water and took her wrist gently in his large hands.

"Ouch," she said, pulling back slightly.

"Sprained most likely. But it needs X-rays to be sure," he said, moving her wrist slowly to assess the damage. "I'll take you into the clinic in town."

"Great, I just got back from town."

"It's the closest clinic. You'll need to be checked by a doctor."

"There are dozens of hospitals near where I lived in San Francisco and I never needed one. Now this. I can't believe it."

"Life on the range," he said.

He rose and headed for the door.

"Where are you going?" she asked.

"To feed the horses and get them settled for the night. It'll be late by the time we get back."

Adam swung by the bunkhouse and looked up the number for Walt Nelson. Jenny Schofield lived on one of the cabins on Walt's land. He'd know how to reach her.

In only a few minutes he was listing the symptoms to Jenny.

"You're right, she needs to be checked by a doctor. She probably has a concussion and will need some attention to the wrist. And at the very least, Doc can give her some pain meds. Do you need me to come over?" she said.

"Not yet. I'll settle the animals and take her into the clinic."

"Val and I are free. It'll only take me a few minutes to get there and I can take her in. That'll give you plenty of time to take care of the animals. It's raining already."

"I'd appreciate it."

"See you in a few," Jenny said as they hung up.

Shelly's head pounded. She brushed against her forehead and her fingertips came away bloody. She moaned softly. Carter sat on the edge of the bed where Adam had been and squeezed out the washcloth. He held it to her. She took it and gingerly pressed it against the burning near her hairline. It stung. Obviously a cut or scrape. She could feel the knot beneath the cloth. She wished she had a mirror.

Holding the cloth against her skin, she tried to figure out what happened and where she was injured. Her head was killing her. Her wrist throbbed in time with her pulse. She wiggled her fingers. They moved, didn't that mean no broken bones? How could she tell? Her entire arm ached.

"Want some aspirin?" Carter signed.

She smiled and then felt tears welling. She was in a world of hurt. Aspirin wouldn't help much. Yet he looked so worried.

"Fine," she returned.

She closed her eyes when he left and tried to breathe through the pain. Riding was definitely not what it was cracked up to be. Before she let herself start feeling sorry for herself, she gritted her teeth and sat up. The pounding grew worse. But she needed to see her face.

She rose on wobbly legs and went to the bathroom. At least she didn't appear to be injured anywhere else, though there was a tenderness on one hip. The scrape was oozing blood, but it wasn't pouring down her face. There was blood on her shirt, however. She clutched the sink with her good hand and gazed at her battered appearance.

That bossy cowboy was so right—she needed a doctor.

By the time Adam returned, Shelly had washed her face, changed her shirt and, with Carter's help, walked back down the stairs. Unable to go any farther, she had sunk on the third step and was waiting.

The rain had started. She heard it pounding on the porch roof. Out the window it looked darker than early evening. She wished the storm had held off. How much worse would it be driving in this than on a clear night?

Adam entered without knocking, surprised to see her sitting on the steps.

"Don't you dare say anything. I'm able to walk—it's my head and arm that hurt. Well, and my hip. I hate the idea of the drive in, but I do need a doctor."

She stood up on shaky legs.

"Change of plans."

Just then a red Jeep pulled into the yard near the house.

He went to the door and in only seconds a tall young woman with long brown hair stepped inside, accompanied by a large German Shepherd wearing a service vest.

"This is Jenny Schofield, a nearby neighbor and a nurse She'll take you into town."

"I'm sorry to bring you out on such a night," Shelly said.

Could Adam not stand to be with her long enough to take her into town?

"Nice to meet you, but not under the circumstances."

She smiled at Carter and stepped closer to Shelly.

"May I?" she asked.

Shelly nodded then wished she hadn't.

Gently Jenny brushed back her hair and studied the abrasion. Then she took her arm above the swollen wrist and gently pressed her fingertips on the swollen area.

Shelly winced but knew the nurse was doing her best not to cause any more discomfort.

"I called the clinic, they're expecting us. We'll stop for something to eat before we come back once she's done there.'

Jenny glanced at Carter then back to Adam.

"Can you take care of supper?" she asked. "Or should we bring something back?"

"Yeah. I'll get a pad and pen to communicate," Adam mumbled.

Jenny's eyes widened. "He's deaf?"

Adam nodded.

She turned and smiled at Carter, signing hello.

Carter smiled back and returned the greeting.

"That's about all I know," she confessed. "Someone needs to explain what's going on."

Shelly did her best with only one hand. Carter seemed to pick up on it and signed he'd be fine with Adam.

Shelly looked at Adam. "Thank you. I thought he'd have to come with us."

Adam nodded. "He'll be fine."

"Let's go," Jenny said. "My Jeep's right out front. It's raining, but it'll only be a few steps. Are you able to walk or should Adam carry you?"

A crack of thunder sounded. Jenny jumped and her service dog pressed against her leg. Adam glanced around, looked back at Shelly, raising his eyebrows in silent question.

She took a deep breath and tried to smile at him.

"Save your heroic efforts. I got this far, I can make it a little farther."

He gave a half smile and nodded.

"Good. You aren't light as a feather."

She started to say something then shut her mouth. He'd carried her up to her bedroom, and from what Carter had told her, Adam had carried her on horseback all the way back to the house. She owed him. What if he'd left her out on the range until help arrived? She'd be soaking wet and probably suffering from hypothermia in the rain.

Before long she and Jenny sat in the warmth of her vehicle as she drove through the storm. Shelly leaned back, trying to get semi-comfortable. Her head pounded and every jarring bounce made it even worse. She gritted her teeth, willing the aspirin to take effect.

The trip passed as a blur—the monotonous swipes of the windshield wipers, the water pounding on the roof, the black asphalt was an endless ribbon stretching forever. Shelly wished time would fast forward and she could get some relief from the pain.

When Jenny pulled into the parking lot of the clinic, Shelly almost burst into tears. Her whole body ached now.

"I think I'm going to be sick," she said when Jenny stopped the truck.

"That's from the concussion, most likely," the nurse said, quickly opening the door to let the dog jump across her and out to the pavement. "Hold it until you're outside if you can," she said, releasing Shelly's seat belt.

Before Jenny could run around to the other side staff members arrived quickly to respond. In only seconds Shelly was lying on a gurney, a young nurse taking vitals. An older woman began to remove the makeshift bandage to check the head wound while Jenny succinctly gave her report.

With all the hustle and bustle, the last thing Shelly remembered, before a whoosh of lightheadedness took over, was asking Jenny to stay with her.

14

"Shelly will be okay," Carter said.

Adam nodded, stirring the meat he cooked for Sloppy Joes. He tried to relax. She'd be okay. Yet the last thing he wanted was a situation like today's. He was trying to escape memories of people covered in blood.

Shelly hadn't been shot, but the blood, the damage to skin and tissue still caused him to remember. Her pretty skin was now scraped and marred. She'd most likely carry a scar near her hairline. She should have stayed in San Francisco and sold the ranch long-distance.

Or he should have moved on as soon as she and the kid had arrived.

He glanced at Carter who stood watching him cook. He knew the kid was worried. His sister was all he had. And if something happened to her, Adam didn't have a clue what would become of him.

Carter would probably get the ranch. That wouldn't be so bad, he thought. The kid was learning fast. And loved every aspect of ranching he'd seen.

Maybe ranchers were born, not made. Did Carter have anything to say about the sale of the property?

Shelly was constant in her goal. She wanted the money.

Adam couldn't blame her. Money went a long way in making the life you wanted.

But it couldn't bring back Brian. Or his mother. Or even budge his grandmother from her flat in Brooklyn. He'd tried often enough over the past four years.

"Jenny?" The doctor came to the doorway.

She turned and rose from the chair in the waiting area.

"How is she?" she asked.

"As you suspected, slight concussion, badly sprained wrist. Some other bruises but she'll be okay soon enough."

They went to the cubicle where Shelly sat in a wheelchair, a bandage on her forehead, her arm in a cast resting in a sling.

"I suggested Ms. Palmer remain here overnight, but she refuses. Can you keep an eye on her at home?"

Jenny nodded. "For a day or two. Beyond that I have another assignment."

"Just overnight should do it," the doctor said. "She said she hasn't eaten, so if you two want to go get a bite before you go home, it'll help. I've given her some pain meds which will kick in soon. Once home straight to bed."

Jenny called Adam while she and Shelly waited for the food at the café. He promised to update Carter on his sister's condition. They'd have Shelly's bed ready for her when she got home.

By the time Jenny and Shelly arrived at the ranch, Adam and Carter had finished dinner, Adam writing out his part of the conversation, Carter speaking his. Once the teen learned his sister was going to be okay, the conversation revolved about the ranch.

The rain blotted out the stars. The lightning and thunder had moved on. Jenny made good time driving on the wet road while Shelly dozed her head leaning against the window. When they reached the house, she woke Shelly up enough for her to walk up the stairs with help from Adam and Carter. Once in her bedroom, the men left so Jenny could help her to change into her nightgown.

Adam and Carter went to the kitchen to wait for Jenny.

While Shelly was likely to go right to sleep, it was early enough the rest of them wouldn't head for bed for a while.

Adam fixed some coffee. The kitchen hadn't changed much from when Mitch had been there. The two of them had usually eaten together in the winter months, more often than not in the bunkhouse kitchen.

When the old man had grown too sick, Adam had prepared the meals here at the house. He hadn't cooked in this kitchen since Mitch had gone to the hospital.

Adam thought about last summer, when the seasonal cowboys had all sat around the big table in the bunkhouse shooting the breeze. Mitch had always had tall tales to tell. A man could learn a lot from listening to others' experiences. He glanced at Carter. Too bad the kid hadn't gotten a chance to know Mitch.

When Jenny joined them in the kitchen, he asked about Shelly.

"I'll stay and watch her tonight. She should be lots better in the morning at least with the concussion. If she needs anything, I'll be right there. She went right to sleep as soon as she got into bed."

"Appreciate your staying. No other job?" Adam asked.

Jenny was a private duty nurse and was in demand, but sometimes had a week or more between assignments.

"I've got the next two days off. I think I'll only need to stay until morning, but if needed for longer, I can manage another day."

He hesitated a moment.

"I was a medic in the army. I have experience with head injuries. More than I ever wanted. I can watch out for her."

"Good. Then we'll see how she is in the morning."

Shelly awoke with a dull headache. She sat up slowly and stared in surprise at the German Shepherd dog gazing at her.

"Hello," she said with a smile.

She remembered Jenny's service dog. Glancing around the room she didn't see her neighbor.

Getting out of bed she was glad to feel almost normal again. Her wrist was in a cast, and as she made her way to the bathroom, she noticed her swollen forehead with a bandage and the beginnings of a black eye.

Great, just what every woman wanted.

She was able to maneuver her clothes, get dressed and slowly went downstairs to the kitchen. The dog must have felt his assignment was over as he'd returned to his mistress' side. Jenny was sitting at the table sipping a cup of coffee.

"Oh, hi, you're awake. How do you feel?" she asked, jumping to her feet.

"So much better than last night. I didn't expect to sleep so late."

"Sleep promotes healing, so get as much as you can. No headache, wrist okay?"

Jenny visually checked her over and must have been satisfied as she smiled at Shelly.

"Hungry?"

"Yes, but I can fix something," Shelly said.

"Take advantage of help while you have it. You'll find a bit of restriction with that arm in a cast."

Jenny quickly prepared scrambled eggs and toast and a hot cup of tea. They chatted while Shelly ate. After a quick cleanup, Jenny prepared to leave.

"I told Adam already if you need anything, I'm just a phone call away."

"I really appreciate your help, last night and today," Shelly said.

"It's what neighbors are for," Jenny said with a smile. "Take care and we'll get together soon for a girl's night out."

When Jenny left, Shelly walked out to the barn to look for Adam and Carter. No sign of them.

She knew she couldn't saddle a horse with one arm. Not that she was that anxious to be riding again. She wandered back to the house and switched on the computer. Unless and until someone wanted to buy this place, she was in charge. Might as well learn as much as she could about this ranch.

Not understanding all the data she was reviewing, after a while she decided to read more of the old journal. At least she was wide awake now and could more easily read the old fashioned handwriting.

It was late afternoon when she heard horses and went to the front porch in time to see her brother and Adam reach the barn.

She walked over.

Adam saw her first. "You doing okay?"

She nodded.

"Much better than last night. Jenny said I should feel close to normal by tomorrow, except for the arm. I made a potato salad and if you'd join us for dinner, and grill some steaks, we could eat in no time."

He nodded, already pulling the heavy saddle off his horse. Carter was at the same stage.

"We'll take care of the horses, clean up and be there."

"And you don't mind grilling the steaks?"

"Not at all."

When the meal was ready, they all began to eat. Shelly immediately found a problem.

"Sorry, I can't cut my meat," she said looking at Adam.

He didn't say a word, but reached for her plate, cutting the steak into bite-size pieces and returning it to her.

"Thank you."

She felt silly. Why hadn't she thought about that? It was going to prove a problem for the next few weeks or until the doctor took off the cast.

When they were almost finished eating, Shelly looked at Adam.

"I thought you were a cowboy born and bred. According to the lawyer, you've only worked on ranches for a few years."

"That's right. So?"

"I was surprised you know so much in a relatively short time. Maybe Carter and I can learn, too. I checked with the real estate office when I was in town a few days ago. No nibbles on the ranch. And then I went by the feed store and saw the posted job opening for a cowboy. No interest there, either, apparently."

"You might find some summer help available with school out. Lots of ranches have kids who attend college and like to work other places to broaden their knowledge," he said. "Your uncle had a college kid last summer."

"He did?"

"He liked younger people. He was always having barbecues for the hands with lots of loud music."

Adam had resisted attending. He'd go sometimes, but more often liked riding out on the range where it was quiet and he could be alone.

And remember.

"So where did you grow up if not on a ranch? Jenny said you were a medic in the Army."

"Can I go see Hank?" Carter signed.

At Shelly's nod, he cleared his place and took off.

Adam wanted to follow him. He had no interest in talking about himself.

"So where?" she asked again.

"Bed-Stuy. It's in Brooklyn," he said.

He wasn't one to talk much about the past, but what could a few facts hurt? He knew what it was like to be injured and unable to do anything. He'd sat with enough wounded soldiers to help them through the night until they could be evacuated to recognize she wanted something to distract her.

"You're kidding!"

He almost smiled at the disbelief in her voice.

"I went to inner-city camps as a kid. First time I saw a horse I was scared to death. First time I rode one I thought I was king of the world. That put me in good stead when I left the army and tried my hand at ranch work."

"Wyoming is a far cry from Brooklyn," she said.

"This life suits me. I'd never go back to the city."

He didn't return even to visit his grandmother. The thought made him break out into a sweat.

She was silent for a while. He was about to clear his place when she spoke again.

"You do the cowboy bit well. Don't tell Carter you came to it late. I want him to go to college and get a good job — maybe in computers."

"Is that what you want to do, work with computers?"

"No."

"Once the ranch sells you won't have to worry about work ever again," he said.

"Is that what you think? Once I have some money, I'll just fritter away my days?"

"What else? I don't know your plans."

Again she was silent. Adam shifted a bit on the hard chair and gazed out the window watching the breeze gently swaying the trees.

"Why didn't you become a doctor when you got out of the army?" she asked. "Seems a logical step for a medic. You could have used the GI bill."

"Decided I didn't like it," he said shortly.

She was right on. He'd chosen the medical field in the Army thinking it would give him a leg up into college and med school when he got out of the service. But the realities of war had changed his mind.

The roiling helplessness swept through him again. He'd gone to save lives and been unable to save the most important one.

"I'm glad you had the knowledge to know what to do yesterday," she said softly.

"Basic first aid."

"Still, you kept your head, knew what to do and did it. I'm grateful. I hate to think what would have happened if it had been only Carter and me."

"Then don't think about it," he said gruffly.

"Tell me something about my uncle. I wish I'd known him after I grew up."

"Why didn't you come to visit?"

"I never thought about it, truthfully. My mother was the letter writer in our family. After she died, there were no more letters. I'm not sure I had an address. Then it was off to college and marriage. I wish I had kept in contact. I never knew he planned to leave the ranch to me. If I had visited a time or two, he would have seen I wasn't suited to ranching."

"You and Carter were his only family."

"Yet he only left the ranch to me. I don't know why. Do you think because Carter is underage?"

"He never mentioned Carter. Did he know about him?"

Try as he might, Adam couldn't remember Mitch saying anything about Shelly's brother.

"I would have thought so. He was six when Mom died. She wrote Uncle Mitch from time to time. Why wouldn't she—"

She stopped abruptly.

"What?"

"Nothing. It hurts my head to talk. You talk, tell me about Mitch."

Adam settled back in the chair willing to give a little. He

started with his first month on the job, how taciturn Mitch had been. And how that had suited Adam to a T.

He spoke for several minutes about the kind of man Mitch had been—old-fashioned and set in his ways, but strong, good to friends and neighbors, with a dry sense of humor that Adam had appreciated.

After a while, he didn't want to talk anymore. He missed Mitch more than he'd expected. Now he wanted to head back to the barn, check on the animals and call it a day.

As if reading his mind, Shelly remained silent when he stopped.

"I think I can manage the dishes one handed. Thanks for the help with dinner," she said with a smile.

15

Shelly had mixed emotions where Adam was concerned. She thought he was bossy, which he was. But he was so good-looking it almost made her stop thinking and start drooling, except she was immune to falling for someone because of her past experience. Shelly was not going to get involved with another heart-stopping gorgeous guy.

When the ranch sold, she'd be a wealthy woman. Even splitting the money with Carter would leave her set for life, with proper investments. If she ever did get involved with another man, it would be a partnership—equals going in the same direction. Not some bossy cowboy who obviously had issues she wasn't capable of dealing with.

For a moment her heart was touched, however. Adam had liked and respected her great-uncle. It was clear in his voice as he spoke of the man. She wondered if he had a father somewhere or if he'd lost his parents years ago.

She'd like to know more about him. But didn't want to pry. Maybe she could talk him into eating with them until she could cut up her own food. Not that she needed him to do that. Carter could.

Still, she could suggest he share at least the evening meal with them. Carter would be thrilled.

Adam was in the kitchen the next morning when Shelly entered. He had cooked a stack of pancakes and a large platter full of link and patty sausages for breakfast. Carter was already eating and she could tell Adam had already finished.

"This is a nice surprise. Thank you."

She wasn't going to protest. How nice to feel pampered.

"As soon as we're finished, Carter and I will get to work."

He looked at her.

"You rest up. If you feel sick, call me on the walkie-talkie in the office. We don't get cell phone reception over most of the ranch, but except for a few pockets the walkie-talkies cover the whole ranch so I'll be in communication range."

"Okay," she said.

"Your uncle was old-fashioned enough to hold on to that old mower but had all his men carry these for communications. I'll try to stay in range."

By the time Adam left, Carter had already dumped his dishes in the sink and headed out, too.

Shelly cleaned up the breakfast dishes one handed. The pain medication helped immensely. Feeling at loose ends, she returned to the office, checked the walkie-talkie and then powered up the computer. Might as well go over things again and hope she made better sense of what she was seeing.

She wasn't sure how long she had been working, but the sound of a vehicle in the driveway made her pause.

Going to the window, she saw a truck she didn't recognize. Hank was near the barn barking. Carter came from the barn and motioned Hank to sit. The dog obeyed but kept his eyes focused on the arriving visitors.

When Paul Simmons stepped down, Shelly stared. She

didn't remember inviting them to visit today. They'd made vague comments, but nothing firm.

Still, she wanted to nurture that friendship for Carter's sake.

By the time she stepped out on the porch, Carter and Suzie were busy conversing while Paul looked on. He spotted Shelly and headed toward her.

"What happened to you?" he asked when he took in the cast and bandage.

"I fell off a horse," she said, hating to admit it.

"When? I'm sorry, I didn't know. Is this a bad time to visit? Suzie and Carter have been e-mailing back and forth already and I had today free so I brought her out. We won't stay, of course."

"No, don't leave. Both of them look happy to be together. I'm glad you had the day off."

Shelly saw Adam come from the barn. The two teenagers turned and headed for him, their hands flying. A minute later the teens came to the porch.

"Can we go riding with Adam?" Carter asked.

"If it's okay with Mr. Simmons and with Adam," Shelly signed. *"He said we can if it's okay with you two."*

The two turned and ran back to the barn. A short time later the three of them rode out and headed for the range. Shelly noticed that Adam was riding Bonny Boy. She was glad he wasn't taking chances with the teens.

"This will be great for Carter. Thanks for letting her go. He loves riding. Come in and I'll make some coffee."

"Let me make it. My wife tells me I'm handy in the kitchen. And you look as if you're about to fall down. Peggy wanted to come but Friday is a busy day at her office, she couldn't get the time off. We still want you and Carter to come to our place for dinner one evening. Looks like it'll be a while, though."

"I feel better than I look," she said. "Once I'm used to the cast, I'll be able to drive."

The rest of the morning passed pleasantly enough with Paul and Shelly sitting on the porch. He told her about Wildcat Creek, how his family had lived there almost as long as hers had owned the ranch.

They compared notes on raising a deaf child in a hearing world.

And he told her about his wife's love for making pies and cakes and entering them in the county fair.

"She says she has to practice, but if I eat all she cooks, I'll be too fat to get in the truck to drive her to the county fair."

Shelly laughed. "I look forward to meeting her."

"Once you are feeling better, we'll plan on a barbecue. Peg's a great cook as well as champion pie maker."

"We'd like that."

"Our place doesn't hold the same appeal as yours, though," he said.

"What does that mean?"

"Horses. Suzie's crazy about riding. We've given her lessons, but don't have a place to keep a horse. All she talked about was how Carter said she could go riding with him and Adam. As long as they're with him, I'm okay. I'm not that good a rider myself."

"Me, either. But Adam knows what he's doing."

"That's one of the reasons I brought her today. That and

the chance for her to be with your brother. He made a great impression on both of us."

"He'll love showing off the place."

Shelly didn't voice her fears that he was becoming too attached to the ranch. Time enough for her to deal with that when they left in the fall.

Shelly, with Paul's help, had lunch prepared when Carter and Suzie came into the house later. Both were pink from the sun. They looked happy.

"*Suzie loves to ride,*" Carter signed. "*Can she come another day and help out? She learns fast.*"

"*Fine with me, but we need to check with her parents and with Adam,*" Shelly returned.

"*And we need better communications,*" Paul signed. "*Today wasn't a good day to come, Shelly is hurt.*"

"*I'm sorry you were hurt,*" Suzie said. "*Carter told me about your fall. There is no wind today so it's hard to imagine.*"

Shortly after lunch was finished, Suzie and Paul left. Carter helped clean up the kitchen and then hung around while Shelly put away the leftovers .

"*Any more chores?*" she asked.

"*Some. I don't think Adam was happy to have Suzie come with us. He didn't object, but seemed a little off. But she rode fine. I know he's in charge, but you own this ranch. Tell him it's okay for me to have friends over.*"

Shelly wasn't sure of Adam's role in this. He wasn't a child-care worker and had probably felt like a babysitter or camp counselor today, in charge of two novice riders. She'd have to clear things with him in the future. It wasn't fair to him otherwise.

But what if he refused? Then what would she do?

"I'll talk to him," was all she promised.

The opportunity didn't come until dinnertime. Shelly heated soup and toasted some bread with cheese. It was as much as she felt like doing. When Carter came to eat, Adam was with him.

"I would have cooked dinner," Adam said, looking at the pan on the stove and the toast squares still beneath the broiler.

"I managed this much, no more."

"Sit, we'll take it from here."

Shelly wasn't going to argue. She was tired and frustrated. She could hardly do anything with her wrist incapacitated. She hadn't realized how much she used her left hand in a day.

"Adam, thanks for watching out for Suzie Simmons. I didn't know they were coming or I would have said something."

Adam had put Carter to work getting the plates and silverware.

"Yeah, Carter explained he'd e-mailed her after meeting her and asked her out here. Forgot about it when you fell. No harm done."

That surprised her. She'd been prepared for a reminder about that not being part of his job.

He caught her eye. "Expecting a different reaction?"

She nodded. Somehow this man never met her expectations.

"It's Carter's home. If he wants friends over, so be it," he said with a shrug.

"He wants her to come again and help out."

"You can use the help," Adam said, setting a bowl of soup in front of her.

Carter followed with the toast.

"How much help would she be?" Shelly asked.

"She could learn—same as you and the kid. Have Carter teach her."

Adam sat down and began to eat.

Shelly stared at him, unable to believe what she'd heard. He'd been so against their staying, not wanting anything to do with either of them. What had changed?

He looked up and caught her staring. She dropped her gaze to the soup. It was steaming slightly. Taking her spoon, she began to eat.

"I checked with Jason at the feed store," Adam said. "There were one or two inquiries about your ad today."

"Really? I thought he was going to let me know if someone showed interest in the job."

"If it gets that far. I told him to push a bit. One of the men is going to call you, I think. Sooner he's on, the sooner I can leave."

Shelly didn't want Adam to go. But he'd been up-front all along about wanting to leave. She'd secretly hoped working with her and Carter would have shown him the advantage of staying.

"I wish you'd remain until the place sells. The new owners may even want to keep you on," she said. "It's not as if you have another job waiting. What will you do until you find one?"

"Might head back to Texas. The winters are better there."

Adam continued eating. Two weeks ago he'd been alone on the ranch missing Mitch and wondering if he should be looking for work. Now he was looking out for a woman, teaching teenagers about cattle and still working until he fell asleep from exhaustion.

The nightmares hadn't been so prevalent lately. He must be doing something right.

It wasn't that Carter was much trouble. The kid was eager to learn everything, Adam could hardly keep up. And he had to admit, Shelly had pulled her share without complaint.

He'd even handled the crisis of her fall, though the flashbacks and memories of other people injured in a rocky place kept crowding his mind. Still, he felt a quiet sense of accomplishment that he'd been able to do what was needed and get her help.

Mitch had said the memories would fade enough to enable him to live a normal life. Adam hadn't believed it at the time, but maybe. At least for this crisis he had reacted appropriately. Maybe he would again if put to the test.

The phone rang. Shelly rose and went to answer it.

"Miz Palmer, this is Pete Trannor. I saw your ad at the feed store for a cowhand. I'm hunting work."

"Could you come out in the morning? I could interview you then," she said. Turning slightly, she saw both Carter and Adam watching her. If this cowboy worked out, would Adam really leave? She didn't like that idea at all.

"Sure thing. Be there around nine."

"Do you know how to find the ranch?" she asked.

"Got directions from Jason. Be seeing you."

After hanging up the phone, Shelly went back to the table. Signing and talking, she informed the two men of the conversation.

"Do you know the man?" she asked Adam.

He shook his head. "Never heard of him. But if he's new to the area, I wouldn't have."

He scraped back his chair and rose, carrying his soup bowl to the stove and replenishing it.

"Do you want to interview him, too?" she asked as he resumed his seat.

"Why?"

"You're much more knowledgeable about the workings of this ranch than I am. You'd know the questions to ask and be able to judge if he's really any good or not."

Adam took another spoonful of soup.

"Guess I could."

"He'll be here around nine."

He nodded.

"That gives me time to look at that mower in the morning. As soon as the ground dries enough, I want to get that hay cut. The forecast is for dry weather the next few days. Sooner we get it cut, sooner we can get it dried, baled and stored."

"Maybe this Pete Trannor will work out and be able to help, too."

"Mitch usually hired extra summer help by this time. Haying's hard work. Once we get it cut, then baled, we have to bring it in from the field to store in the back part of the barn to keep it dry. Sell the extra bales."

Shelly took a moment to sign the conversation to Carter. He nodded, his eyes alight with the thought of new challenges. She was happy at the possibility of another influx of cash. The clinic charges hadn't been cheap.

Adam left right after he and Carter cleaned up. Carter went into the office to use the computer and Shelly walked out onto the porch. She still didn't feel back to normal, but it was too early to go to bed.

Hesitating only a moment, she started walking over to the bunkhouse. She wanted company after being alone all day.

She heard the clang of metal on metal coming from behind the barn. Changing direction, Shelly followed the sound and soon found Adam deep in the works of an engine that had to be the mower. The large machine showed patches of rust and scraped paint. It was old, but if it worked, so what?

Adam swore and hit the metal again. Shelly stifled a giggle. This was not a happy man.

"Trouble?" she asked.

He lifted his head to look at her.

"You might say. This engine is a piece of junk."

She came closer and peered inside. The only thing she recognized was the grimy dirt clinging to every part.

"No wonder it won't work, it's filthy."

"Gets that way. Can you manage to climb up into the driver's seat and try to start it?"

She eyed the mower dubiously. Stepping gingerly, wishing she had use of her left arm, she soon sat on the hard driver's seat. She was up high. Glancing around, she wondered what it would be like to drive the mower.

"See the button to the right of the shaft?" Adam called. "Push it and hold for about three seconds."

She complied. There was a grinding sound.

"Okay, stop!"

Shelly waited a moment, but when he didn't speak again, she got down and went to stand beside him. Several tools were spread on the ground, a couple balanced on the edge of the engine. She peered over his arm. He seemed to know what he was doing, but she was totally baffled. How could any one person learn enough to run a ranch?

There wasn't a service station nearby, so Adam had to do the work. She couldn't even imagine a tow truck large enough for this piece of equipment.

"What happens if we don't cut the hay?" she asked.

"It'll go to waste. We need hay in the winter to keep the cattle alive."

"Maybe I'll sell the herd, then we wouldn't need it."

"You could sell the hay if you sell the herd," he said, still working on some connection in the engine. Finally he gave another shove to the tool he was using and the bolt moved. In only moments he held the part in his hand.

"Needs cleaning. Let's hope it works when that's done." He turned around and walked into the barn.

Shelly walked beside him.

"How do you know how to do that?" she asked.

"Learned engines as a kid—on cars, but this is similar."

Going to one of the storage shelves in the barn, he pulled out a glass jug marked Kerosene. Pouring some in an old coffee can, he dropped the part in. "By morning we'll know if that'll work or not," he said.

She watched as he wiped his hands on a grimy towel.

"What made you decide to become a cowboy?" she asked.

16

"I wanted a change from the city. After I got out of the Army, I headed west. No particular destination in mind. Then saw an ad for a cowboy at a ranch in Texas. I applied. The man who hired me thought I'd last a day. I stayed nine months, then found something better. Learned all I could at every job."

"When did you come here?"

"Over two years ago. I was still green. Mitch taught me a lot."

He placed the towel back on the hook and looked at his hands. They weren't much cleaner.

"I need to go wash up."

"I want to hear more," Shelly said.

"About what?" he asked, turning to look at her.

"About you, learning to be a cowboy, the army. My father was career Army. I have to say I'm not any where close to being as gung ho as he was."

Adam nodded. "I was never gung ho Army."

"Why did you join?"

"To get out."

"Out of what?"

"Brooklyn. The neighborhood I grew up in wasn't the

best in the world. We saw the army as our ticket to better things."

"We?"

His expression closed. "A friend."

"Where is he now?"

"Dead."

Adam turned and walked away.

Shelly stared after him. She hadn't known. Apparently they'd been close. Had it been a woman? Most likely a buddy.

She didn't think she imagined the bleak look in his eyes. Sighing softly, she wandered back to the corral and leaned against the fence, gazing at the horses. One ambled over and put its head on the top rail. She rubbed its nose gently.

"I was looking for company," she said to the horse. "Were you as well?"

After a moment, curiosity satisfied, the big animal moved away.

"Guess not. Or at least not with me."

She watched them a bit longer. The sun had set; twilight grew darker.

She turned and went back to the house.

Getting some water in preparation to go up to her room, Shelly was still by the sink when Carter came in. He immediately saw her and began signing.

"*Wayne's summer plans changed. His mother is pregnant and sick all the time, so they are not going to Hawaii. Can he come here? He wants to come. I told him how much I'm doing and he wants to help out. Adam said we'd have lots of work including cutting hay. Wayne could help. If Suzie comes out, that's one more who can help. And you won't be able to, so they could do your work.*"

Shelly's initial reaction was to refuse. But she asked him about Wayne before turning him down. And the more Carter told her about his friend, the more she began to wonder if he could come to visit—and actually be of help. She was going to be almost useless for the next few weeks while her wrist healed. If they hired Pete Trannor, that would ease some of the burden for Adam.

But having teenagers around—would that help or hinder?

Yet kids had been working ranches over the summer for years. It would be good for the boys and they could help move the bales of hay if nothing else. Adam had said that Mitch had hired college kids. Wayne and Carter were only a few years short of college.

"*Let me think about it. And talk to his parents. And discuss with Adam.*"

They might be horrified at the thought of their son going to Wyoming and working on a ranch. She wasn't sure she'd let Carter go off with people she didn't know.

Would Adam see the visitor as more work or a help?

Or would he even be around if Pete hired on?

Shelly sat on the front porch the next morning when the dusty pickup came down the drive. She watched as an older man of about fifty climbed out and glanced around. In a moment he turned toward the house.

Adam appeared in the large opening to the barn, then also headed for the house.

Shelly rose to greet Pete when he reached the porch. Once introductions were made, she invited both men into the office.

She knew nothing about hiring a ranch employee, but the man looked the role, the hat well worn, yet clean. Boots, of course, but polished to a shine. The jeans and shirt looked new.

"I asked Adam to join us," she explained when they all sat in the office. "I know very little about ranching. And I'll be up-front with you. This place is for sale. I can't guarantee any length of employment."

Pete nodded, looked square at Adam.

"Been working for a lot of years. Know most of what needs to be known," he said.

Adam nodded. "Tell us where you worked."

The interview had started. It was almost two hours later by the time Adam glanced at Shelly and gave a small nod.

She smiled. She liked everything Pete had said but left the final decision to Adam. She was glad he approved.

"Want to look around the place?" Shelly asked. She'd love for him to join them, but was cautious enough to be sure to call and verify all references before making an offer.

"I would," the man said.

Adam rose. "I'll show him around."

"Thank you. It was nice meeting you, Pete. I'll call these references while you two look over the ranch."

As she had hoped, all references were sincere and glowing. One rancher said he kept hoping Pete would come back. When asked why he left to begin with, the man said he had only a limited number of year-round positions and those were filled with family men who had been with him for years. But if one of them left, he'd want Pete to take over.

She then called Nathan to let him know what she was doing and to get a range of salary to offer.

"If Adam will stay, I'm making him manager," she said.

"Hmmm," the lawyer said. "He knows the place. Doesn't have that much experience, however."

"He knows more than I do."

"Your choice, Shelly. There's money enough for the time being."

"We're cutting hay soon. If there's extra, maybe we can sell some of that."

"Every bit helps. Come fall you'll have a lot of cattle to sell, that's your primary source of income."

Shelly went outside to offer Pete the job. She didn't see the men. When she entered the barn, it was empty. Checking the corral, she noted all the horses were gone. Obviously when he said he'd show Pete the ranch, Adam had meant the entire spread. Carter must have gone with them.

It was late afternoon when the three men returned. Carter was becoming very proficient at riding, Shelly thought, spying them from the window.

She wrapped up the work she was doing on the computer and checked on the roast she had in the oven before going outside. Waiting on the porch, she watched as they all came from the barn. It was like seeing three generations of a family. Pete was older, yet carried himself like a fit younger man. Adam was in his prime, walking with that special cowboy gait. Carter was the youngest, but he was already beginning to resemble the others in the way he wore his hat and carried himself.

"Nice place you have here," Pete said when they drew closer.

"Thank you." Shelly smiled at him. "Want to work with us?"

"Be pleased to."

"Then you're hired. When can you start?"

She told him how much she could afford and that the job came with room and board.

"I'll need to pick up my horse where I've been boarding it. I could get back here late tomorrow."

"He can bring his own mount, which helps you out," Adam said. "You'll need to buy another one or two before fall if you're still working cattle."

She looked at him. "I'd like to speak to you about that if you have a moment."

He nodded warily.

"Pete, can you stay for dinner? It'll be ready at six."

"Be pleased to. Maybe Carter can show me the bunkhouse while you and Adam talk."

A moment later Shelly faced Adam. He didn't look precisely welcoming, but she was determined to get this over with.

"What?" he growled.

"I want to offer you the position of manager of the Triple L Ranch," she said formally.

Adam stared at her. He was leaving. He'd told her that enough times. What part of it didn't she get?

"Before you say no, think about it. From all the people I talked to today, Pete is a good worker. Carter is learning fast, you said so yourself. We'll be here through the summer unless the ranch sells first. You don't have to leave. I know you don't like being around me and I'll try to stay out of your way. But the ranch really needs you."

"I don't dislike you," he said.

What was he doing, discussing the situation? He needed to get packing, figure out where to head to next. Get away from Shelly, her brother and the memories of Mitch. He wasn't considering her offer.

"Please, just think about it for a few days. You'd be totally in charge. You could make changes if you think they are warranted. Hire as much help as the money allows. I'm coming to the realization this place isn't going to sell fast. I need someone I trust to run it properly. Someone who cares about the ranch as much as Uncle Mitch did."

"It's your ranch, you run it," he said.

"I don't know enough."

"Neither do I."

He watched her indecision.

"You know more than I do. And I think you're the type to search for answers to what you don't know. Anyway, that's my offer."

"I'm not your man, Shelly. Until four years ago, the only time I'd been on a horse was when I was sent to inner-city camp programs."

"I expect my uncle was teaching you every single day."

Adam lifted his gaze to the land. The rolling hills touched his soul. Taking a breath, he could smell the grasses and cattle. He was a city transplant who had thrust down deep roots. No matter where he worked, he'd want it to be outside. He liked this part of the country. And she was right. He had picked up a great deal of knowledge from Mitch. They'd never ridden out without the older man regaling him with stories that imparted wisdom and knowledge.

But to even consider staying would mean he was getting

involved. How much more would the place come to mean to him if he actually managed it?

He didn't want ties.

He started to refuse. But something kept him quiet. It wouldn't hurt to think about it for at least a day.

"I'll let you know," he said.

Shelly nodded and went inside to check on her roast. The meal was ready to dish up a short time later when the men filed into the kitchen.

"Do you need some help?" Pete asked, as he watched Shelly try to serve the plates one handed.

"I guess I do," she said.

Everyone served himself and Carter heaped food on a plate for his sister.

"I can't eat all that," she signed.

"You have to get your strength back, that's what Adam says."

She glanced at the man already standing by the table. Was Carter going to start spouting words of wisdom from Adam? He couldn't choose a much better man, she mused, thinking of their father and Thomas. Carter hadn't had stellar role models in his life until now.

Once seated, Shelly asked Pete about the last place he'd worked. He proved to be entertaining as he described the other men on the ranch, and some of the cantankerous horses.

Shelly signed as Pete talked so Carter could enjoy the stories as well.

After a few moments, Adam reached over and caught her uninjured hand. "Eat, before your food gets cold. We won't talk until you can translate again."

"Oh, sorry, I didn't even think," Pete said.

Shelly could hardly think herself. She wanted to wrap her fingers around Adam's hand and hold on. His touch was warm. His hand, rough from the work he did, offered security. He squeezed hers slightly and let go.

Carter watched intently. *"What did he say?"* he signed.

"To stop talking and eat."

He grinned and nodded.

The next few moments were silent as they continued the meal.

Shelly was touched that Adam had thought enough about both her and her brother to stop talking so she had a chance to eat and Carter wouldn't be left out. Their own father had never done that.

How hard had life been for her brother? she wondered. She'd left home only a couple of years after her mother died. She'd never really considered how difficult it must have been for Carter.

17

Pete left after dinner with a promise to return the next day as soon as he got his horse.

Adam headed off—probably to work on the numerous chores that never seemed to end, Shelly thought. Carter did the dishes. She was left with little to do.

She wanted to wash her hair. The scrape on her head was starting to itch, a good sign of healing, but it was driving her crazy. There had to be something she could do to get relief.

She went up to the bathroom, eyeing the old-fashioned tub. No handheld shower device. So unless she wanted to risk soaking everything, she couldn't really use it. And how would she wash her hair one-handed?

She'd ask Carter. Maybe they could use the kitchen sink.

When she returned to the kitchen, it was empty. She checked in the office, but he wasn't there. Had he gone out to the barn? Feeling grumpy, Shelly headed outside.

Carter had already saddled his horse. Adam was nearby.

"Where is he going?" she asked. "I don't want him riding off alone. He could fall or something like I did."

"Relax, he's just going in the field behind the barn with Hank to practice. We brought a couple of steers down with us this afternoon. He'll be fine. We'll be right here."

Shelly watched as Carter checked the cinch, then swung up on the horse's back as if he'd been doing it for years. She smiled. He really was having the best summer of his life, she thought.

"You want something?" Adam asked.

"I was going to ask him to help me wash my hair. I don't want to get the stitches wet, but I really want clean hair."

The minutes ticked by. Then Adam said, "I could help."

She looked at him, feeling an unexpected warmth wash through her. For an instant she pictured this large cowboy with his hands in her hair, lathering it up, running his fingers through when rinsing to get the shampoo out. She'd never had anyone wash her hair except salon workers. Could he really do that?

She was desperate.

"You're on," she said.

Adam could wash her hair right now. She'd have to wait another few hours for Carter.

Shelly led the way inside, going upstairs to get towels and her shampoo. When she returned to the kitchen, Adam had started the water and gotten it warm. He'd also taken off his hat. He must have run his fingers through his hair a few times because it stuck up in a couple of places. She squelched the urge to smooth it down. They were here to wash her hair, not his.

"I can't get the stitches wet," she said.

"I know."

Nervous, she set the shampoo on the counter and looked at him.

"So how do we do this?"

"I thought you could kneel on one of the chairs and hold a towel against the stitches to block any water. Then I'll use the sprayer device in the sink to wet your hair, lather it up and rinse."

"Sounds like a plan."

He brought over one of the chairs and soon Shelly was leaning over the sink, a towel pressed against her forehead to keep it dry.

The warm water felt heavenly. In only seconds she could feel his fingers massaging her scalp as he worked in the shampoo. She closed her eyes, resting her arms on the edge of the sink, and gave herself up to the blissful experience.

Surprisingly, Adam seemed to know exactly what to do to keep the water from her scrape. He carefully rinsed her hair, and lathered again. This time he seemed to thread the strands through his fingers as if giving each one special attention. She could become addicted to having her hair washed this way, she thought.

The warm water of the final rinse had hardly stopped when he wrapped her head in one of the towels she'd brought.

"Face still dry?" he asked.

She nodded, scooting off the chair and standing up. She wrapped the towel more securely.

"Thank you. With only having the use of one hand, I couldn't do it myself."

"I'll comb it out for you," he offered. "Where's your comb?"

She hadn't thought that far ahead.

"Upstairs, I'll go get it."

"I'll wait on the porch. The warm air will dry it fast."

A few minutes later, Shelly sat on a bench while Adam stood behind her, gently working through her tangled hair with a light touch.

"You've had experience," she murmured.

It was pleasant on the porch. She couldn't see Carter, but she could hear the thumping of the horse as it ran, stopped and resumed. Hank barked once or twice. What she could see were the vibrant colors in the sky as sunset approached. The mountains in the distance were mere smudges.

"I used to brush my grandmother's hair," he explained "She has arthritis and it's difficult for her."

"Where does she live?"

"Back in Brooklyn."

Shelly couldn't picture this tough cowboy as the kind of boy to patiently brush his grandmother's hair.

"She must have enjoyed that. Who brushes her hair now?"

The silence was momentary, but Shelly suspected she'd hit a sore spot.

"No one, I guess. She must do it herself."

"Maybe your family rallies around," she said.

"There's only the two of us left."

"Are you close?"

"I haven't seen her in more than four years," Adam said.

The steady movements of the comb were hypnotic. Shelly closed her eyes, enjoying the sensuous moment. And fascinated by the bits Adam had revealed of his life.

"Invite her to visit," she suggested.

"I have. She thinks anything beyond New Jersey is the wilds of the old west. She won't come."

"And you don't want to go there to visit her?" she asked.

"Not yet," he said. "Maybe one day."

He reached over her shoulder and handed her the comb.

"Your hair is tangle free."

Shelly knew he was going to leave. She didn't want him to.

"Stay a little longer," she said. "I could get us some iced tea or coffee."

"I don't need anything," he said.

He pulled one of the chairs from against the wall and sat in it. Rocking back on the rear legs, he adjusted his hat low on his face and gazed out over the ranch.

"It's so peaceful here," she said, almost afraid to say anything that would break the shared intimacy.

He nodded.

"Did you and your friend Brian want to be cowboys?"

He slanted her a glance. For a moment Shelly didn't think he'd answer.

"It never came up. We thought we'd do our stint in the army, go to college and become millionaires."

"Only he didn't make it out," she said softly. "Were you there when he died?"

Adam nodded. She could see the muscles in his cheeks tighten.

"That must have been devastating."

Adam rose.

"All war is hell. Brian was just one in a long list of dead. He never had a chance."

He crossed the porch and stepped off.

Shelly surged to her feet.

"Don't go. I won't ask any more questions if you don't want."

He turned slightly.

"I don't talk about the war."

"Maybe you should—get it out…lose some of its horror."

"That'll never happen. War is all about horror."

"My father used to talk to my mother about the places he'd been. She was a good listener. I remember him saying once that he didn't know what he'd do if he had to keep everything bottled up inside."

"So are you some pop psychologist?"

"No, just someone who could listen."

"I'll remember that if I ever want to talk."

"You do that. I'm going to have some ice cream. Do you want some or would you rather walk off in a snit?"

"I'm not in a snit. I choose not to discuss the past with anyone."

"Ice cream or not?"

Adam turned and walked back until he stood right in front of her.

"What kind?"

He was deliberately crowding her space. She took a step back. He took a step forward. When she bumped against the door, she couldn't retreat any farther. He was hardly a hand's width away. If he was trying to intimidate her, he wasn't succeeding.

The feelings he was causing had nothing to do with fear.

"Chocolate, Rocky Road or Butter Pecan?"

"Rocky Road's my favorite, Butter Pecan was Mitch's. He kept a supply all summer long."

"So some of this could be months old. Does ice cream ever go bad?"

She didn't dare take a deep breath, afraid she'd brush up against Adam. From the dancing lights in his eyes, he knew he was making her uncomfortable and was amused by her reaction.

Maybe she should turn the tables.

She put her good hand on his chest and pushed. The resistance beneath her palm surprised her. He stepped back easily enough, then caught her hand. For a moment they stared at each other. As his head lowered, Shelly drew a breath, taking in the scent of the man, feeling the warmth of his skin as he brushed his lips over hers.

18

Adam didn't want to let go. Shelly was warm and sweet. Her mouth moved against his and long-dormant desire spiked. He tightened his embrace, imprinting the feel of her against his body, soft where he was hard. He'd been too long without female companionship. But it hadn't bothered him before.

Now, with this sweet woman in his arms, it did. He wanted more than some sweet kisses. Much more.

Her brother was in the field and could ride into view any second. It was broad daylight. But none of that mattered. Just a few more moments of pleasure, her arms tightly around him, her mouth driving him wild. Her scent imprinted on his soul forever.

A sound from the barn penetrated and Adam slowly ended the kiss. He didn't want Carter coming out and seeing them. Who knew what conclusion the teenager would jump to.

He eased back, his arms still around her. Shelly withdrew almost as carefully. When he let his arms drop, he felt empty.

She stared at him, her eyes wide with questions. He wished he had some answers.

"Probably a dumb idea," he mumbled.

He needed to get away. Return to the bunkhouse and make plans to leave. With Pete starting, Shelly wouldn't be left in the lurch. She'd be able to get another capable hand before long.

"Probably."

Her hand rested on his chest, her fingers moving slightly, sparking excitement in every cell of his body. He caught her hand, brought the palm to his mouth. Kissing her, he watched the emotions flare in her eyes. She wanted him as much as he wanted her.

"I'm heading off now," he said.

It was safer. Staying around Shelly would prove too hard to resist.

For a moment he saw disappointment in her gaze.

"Stay for ice cream. That's all. Carter will be in soon. He'll want some, too."

He kissed her hand again.

"Just ice cream, then."

She nodded. Pulling her hand free, she turned and scooped up her comb, which had fallen.

"Want me to bring it out here?"

"That might be best."

He needed to back off. Shelly was not the kind of woman to want a casual affair. And he wasn't going to get involved with anything long-term.

He leaned against the railing. Things were changing too fast. The reason he was here hadn't altered. He'd let Brian down. He'd fled the memories he hated. Becoming attached to the Palmers was as stupid as trying to hold on to Brian.

"Rocky Road," she said, coming out with two bowls of ice cream. She'd chosen Butter Pecan.

"Thanks." He sat on one of the chairs and began to eat Glancing at Shelly, he saw she was watching him.

"I really want you to consider the manager's job," she said He took another bite of ice cream.

"Told you I'd think about it."

She took a deep breath. He could still feel the imprint o her against his chest. He looked away. For the first time in a long time, however, he didn't relish the thought of the privacy of his room. He wanted to stay—a little longer anyway.

What was the proper protocol? Did he apologize fo kissing her? Make some comment about how fantastic it hac been? Or ignore it as if nothing had happened?

It didn't make a lot of sense. His life the last four years had been solitary. He liked it that way. No ties, nc complications, no risking any connections because he knew firsthand how fast a friend could die.

As soon as he was finished, he'd check on the boy anc then turn in.

She ate tiny scoops of ice cream, making a sound of pure bliss as she slowly savored each spoonful.

Scowling, he looked away and concentrated on mentally listing the tasks ahead.

"I'm not getting involved with anyone," Adam said.

Might as well make that perfectly clear. Even though she'c said she was going back to San Francisco, and he talked abou moving on, he wanted no misunderstandings. No clinging, nc crying goodbyes.

Shelly looked at him.

"A kiss isn't a lifelong commitment. Even a marriage isn' a lifelong commitment these days. I'm not too high on men right now. I learned that lesson the hard way. I'm happily single again, as the saying goes, and plan to stay that way."

That surprised him. "You don't want to get married?"

She shook her head.

"What happened?"

"He fled the country about two steps ahead of the law and a boatload of angry clients. Seems he felt he could enjoy life better in the islands somewhere—using other people's money."

Suddenly she laughed.

"Oh, the irony just struck. If he'd stayed honest a couple of years longer, we'd still be married. And could expect six million dollars from the sale of the ranch. Oh, how I wish I knew how to contact him to tell him!"

"You don't know where he is?"

"I do not. But even if I did, the law gets first dibs. One day we were visiting with friends, the next he was gone. Two days later the cops descended."

Adam wasn't sure what to say.

"He hasn't been caught?"

"There are some places in the Caribbean where they don't honor U.S. extradition. Guess he found one of them. All I know is he left me holding the bag. It took months to get squared with the law, for them to believe I had no idea of what he'd been doing or planning. If I ever get my hands on the man, he'll rue the day he left me with his mess."

"Tough break."

"Shows me I can't trust my judgment in people. I tried going into business for myself—doing events planning. I can throw a mean party."

Adam asked, "What happened?"

She shook her head. "I didn't have any money after Thomas took off. And not a lot of experience in anything but throwing parties. I might have done all right if my second client hadn't bilked me and then bad-mouthed the services I provided."

"Bilked you how?"

He was growing fascinated by her story.

"I threw this lovely pool-side party for fifty at the woman's estate in Woodside. Elegant hors d'oeuvres, wonderful wine, all the trimmings. Everyone said it was a great success. When I tried to collect, however, she said it wasn't up to her standards and she refused to pay for anything. She even began spreading the word that my services were poor and not worth the time or money. Who knew if I might steal something from clients like my husband had? Just thinking about that makes me want to scream."

"But there must have been a contract or something binding that protected you," Adam said.

Shelly shook her head slowly. "I wasn't smart enough then to have a contract. I couldn't pay all the vendors as promised. It took me six months to get them paid off. In the meantime, no one would extend me more credit when I couldn't pay on past orders. So goes a budding career."

"So what did you do?"

"Waited tables."

"A waitress?"

"I'm pretty good at it and the tips are fantastic. I'm not qualified to do much else and jobs are at a premium in the Bay Area. I want to stay there because of Carter."

"What about your parents?"

She took a deep breath.

"My father died just before Thomas took off. His Will had been made after my marriage and he thought I was set for life. He left almost everything to his wife."

"Not your mother."

"My mother died when I was sixteen."

Adam thought over what she'd said. "What about Carter?"

"What about him?"

"Didn't your father leave him provided for?"

"A small stipend only—to supplement his schooling at the California School for the Deaf. It's a state-run school that costs nothing for Carter to attend."

"Why not an equal share with his wife?"

She shrugged.

"There had to be a reason."

"I guess."

"And it is?"

"Stop pushing. It's none of your business."

"Most of what you told me wasn't my business. You wanted to let me know. So what's the hang-up with Carter?"

"My father wasn't Carter's real father," she blurted out.

That did startle Adam. "Who was?"

"I don't know. I found out when my mother died. I don't think Carter knows. He just thinks our father was a cold, unfeeling military man. Being at the school for the deaf helped since he was away from home most of the year."

"But your father took care of him on vacations?"

"Mostly. I don't think he wanted his fellow officers

knowing. That's why it's so important I sell the ranch and get some money. I'll be the only one responsible for him until he's old enough to earn his own living. And you know that won't be as easy as for some kids."

"I don't know about that. He's a good worker. Learns fast. Once he settles on something, he'll excel."

"He thinks he wants to be a cowboy," she murmured.

"And that would be a problem because why?" Adam asked.

She looked at him. "I always thought of him working with computers or something, making lots of money."

"Maybe money isn't as important to him as it is to you," Adam suggested.

She flared up at that.

"Money is important to everyone. Do you know how hard it is to earn a living if you're not skilled or have some kind of special education? I want him to have choices."

"He has choices. Just because he's only sixteen doesn't mean he isn't starting to become a man. He'll have to try things to know what he wants. So far he takes to this work like he was born to it. He's always asking questions. But never the same one twice. Give him some slack, Shelly. He could make a good rancher."

"What did you want to do when you were sixteen, become a cowboy?" she asked.

"No, at sixteen, I was car crazy. There was a man at a garage who gave me a job—taught me all about engines. Back then I thought I'd open a service garage myself maybe or work for him all my life."

"Now you work cattle, a far cry from cars."

"Life has a way of changing plans. I'm not saying ranching is the right thing for your brother. But I do think it's his decision, not yours."

"I guess. I just—I don't know, I thought we'd both get jobs in some city and see each other more often than we do when he's at school. I know he's ten years younger, but he's all the family I have. He'll feel differently when we sell this place. Then he'll be able to do anything he wants."

Adam didn't argue the point. If in fact Carter wanted to be a cowboy, having several million dollars behind him wouldn't hurt.

He rose. "I'll take the bowls inside," he offered.

Time enough to move on. Hearing Shelly's past made him yearn for things that couldn't be. They were scarcely friends. Would never be more. He had too much baggage to get involved with someone. And she had different dreams than he did. A few more weeks together—if he stayed around—and they'd go their separate ways.

Shelly watched Adam walk to the barn a few minutes later. She wished he'd stayed longer. That he'd told her more about his past than the fact he'd liked cars at sixteen. Still, it was the longest conversation they'd had, so maybe it was a good sign.

"For what?" she asked herself.

His kiss had been wonderful. For the first time in a long time she'd felt desired and cherished. Not that she was interested in any kind of long-term relationship. Her trust in others was shaky. She and Thomas had been married nearly six years. And he'd totally fooled her.

Adam was not interested in her in that way either. It was just chemistry or something.

Feeling deflated, she stood up. She was tired, her head ached and her wrist throbbed. Time for bed.

She had enough on her plate without worrying about a cowboy she'd only met a couple of weeks before. Knowing she was being impatient didn't stop her from wanting faster action on the sale of the ranch. She was worried Carter would totally learn to love the lifestyle he saw here and not want to return to California. Where would that leave her?

19

At breakfast the next morning, Carter asked again if his
friend Wayne could come for a few weeks.

"*I'm not up to it*," Shelly said, holding up the cast.

"*We'd be a help—we can cook. And there's lots more to do around
here with haying starting*," he countered. "*I bet Adam would like the
extra help.*"

"*Has Wayne ever cut hay or baling?*"

"*No, but he could learn as fast as I will. And Suzie said she'd come
out and help. She could even stay here a few days, save her parents
bringing her out and back.*" Carter's expression pleaded.

"*I'll ask Adam. He might not want teenagers around.*"

"*This is your place. Just tell him.*"

"*That's not how things work. I asked him to be manager. It could
take years to sell the ranch. I need someone who knows how to run a
ranch to be in charge. If he is in charge, he gets veto vote to visitors.*"

Carter frowned at that, but didn't argue. "*Ask today, okay?*"

Shelly didn't respond immediately. She didn't know if
Adam would accept the position. Asking him to put up with a
couple of other teenagers didn't seem like a good way to tip
the scales in her favor.

Yet, if Carter wanted his friends here, what would it hurt?
She liked Suzie. She was sure she'd like Wayne.

"I'll ask. Get me Wayne's parents' phone number. I'll need to discuss things with them as well."

He jumped up and ran from the room, not wasting a second.

Shelly hoped Adam would say yes—both to staying and to having visitors.

When Shelly went out to the barn in the early afternoon, it was deserted. Two of the horses were gone. Adam and Carter had left her behind. Not that she felt up to riding. Bonny Boy came to the corral fence and put his head over.

She rubbed his nose.

"I know you didn't mean to toss me, but I'm not up to riding again for a while. One day, I promise."

He blew on her hand and then ambled away.

When she walked into the cool barn, she saw a piece of paper near the door. Adam had written a note to Carter, telling him of the chores that needed to be done, and then asking Carter to bring his horse to the hay field. Adam had taken the mower out to see if it'd work.

Shelly smiled, knowing Carter would have followed every instruction to the letter. A couple of weeks ago he'd never been on a horse. Now he could ride, was working with a cattle dog and was helpful enough to go out to meet up with Adam. She could see a growing confidence in her brother since he'd been on the ranch.

Maybe being a cowboy wouldn't be the worst thing Carter could do. It sure suited Adam.

She wondered what he'd been like as a boy. Car crazy at one point. Weren't most teenage boys? What would he have done if he hadn't been sent to a war zone? He'd been a medic, maybe he'd have studied to be a doctor.

Hearing a truck, she went outside to see Pete arriving pulling a horse trailer. She wished she'd had Adam's answer before the man arrived. She'd like to start off with Pete reporting to Adam. Oh well, for sure life didn't always go the way she wanted.

Pete quickly unloaded his own horse, put away his things in the bunkhouse and spoke briefly with Shelly. He got general directions from her, saddled up and rode out to find Adam and get started.

Shelly went to the office. The last couple of days had given her time to figure out the programs her uncle had used. Now if she only knew what things meant. Was it good to have the number of head of cattle she had or should she decrease the herd? Or increase it? Was she going to be able to sell some of the hay for a quick source of income, or have to find some other way to stretch money until the fall sales?

She called Wayne's parents and reached his mother. Explaining who she was and why she was calling, she was surprised at the easy compliance in Mrs. Bronson's attitude.

"Wayne is so disappointed we're not going to Hawaii. When his friend invited him to a working ranch, we thought that was wonderful. He and Carter have been friends for several years, you know."

Shelly murmured an appropriate response. She didn't know Carter's friends. First she'd been too tied up with Thomas to visit his school often. Then too tired from working long hours making a living.

"Would he be able to fly there? I know Carter said you drove out, but that would be really difficult for us," Wayne's mother continued.

Shelly hadn't even thought about that. Where was the nearest airport?

"We'd have to check, but I think he could fly into Casper. We could pick him up there and bring him to the ranch."

Good grief, it would take a day to get to Casper and back. And she thought Wildcat Creek was far.

"He doesn't know much about horses or cattle, but Carter said he could learn. We've all read Carter's e-mails, he sounds like he's having a wonderful experience. What a special summer it would be for Wayne. He needs something like that about now. I'm pregnant and it's changing everything."

"I still need to make sure my manager is okay with the idea. He'd be the primary teacher for the boys," Shelly cautioned.

She knew both boys would be thrilled. She didn't think Adam would be, however. But somehow she had to make him see it was a good thing.

After promising to call later to confirm dates and all, Shelly hung up.

No sooner had she replaced the phone than it rang again.

"Hello?"

"Shelly? Sam Hardman here. Calling to see how Hank's doing."

"Just fine. Carter's working with him and the two of them seem well suited. He responds to hand signals now."

"I didn't know at first the boy was deaf. He's working out well, according to Adam. A good worker. Looks a lot like your mother."

"He does. More than I do."

"She was a wonderful woman."

"I miss her a lot."

"The thing is, I have some pictures from that summer you two stayed with Mitch. Thought maybe someday you'd want to see them."

"I'd love to. Why not come to dinner here one evening. Even though it was before Carter was born, I'm sure he'd love to see pictures of our mother."

Shelly had a startling thought. Carter had been born the spring after their visit to Uncle Mitch. If Sam had photos, he must have seen her mother often. Maybe he knew if she'd been partial to someone that summer. Maybe her mother had fallen for some cowboy.

Or even Sam himself!

She swallowed. Was she actually talking to Carter's father?

They arranged for an evening a couple of weeks later and Sam hung up. Shelly stared at the phone. If Sam was Carter's father, would he storm in and demand custody?

Maybe she should call back and cancel.

Or maybe, a small voice said, you could see what he has to say.

As soon as dinner was over that evening, Shelly asked Adam if she could talk to him in the office. Carter smiled as he watched them leave, his excitement obvious. She hoped Adam would agree to working with Wayne–if he came to stay for a few weeks.

Once in the office, Shelly shut the door. Nervous, she went to sit behind the desk, then wondered if that had been the best tactic.

He stood near the window, watching her.

"I know you may not have thought fully about my offer,' she began.

"I thought about it. I'll stay."

She blinked. She felt certain she'd have to argue the point offer more money, or accept defeat.

"Oh, good. Thank you."

"I probably won't be doing things much different from your uncle Mitch," he added.

"Sounds fine to me. I'll rely on you." She cleared her throat. "There is one other little thing."

Adam said nothing. She could have used an encouraging nod or something.

"Carter would like to invite a friend over."

"Suzie?" he asked.

"Well, yes, Suzie, too. She's dying to come ride some more."

"Suzie, too? Who else?"

"There's this friend of Carter's from school, Wayne Bronson. Actually, Carter thought he could come and help out around the ranch. You'll need men to load the hay on the wagon and bring it to the barn. They'll need some training, but they're both young and strong and anxious to help."

Adam narrowed his eyes. "You're asking me to take on another deaf kid? Teach him and Carter about ranching? Make that three if you're including Paul Simmons's daughter."

It did sound a bit daunting when he put it like that.

"The only difference between those kids and any other kids is the way in which they communicate—visually rather than aurally. They're young, intelligent and excited about the chance to spend the summer working on an actual ranch. Carter has been some help, hasn't he?"

"Sure, but he learns fast. Plus this is his family's ranch. He wants it to succeed. But it's a dangerous business. What if one of those kids falls from a horse like you did, only with more severe results. Then what?"

"What if they don't? What if they do exactly as they are instructed and blossom from a summer of work in the sunshine and fresh air. They'll learn new things, like riding and cattle and...and hay!"

Adam's lips twitched.

"Yeah, hay is important to learn. I can't do that, Shelly."

"Please, Adam. I promise they won't be trouble. I'll get a release signed by their parents. You won't lead them into any deliberate danger. Everyone understands there are some inherent risks in life. Think what a wonderful summer these kids would have."

Adam stared at her. She was serious. For a moment he flashed back to the kids on the dusty road in Afghanistan. They didn't have a wonderful summer. Heck, some wouldn't have any more summers. Dead by roadside bombs. From their own people. Limbs blown off, eyes staring at nothing.

He swallowed and looked around, grounding himself in the mundane aspects of Mitch's office.

He'd tried to save the children, but too much trauma, too much blood loss had made it impossible. Now she was asking him to be with kids, take them out where danger lurked. Risk their lives when they were safe and whole. He couldn't do it.

"Please," she said softly.

He shook his head. "I can't. They wouldn't be safe."

"Yes, they will be. If you don't want to, can I ask Pete? Please let these kids do this. It will be good for them, really."

He didn't want this. If they came, he'd leave.

Wait. He turned and gazed out the window. He'd just told her he'd stay as manager. Now he was ready to run. Mitch had told him the pain would ease. It hadn't. Adam could still see those women and children. Still hear the wails of the mourners. He could feel the warm sticky blood on his hands, as he tried so hard to save just one.

"Adam?"

He looked at Shelly. What didn't kill you made you stronger.

"All right, if Pete says he'll work with them, then fine. Keep them away from me."

With that he left. He needed to get out into the sunshine, ground himself that he was in Wyoming, not some dusty roadside on the other side of the world where death and destruction was only a mortar shot away.

He walked out to the barn. Pete and Carter were working in the yard with Hank. The dog glanced his way, but his training held and he stayed with Carter.

Adam kept walking.

Shelly scarcely saw the men during the next few days. They rose early to feed the stock and do minor chores, then headed for the hay fields. By the second day she felt well enough to try to ride. Carter saddled Bonny Boy for her. If she brought the horse to the steps leading to the porch, she could use them to give her enough height to swing up with minimum effort and no undue strain on her healing wrist.

Her heart was in her throat when she perched on the horse's back. But a couple of turns around the yard and her confidence returned. She could do this.

The next morning she had Carter saddle her horse before he took off. By late morning she packed lunch for all the men, then headed toward the sound of the mower. The faint hum grew louder as she approached until she wondered how the men could stand it without going deaf!

Carter was unconcerned, but both Pete and Adam wore bright red ear coverings.

Pete stood beside Carter as they watched Adam in the distance make the turn with the mower and rumble back toward them. Adam saw her first. Slowly he brought the machine to a halt near the other two and turned it off.

"Giving trouble again?" Pete called.

Adam shook his head and nodded over to Shelly, who urged Bonny Boy closer now that the loud racket had ceased.

They were appreciative of the lunch and especially the cold beverages.

"Next time, bring a barrel of cold water," Carter signed. *"This is the hottest it's been. Adam says it's one of the worst jobs a cowboy has to do but it needs to get done."*

She flashed a look of gratitude at the cowboy, now walking around the mower, studying different sections. If nothing else, the man was a strong role model for hard work.

She'd never seen him relax, much less goof off. He was nothing like—

Stop! she admonished herself. She could not compare all men to Thomas. She knew he wasn't the norm. But it was hard after living with the man for so long.

That day set the pace for the ones that followed. Shelly could see the difference to the field each noontime. More and more hay was cut. Once that was done, they would rake it into rows, turning it a bit and letting it air dry. Then the old baler would follow the windrows and pack it into bales for transportation.

20

Ten days after her accident, Shelly drove to town to have the stitches removed and to have the doctor check her out. She didn't tell Carter or Adam she was going. They were at a critical stage with the hay and she was capable of driving herself.

The doctor's visit went smoothly. The stitches were removed and he pronounced her wrist to be healing nicely.

Planning to stop for lunch before returning home, Shelly headed for Rosie's Café.

Upon entering, she looked for a seat. It was crowded.

"Shelly?"

Sam Hardman beckoned from one of the booths where he sat alone.

She smiled uncertainly and wound her way through the tables. He was coming for dinner at the ranch in a couple of more days. She hadn't expected to see him before.

"Join me?" he invited, standing as she approached.

"Thank you. I should have realized lunchtime would bring a crowd, but I didn't expect this."

She slipped into the booth opposite Sam.

"I've just ordered. Let me get the waitress back here. Then you can tell me what happened."

He gestured to the cast.

Once Shelly had placed her selection, she looked over at him and explained about the accident.

"I came in to see the doctor today to get the stitches out. In three days I'll be driving to Casper to pick up a friend of Carter's who is coming to stay for a few weeks—to learn all about ranching."

"Another deaf boy?" the rancher asked.

"Yes, they attend school together."

"You know Paul Simmons's girl? Suzie, I think her name is?"

"Sure do. She's been out to visit and is coming again when Wayne does."

Sam looked at her for a long moment.

"Quite a group you'll have," he said.

She nodded.

"Need any help?" he asked.

She glanced up. "Doing what?"

"Whatever you need. Maybe some more horses. I have a couple of old ones that work well, but aren't up to the strain of a full-time ranch hand. Think they'd be perfect for kids still learning. Tack would go with 'em. Might come over and lend a hand. That Adam seems a loner. Never much participates in things in town. He okay with this?"

"He's been helpful to me and Carter. Still, I'm sure he'd appreciate some additional resources. The kids each need a horse and I'd like to be able to ride out and watch as well."

Had Adam thought of that aspect? She bet he had. What were his plans to make sure everyone had a horse to ride? Maybe she should double-check with him. But ever since he'd reluctantly agreed to have the kids for the summer, he'd kept his distance.

Or was it the kisses? She still thought about them each night before falling asleep.

Sam was looking at her oddly. She dragged her thoughts away from Adam and his kisses.

"Did I miss something?"

"I said I'd bring two horses over when I come to dinner day after tomorrow, if that suits you?"

"Yes. I really appreciate your offer."

She smiled as she studied Sam's features to see if she saw anything to suggest that Carter might be related to this man. His gray hair had once been dark, like Carter's. But dark hair was the rule rather than the exception in hair color.

"Want me to go with you to Casper?" Sam offered. "Long way for a girl to go alone."

Shelly almost smiled. She was more than capable of making the trek and she'd long ago stopped being a girl. But she didn't take offense.

"Carter's going with me. We'll be fine, but thank you for the thought."

Their meal arrived and when they began to eat, Sam asked how they were settling in at the ranch. She told him and turned the conversation to memories she had as a child. He spoke warmly about her mother, but gave her no clue to indicate the two of them had had a closer relationship than casual acquaintances.

Shelly wished she had just one conclusive piece of evidence. Would Sam's pictures offer anything?

Shelly stopped at the local supermarket before heading for home, picking up a cake mix and frosting to bake a welcome cake for Wayne and Suzie when they arrived. She chose several baskets of fresh strawberries and then some fresh vegetables. She tried to get an assortment of things to appeal to everyone.

She was picking Suzie up on the way back from the airport. The young girl would be spending a week or longer. Shelly hoped the adventure would work out.

As long as Adam was in charge, she didn't worry about things going wrong.

She had not taken lunch out to the men, telling them earlier they were on their own that day. When she unloaded the groceries, she noted the kitchen was not as pristine as she'd left it. They must have returned home to eat lunch.

Shelly was getting quite proficient with her cast and soon had a huge pot of spaghetti sauce simmering.

When the tired men trekked into the kitchen shortly after six, she took satisfaction from the look of delight on their faces with the aroma filling the air.

"My favorite!" Carter signed.

"What he said," Pete added.

They had all washed up in the bunkhouse, so were ready to eat.

"Which was what?" Adam asked.

"Don't know, but he looked happy as a clam, so I figured it was something about how great the grub smells. I thank you for including us in with your meals," Pete added to Shelly.

"Carter said spaghetti is his favorite," Shelly explained. "And I'm happy to have you and Adam with us each night."

She began to pass out the plates so they could serve themselves at the stove. Her arm wasn't up to heavy lifting, so it made things easier this way.

Adam let the other two heap their plates, then gestured for Shelly to go.

"You next, you fixed it all. Where were you when we came in at lunch?"

"I went to town to have the stitches out. And stopped at Rosie's for lunch. I saw Sam Hardman there. He's coming to dinner the night before we go to pick up Wayne. He said he'd bring a couple of horses for the kids to use."

Adam nodded. "I'll call him tonight and see what he's bringing."

"I told him you were in charge."

She handed her plate to him.

"Would you mind? I want lots of sauce on my noodles. I'll put the garlic bread on the table. The salad is already there."

"What did the doctor say?" Adam asked as he finished filling her plate.

"That I could wash my hair myself now, as long as I wrap the cast in plastic," she said, smiling brightly at him. "I've been doing that for my showers, so not a problem."

She would miss Adam washing her hair. He'd done it a half-dozen times now. But there had been no more kisses like the first time.

"Maybe I should wash it once more—just to make sure."

The look in his eyes made her knees go weak. The intensity surprised her as did the flash of desire. For a moment she wished her brother and Pete were out with the dog so she and Adam could have been alone.

Their gazes held for a long moment.

Finally he broke contact and taking her plate to the table, he placed it down and held her chair for her. Then he got his own dinner.

Shelly was aware of every move Adam made. She tried to keep the conversation going, but as at other meals, he suggested she eat first and then interpret for Carter.

"Carter's teaching me to sign," Pete said.

He glanced at Adam. "I think the boss man's learning, too."

Adam scowled. "None of that, Pete."

The old cowboy laughed.

"Doesn't want to be boss, missy," he said to Shelly.

"He agreed," she replied calmly, her heart jumping.

Surely he wasn't going to change his mind.

"And as boss, if you don't do what I say, I'll assign you stall clean-out forever," Adam growled.

Pete laughed, mimicking the action so Carter could catch on. The teen laughed as well.

"In a couple of days, we'll have three signing kids around. Watch the conversation then," Shelly said.

When dinner finished, Pete said he was going to the bunkhouse to watch a show he wanted to see on TV. Carter was off to use the Internet to talk to Suzie and Wayne and finalize plans. They'd both be on the ranch in a few days.

Adam didn't get up from the table right away. Shelly looked at him quizzically.

"Not anxious to be somewhere else?" she asked.

"It does seem as if everyone deserted," he said.

"Want some more iced tea?" she asked.

"Sure."

She brought some fresh ice from the freezer and filled his glass. She added some iced tea to her own glass and sat back down.

"That was a good dinner," he said, twirling his glass around and around with his fingers.

Shelly thanked him. "How's the hay coming?"

"Ready to bale starting tomorrow. Pete and I drove the machine to the field. Brought back the mower and rake. When I have some time, I want to tear down those engines and really work on them. Might get another year or two out of them."

She didn't state the obvious, that in two years she hoped this ranch belonged to someone else. Thinking about that seemed surreal. She had the day-to-day activities to take care of.

"You want to talk to Sam while I do the dishes?" she asked.

He nodded. She brought him the cordless phone. Taking the last of the items from the table, she quickly ran hot water over the dishes. Using her right hand, she washed them with a soapy rag and then put them in the drainer in the side sink. Once finished, she sprayed everything with hot water. Best she could do and so far no one had gotten sick.

She listened as Adam discussed horses with Sam. The other man must have offered help because Adam made some suggestions on where he needed backup.

He finished the conversation before she finished the dishes, but didn't leave. Shelly wiped down the counters, rinsed out the dishrag the best she could and draped it across the edge of the sink.

"All done?" he asked.

She turned and nodded. He was still at the table. Rising he grabbed his hat and headed toward the front of the house

"Let's sit on the porch and talk," he said.

Her heart jumped again. She hated it when people said let's talk. It was never good.

Once she was seated on the porch, she smiled brightly, as if that would ward off bad news.

"What's up?" she asked.

"Do you know what you're doing having these kids out? Look at you, second or third day riding and you conked yourself on the head, needed stitches and almost broke your wrist. How much better do you think these kids are going to do?"

"Probably lots better. Carter has been working with you or Pete almost every day, and he hasn't had a mishap. Don't assign them anything dangerous. They'll love working and helping. That's all most people want—to be needed. You said normally by this time of year Uncle Mitch had hired on a bunch of extra hands—including a college kid. We can use the help, right?"

"How much help are green kids going to be?" he argued.

"More than no help at all. Or even me with my wrist. I can't do much until it heals, but I can keep the meals coming. The kids can help with the haying. Or is that too dangerous because of the machinery?"

"Being around horses and cattle isn't a walk in the park,' he said.

"I know, but I have to believe they'll be fine. They really want this, so they aren't going to ignore rules. Just make sure you train them the right way. I can't think of a better role model for teenagers than you."

Adam stared at her for a long moment.

"You're crazy. I'm no role model. I can hardly make it through the day on my own."

"Now you sound crazy. You're the most together man I know."

Adam took off his hat, ran his fingers through his hair and replaced the Stetson. He shook his head.

"I'm not. If you think I'm going to have much to do with these kids, you don't know me at all. I want to stay away from people, not become a role model or work with others. I'm a loner."

"Keep telling yourself that and maybe one day you'll believe it," she said.

"It's the way things are."

"There must be a reason. You said you and your friend Brian—oh, because he died? Is that it? Don't get close to someone because if they die, you'll be hurt?"

Adam rose and went to the railing, then leaned against a post. He stared out over the land.

"Don't try that psychology on me. I have my reasons."

"I'm not asking you to be friends with Carter and Wayne and Suzie. Just teach them some skills for riding and working cattle. They'll give you their very best in exchange. And if they get hurt or something, you'll know what to do."

"Knowing what to do isn't always enough. Sometimes nothing is enough."

Shelly was silent for so long, Adam turned to look at her. She was studying him with a speculative expression.

"Tell me what happened to Brian. Help me understand, please."

"He died, I told you."

"Were you there?"

He turned his back. It was still daylight. He could get a horse and ride until he was too tired not to sleep. He could check on fencing, make sure the water pumps were working, make sure—

"Adam, were you there?"

21

"Yeah, I was there. I had my hands on two of the bleeding wounds, but they were more than I could staunch. He bled to death. I couldn't stop the blood. I couldn't save my best friend. All the medical training I had was worth spit. I couldn't save him. Or the children. Man, the children, shattered by car bombs, shot by their own side because they waved at us or took our candy. They never had a chance. They should be running in some playground, attending school, dreaming of what they could be when they grew up."

He closed his eyes but snapped them open again. The scenes engraved in his mind made him feel sick. Would he ever forget the faces, the futility of trying so desperately to save those kids, even when his CO had ordered him to step away? He had to save them.

Clenching his hands into fists, he willed away the images. Yearned for peace.

He felt her hand against his arm, gripping for comfort. Only there was no comfort from the nightmares and memories. Nothing to ease the pain of not saving Brian.

"I never even went home to see his mother," Adam said.

Why was he telling Shelly this? He hadn't told anyone else, not even Mitch. Maybe because he needed to make her see that he wasn't the man to run the ranch, to teach children.

"I mustered out at Langley and headed west, as far from the old neighborhood as I could get. Never even saw my grandmother or Ellie, Brian's mother. She was like a second mom to me as I grew up and I never even went back."

"It would have been too hard," Shelly said softly, rubbing her fingers against his arm.

Adam turned and looked at her. She was soft and sweet and looked as innocent as a newborn. Except her life hadn't been the perfect storybook tale as it should have been.

He pulled her into his arms, clinging to her, feeling the contact, knowing for once he wasn't alone. It was a gift bigger than he deserved.

"I'm sure she understood. She would have been weepy and clingy and that was the last thing you needed," Shelly murmured, rubbing his back, leaning against him.

"Maybe some day you can visit or call her. Just to talk. You both loved her son. She'd understand."

"I should have gone home. Should have told her I tried my best to save him."

"She knows that. Both Ellie and your grandmother know you tried your best. If anyone could have saved him, you would have. You know that, too, Adam."

"There wasn't anything I could do. Two other medics helped. Nothing. He was dead in minutes. Gone forever."

"I know. Death is so final."

He heard the sympathy in her voice. One part of him wanted to thrust her away and go off alone. Another part wanted to continue holding her, breathing in the scent of her, feeling her warmth thaw some of the ice around his heart and soul. Could the words she was saying be true?

Did Ellie know he'd done his best? There was a gaping hole where he should have been. There was no one to talk to late at night. No one to share the satisfaction he derived from working on the land, mastering a horse. No one to reminisce with. No one to go out with and get rip-roaring drunk.

"I can't imagine the horrors of war," Shelly said. "I do rest easier knowing you have a medic background. You were so cool when you found me and knew exactly what to do. Not every ranch has that and they still hire on workers."

"Not kids."

"These kids are two years away from being old enough to live out on their own. How will they get the experience they need if someone doesn't give them a chance? It's only a few weeks, Adam. It'll work."

"And if not?"

"We'll cross that bridge when we get to it, I guess."

She shifted slightly and Adam was instantly aware he was holding a beautiful woman in his arms. The need for comfort fled as a new need took its place. He buried his face in her silky hair. It smelled like flowers and Shelly.

She had her own baggage. Her husband had left her with a mess and probably a strong distrust of men.

Yet she trusted him. At least on the ranch. Would she trust him with more?

What more was he willing to risk?

She pulled back a little and looked up into his eyes.

"Don't you truly think we can make this work?"

He stared into her blue eyes, wishing they were alone on the ranch, that he had put clean sheets on his bed. That she'd smile at him the way she often smiled at her brother. No, not quite like her brother, but with desire and want in her eyes.

"What, the kids or us?"

She blinked.

"Us?" she almost squeaked.

He didn't respond except to kiss her.

He felt the hesitation before Shelly kissed him back. Her mouth was sweet. Her tongue met his when he traced her lips. He could feel the strength in her arms as she held on tightly. The unforgiving feel of her plaster cast dug into his back. He didn't mind—he was holding heaven in his arms.

When she pulled back, Adam half expected her to ask him to leave. Instead, she smiled at him and threaded her fingers up through his hair.

"Sometimes you run your fingers through your hair and leave it in spikes. I always want to smooth it down."

He drew her hand to his mouth and kissed the palm, then wrapped his fingers around it and held it against his chest. "So do it."

She giggled softly. "Right in front of Pete and Carter? Like that sure wouldn't cause comment."

"Where do you plan to put these teenagers you have arriving?" he asked slowly releasing her hand and stepping back.

"What do you mean?"

"I thought the boys might like to stay in the bunkhouse with me and Pete. Give them the real flavor of being a cowboy. You'll still be doing meals, right?"

"Of course. That's a fantastic idea. They'd love it. Then Suzie could have the room Carter's been using. There's another bedroom I started cleaning before my accident. And the one Uncle Mitch had. But I know they'd prefer to be out with you and Pete."

"Two rooms in the bunkhouse can be cleaned tomorrow. I'll hold off another day or two before baling the hay, give it more time to dry. Weather should hold."

"Sam Hardman's coming to dinner on Friday," she reminded him.

Adam nodded. "He and I spoke about the horses he's bringing. He offered to help in other ways, too. Odd, that. Never knew he offered to help Mitch. Of course Mitch probably forgot more than Sam knows. Not the case with me."

"He probably feels ranching is too much for me. I'm not Mitch," she said.

"I noticed," Adam said.

For a little while he was just a guy with a girl. He took a breath. It was nothing like New York. But also nothing like Afghanistan.

He tugged her closer. "I'll have to get back to the bunkhouse. See what those guys are up to."

"Good night, then," she said, raising her head for another kiss.

When Shelly awoke the next morning, she hesitated a minute before getting out of bed. Had last night changed anything? A few kisses weren't that much of a commitment. Or even a declaration.

Should she act cool, as if last night was just like any other night? Or should she expect their relationship to change? Would he be distant again or a bit more friendly?

Maybe they needed to discuss things.

Or maybe she could see how things went. That was an easier option and the one she voted for.

When Shelly arrived in the kitchen, she saw someone had started coffee and there were toast crumbs on the counter. But Carter wasn't there. He'd already gone out to see the horses, she had no doubt.

She prepared a large hot breakfast and waited for the men to come in.

Pete showed up at six, Carter on his heels.

"Where's Adam?" she asked, starting on the next pan of eggs.

"I don't know," Pete said, sitting at the table and pouring a cup of coffee. "He wasn't around when I got up and his truck's gone."

Her heart sank.

"Gone?"

Had he left, just as he'd said he would?

She stirred the eggs, not seeing them, seeing only the dark eyes that had witnessed too much. The reserved man who didn't want to get involved. The hurting individual who hadn't been able to save his friend.

He couldn't be gone.

"Seems unlikely he'd take off without telling someone," she said, trying to think.

"Maybe. He's a hard man to get to know. Keeps himself apart, you know what I mean?" Pete asked.

Shelly nodded. She had thought they'd breached that

barrier, but apparently not. Where could Adam be?

She went through the motions of serving breakfast to Carter and Pete and even poured another cup of coffee for herself, but she couldn't drink it. She felt her world tilting off center.

"If he's gone, we'll have to look after things ourselves," she said.

Pete glanced up. "Gone as in for good?"

"You said his truck was missing."

"I thought he went to get a part or something. Why would he leave?"

The older cowboy looked puzzled.

"What?" Carter signed.

Shelly thought of the many times Adam had told her he wanted out. No one else knew that. Could it be he just went on an errand? Without telling anyone?

"I'm wondering where Adam went," she signed.

"Probably to get the part for the engine that keeps cutting out," he said, finishing the last of his meal.

Shelly stared at him. *"I thought maybe he left, moved on."*

Carter frowned. *"Why? This is his home. He works here."*

She nodded, hoping Carter was right.

If he returned, good. If not, she'd deal with it. She began to clear the dishes.

If he had only gone on an errand, she might fire him for giving her such worry.

Once the dishes were stacked in the sink, and Carter and Pete back in the barn, Shelly left the house and crossed quickly to the bunkhouse. She had to know.

She peeked into each bedroom—there were six in all.

Most were dusty with a blanket thrown over the beds. Two were occupied, one obviously Pete's. The next one had a neatly made bed and not a single item of personal belonging showing. But looking into the drawers, she saw jeans and shirts. There was another pair of boots in the closet and a new hat. She drew a deep breath of relief and smelled Adam. This was his room, and his clothes were still here. He was coming back.

Leaving quietly, she slipped by the barn and hoped no one had seen her. At least she could get through the day knowing he hadn't gone for good.

22

It was late afternoon by the time his truck drove past the house. Shelly was in the office and almost dashed outside to confront the cowboy who had given her hours of worry. But she remained at the desk, listening, hoping he would come in and tell her where he'd been.

By dinner time she was ready to throw in the towel and go find him. When the men came in to eat, Adam was right behind Pete. But he didn't even look at her. She served her plate and left the rest for the men to serve themselves. Sitting down, she waited until the others were ready before beginning to eat. She glanced at Adam.

"I didn't know you were going off today," she said.

Proud her tone sounded casual, she clenched her good hand in her lap and waited.

"Needed a part for the baler. Thought they might have it in Wildcat Creek, but no luck. I tried Coleville and ended up having to go all the way to Casper."

She nodded and began to eat. Relief swept through her. He hadn't left.

Two days later Sam arrived late in the afternoon as promised towing a four-horse trailer. Carter and Pete were on hand to unload the horses—all four of them. Shelly heard the commotion and came from the house to see what was going on.

"Hello," she called as she hurried to join them.

"Howdy. Brought a couple of extras. Know those kids will be running these horses ragged. All are good steady mounts. I talked to Adam about them."

Sure, Adam was talking to Sam. He had hardly said two words to her since he'd returned the other day. And when she'd said she wanted to talk with him last night, he'd pleaded extra work and disappeared so fast she almost hadn't seen him go.

She watched as Pete and Sam backed the horses down the ramp, handing the halter lines to Carter, who then led them into the corral. They ambled away once released, checking out their new abode.

Once all were in the corral, Sam closed up the trailer.

"Come in, I have iced tea. Dinner won't be for a little while," Shelly said.

"Let me get the pictures from the truck."

He pulled out two fat photo albums and turned to walk with her back to the house. Carter was already in the corral, patting one of the new horses. Hank sniffed around the hooves.

"They won't kick the dog, will they?" Shelly asked.

"They're used to cattle dogs. And Hank's used to staying out of their way. They'll be fine."

"If you don't mind the kitchen, come on back so I can finish dinner while we visit," Shelly said.

"Smells mighty good," he said when they entered the house.

"Pot roast. I've learned to fix hearty meals here. Adam turned his nose up at one meal that was all salads, eating rabbit food as he called it, and he ended up fixing a huge sandwich with half the ingredients in the refrigerator."

"We work hard, like to fill up," Sam said.

He put the albums down on the counter out of the way. "We can look at those after dinner."

"Have a seat," Shelly said, pulling out a chair for him to use.

She quickly poured iced tea for her guest and went back to the biscuits she was making. It had been hard to roll out the dough with her cast on, but she'd managed. Every time she accomplished a task, she felt better.

She was beginning to hope the place wouldn't sell fast. Carter wasn't the only one having a wonderful summer—despite her wrist.

"You sure look like your mother," Sam said with a sad smile.

"Thank you," Shelly said. "I always thought she was beautiful."

"Me, too." He took a sip of tea. "I remember her that summer you two spent here. She loved riding, swimming in the river, cooking over a campfire. Guess traveling around the world with your father made her adventuresome."

"I remember riding horses that summer, going out with Uncle Mitch and watching cattle walk around. I'm sure we were doing more, but that's most of my memories. And the swing on the tree near the barn."

"I put that up for you," Sam said. "Mitch suggested it, but I was a much younger man than he was back then."

Shelly hadn't remembered Sam from that summer.

"Did you come to visit a lot? I don't remember."

"No reason you should. I came a lot the last few weeks you were here."

He turned his glass on the table.

"Do you know why your mother brought you here?"

Shelly shrugged.

"To visit. We were between moves, I think. Seemed like we moved every two or three years in those days. After Mom died, we didn't move as much. I guess my father put in for transfers in earlier years and then stopped."

She hesitated. "Was there another reason?"

He looked at her. "If there were, I'm sure you would have known. Your uncle sure was happy to have you stay for so long. I suspect your mother was always his favorite relative. He would have left the ranch to her had she still been alive."

Shelly nodded, knowing Sam probably didn't realize the place had been left solely to her. She planned to share it with Carter, so there was no problem there. But it was odd that Mitch had left it to her alone.

Dinner was delicious. Each of the men complimented her on the savory pot roast and fresh vegetables that were steamed to perfection. When she brought out strawberry shortcake for dessert, there were groans of delight.

Adam didn't say much during the meal, but Shelly caught him studying Sam several times. The rancher seemed to fit in perfectly. He and Pete swapped stories, trying to top each other with more outlandish tales. Shelly was kept busy translating for Carter so he wouldn't miss out. He laughed at many of the antics.

She even caught Adam laughing at one point. It changed his entire appearance. She stared until he caught her eye, his smile fading as he turned away. She was transfixed with the change. Sam said something else that was funny and she turned back to translate for Carter.

When the meal ended and they were ready to push back from the table, Sam offered to bring over the albums. Pete and Adam decided to stay to see the photos as well, so dishes were cleared and the large books brought to the table.

The first picture showed Maureen Palmer up close. She was laughing at something and her eyes sparkled in the light. Shelly felt a pang. Her mother seemed so young in the photo. She'd only been a few years older than Shelly was now.

Involuntarily, she reached out and touched her cheek. "Mama," she said softly.

Carter signed, *"She was pretty, wasn't she? You look a lot like her."*

Shelly nodded, glancing up to catch Adam's gaze. He said nothing, just looked at her, then back at the picture.

"Look how happy she was—I don't remember her that way," she said, studying the photograph again.

Sam cleared his throat, as if covering for a display of emotion, then flipped the page. There was Maureen with Shelly. The little girl sat on a horse that looked way too big for her. Maureen was smiling up at the young Shelly, who beamed from ear to ear.

"You started riding early," Pete said.

Adam glanced at Carter, then Sam. "Nice pictures. You take them?"

"No, some Mitch took, gave me copies. He probably has a box of pictures somewhere around."

Shelly flipped slowly through the album. She remembered her mother as a rather sad woman who put up with the military manner in which her husband ran their home. Shelly thought back, remembering her mother's laughter—rarely heard after Carter was born. Had she mourned the fact her baby was deaf? She'd never indicated that to Shelly. But why would she? Maureen had been the adult, Shelly the child. Or had she been mourning the loss of Carter's father? Shelly had never considered that angle before.

There was a picture of Sam and Maureen. For a moment, Shelly didn't recognize Sam. He didn't look much older than her mother in the photograph. With his cowboy hat and snug jeans, he looked hot. Had her mother thought so?

"Did you spend a lot of time with them?" Shelly asked, hoping her voice sounded casual.

"Mitch and I had been friends for years. My wife had recently died when you two came for the summer. I guess I spent a fair amount of time over here. Sometimes you and your mother came to my place for dinner. Once I took her into town to see a movie."

It didn't sound like a passionate affair to Shelly, but he would hardly admit to such a thing after all these years.

When she turned the page again, she saw her mother and another cowboy, this one younger, and even from the photograph, Shelly could almost feel the sex appeal.

"Who is that?"

Sam frowned. "Stan Elliot. He worked for your uncle that summer. Left right before your mother did. Just worked in this area that one summer."

Shelly stared, mesmerized. She couldn't tell the cowboy's

hair color, but he was tall, like Carter, and lanky. Another photo showed Stan with Maureen. And another. They were clowning around, and once again Maureen was laughing. More of Shelly and her mother and Uncle Mitch. Good grief, he'd looked ancient in those days. He'd been in his seventies back then.

The photographs finished too soon for Shelly. For a little while she could wrap happier memories around herself and relive that summer.

"You had a mighty pretty mother, Shelly. You favor her," Pete said, rising. "Sam, want to come see how Carter does with Hank? They're working real well together."

"Don't mind seeing that," Sam said.

He smiled at Shelly. "Keep the books for a while. I want them back, mind, but can lend them for a while."

"Thank you."

Adam hung back when the others left. Shelly got up from the table to start the dishes. She ran water in the sink.

"We need to talk," she said.

"About?" he asked.

"The other night."

"What about it?"

She turned and looked at him.

"That's what I wanted to ask you. Is this something to explore?"

She held her breath. She hoped they might draw closer.

He sighed and looked across the room at her.

"You own a ranch, I work here. We had a few kisses. I can apologize if you like. Nothing to explore. There's too much baggage in my life to do anything but get through each day. You'll sell this place and return to California. Let's leave it the way it is."

"And how is that?"

She held on. She would not give way to the sudden sadness that swept through her.

"The way it's been."

Turning back to the sink, she turned off the water. She'd wanted to talk, she just didn't like the way the conversation was going.

"Is Sam Carter's father?" he asked.

She almost dropped the pan she'd picked up.

"Why would you ask that?"

"The way he kept looking at Carter during dinner. And there's something around the eyes, the way they both smile. They favor each other."

She bit her lip and began washing the pan.

"I don't know," she said at last.

"But Carter's not your father's son?"

She shook her head.

"I learned that when my mother died. Carter was in the car crash, too, and needed blood. He and my father weren't compatible. My father was never the same toward Carter after that. But Carter was so little, I don't think he noticed. At least I've always hoped he didn't. Dad supported him. His name's on Carter's birth certificate. I think it was a face-saving tactic—don't let anyone know the son wasn't his. But he left him next to nothing in his Will. Dad couldn't bring himself to leave another man's son a legacy."

"Sounds like he didn't leave you anything either," Adam said.

"I was married to Thomas when he wrote his Will. I guess he figured I was taken care of."

She didn't need to voice the hurt she'd felt when the will had been read.

"So what did he think would happen to Carter if he died before the boy was earning a living?" Adam asked.

"Schooling is pretty much taken care of, so I guess he thought I'd take him during vacations. He was right. He's my brother no matter who his father is. Do you think it could be Sam?"

"Maybe. I'm thinking Sam's wondering, too. Is it possible?"

Shelly draped the drying cloth over the edge of the counter.

"Carter's birthday is in early May. I suppose it's possible. I never really thought about it until after I found out. Mostly, I couldn't believe my mother had been unfaithful. It was a shock. I was sixteen and she was my idol. I loved her so much. Much more than my father. Is that horrible?"

"Not especially. You must have had your reasons."

"My mother was a loving, warm, wonderful person. My father thought he was in the ranks of the military at home and at the front. It wasn't a harmonious household. In retrospect, I think getting away from my father was a big factor in rushing into marriage with Thomas. He was the exact opposite of my father—a charmer from the word go. That's why he was so successful in scamming so many people."

"Does Carter know?" Adam asked, rising from the table and coming to lean against the counter, arms folded across his chest.

"Not that I'm aware. He hasn't asked any questions and Mom died ten years ago when he was six. A drunk driver smashed her car and killed her instantly. The blasted driver walked away unscathed."

"Tough break," Adam said.

Shelly nodded.

"That cowboy in the later pictures sure seemed to have a thing for your mother."

"Sam asked if I knew why Mom had come visiting that summer. Could that have anything to do with it?"

"Ask Sam."

"I can't just come out and ask if the man had an affair with my mother—oh, and could he possibly be the father of my brother?"

"I guess that is a bit awkward. I'm betting a man who's kept a secret for this long isn't going to let anything slip."

23

The next morning Shelly was up early. She and Carter were going to pick Wayne up at the airport in Casper, then swing by the Simmons's home in Wildcat Creek to pick up Suzie. By dinner tonight, there'd be a full table in the kitchen.

Adam had left for the hay field before Shelly was even up. He'd gone to the bunkhouse as soon as Sam had left last evening. So much still had to be said, but he was avoiding her. He told Pete he wanted to analyze the hay, then get back to put the part in the baler and start it up.

Shelly wished Adam had stayed to see them off. She liked being with him, yet was cautious about letting herself trust anyone. He couldn't get past his experiences from the war and he made sure she knew there was no future for them. He knew she was only in Wyoming for another couple of months, then would return to California.

To what she wasn't sure. Especially if the ranch hadn't sold by then. If she could just find an inexpensive place near Carter, find work and earn enough to go back to school, at least she'd have a plan for the future. She liked working with people and might pursue something in the travel industry. If, as Geoff had said, it took years to sell the ranch, she'd be foolish not to make plans for the fall.

There wasn't a future between her and that cowboy. Much as she wished there could be.

As they drove east toward Casper, she gazed at the land. There was so much of it that showed no signs of man. So different from the crowded Bay Area with homes and businesses lining every square inch. The traffic was hardly noticeable compared to bumper-to-bumper back home. She knew Montana had the nickname big sky country, but it could equally be applied to Wyoming. She loved the huge blue dome overhead.

She suddenly had no desire to return to California's congestion. The thought shocked her.

At the airport, Carter and Wayne were glad to see each other and their hands flew as they caught up on news. They were in the same class at California School for the Deaf and had been friends for years. Wayne was excited about working on the ranch and Carter quickly began telling him all he'd learned so far.

They sat in the back seat together so it was easier to communicate. Several hours later, Shelly stopped for Suzie. The three teenagers quickly fell into conversation. Suzie sat in front but turned around to sign with the boys. It was late by the time Shelly reached home. She was tired from driving all day. There was still supper to prepare.

"Boys in the bunkhouse, Suzie upstairs in the main house with me," Shelly signed. *"Segregation—boys with the cowboys, girls together. Carter, you and Wayne take Suzie's bags upstairs, then go find out from Adam where you'll be sleeping. Dinner as soon as I can fix it."*

The three teens scrambled around to follow Shelly's orders. In no time, Suzie's things were in the room Carter had used and the boys were lugging Wayne's suitcases to their living quarters for the next few weeks. Suzie following to see where they were staying.

Shelly washed her face and brushed her hair before heading for the kitchen. A large sheet of paper was taped to the cabinets.

"Dinner on us in the bunkhouse," a bold hand had written.

"Thank you!" she said softly and turned to head outside.

The aroma of cooking meat met her as she rounded the corner of the barn and approached the bunkhouse. A large grill stood nearby and she could hear the sizzling as she walked closer. Pete and Adam stood over the grill. They looked up when she came into view.

"Glad you're back, we were getting worried," Pete said. "We thought we'd save you fixing dinner."

"And we wanted to fire up this old grill," Adam added. "If we're having a barbecue with neighbors soon, I wanted to make sure it worked."

He glanced at her, then back at the meat cooking. She tried to ignore the prick of hurt. The closer she got, the more aware she felt around him. She wished he'd lean over and kiss her. Whoa—maybe not that far. A friendly smile would be welcome.

When the teenagers came out, they gravitated immediately to the cowboys. Carter introduced Wayne and Suzie. Shelly translated softly in the background. Adam and Pete shook hands with the visitors. Shelly was glad Adam showed none of his trepidation to Wayne's visit. She knew he felt they didn't belong, but she was happy for her brother to have some friends to hang out with. If things worked out, Wayne could stay the rest of the summer.

Both visitors were taken with Hank. Carter proudly showed off some of what the dog could do.

Shelly was ready for bed long before anyone else was. She told Suzie the main door would be unlocked and to come in when she was ready for bed, but not to stay out too late. Morning came early on a ranch.

Bidding the others good-night, she headed for the house. Glancing back, she felt wistful. She'd hoped Adam might have walked with her, but he was describing the next day's work to the kids, drawing pictures in the dirt with a stick.

She should be glad he was dealing with them so well. But she wanted some attention from the cowboy herself.

The next day everyone was up early—Wayne and Suzie excited beyond belief. Shelly made sure they ate a hearty breakfast, gave everyone two water bottles, and watched as Pete and Adam led the cavalcade out to the barn.

Her wrist didn't ache as much as it had. The scar on her forehead wasn't as noticeable as earlier. She was getting better. Maybe she'd ride out with them later in the week, once she felt caught up with the household duties.

Mid-morning, Shelly began working on the books again. She was learning more and more about the operation of the ranch by seeing what time of year her uncle incurred expenses or deposited large sums of money. The place was profitable, no doubt about it. The extraordinary medical expenses prior to his death had run it perilously close to the red, but if Adam could keep the business going this year, it should resume its healthy profitability. She and Carter could earn a comfortable living from the ranch.

Maybe instead of planning to return to California when Carter did, she should think about staying. She had a home. She could wait for the sale here as easily as in some apartment in the Bay Area. It'd mean Carter wouldn't have any family close by, but as long as they owned the ranch, he could come for school breaks.

She'd have to give that some thought. It was so far from what she'd envisioned when she first arrived that she wanted to make sure it wasn't tied directly to her wish to stay near Adam. Not a very wise reason to change her future plans.

Yet, she had no one close in the Bay Area except Beth and they'd proved this summer that e-mail worked well. She could invite Beth to visit, catch up with all the news and show her the new Shelly.

Could she make it work?

Hearing a loud noise, Shelly went to the window. Adam had obviously gotten the baler working. She watched as he maneuvered the awkward machine away from the storage area and out toward the fields.

Pete was working with Wayne in the corral, having him mount and dismount. Earlier he'd been learning the different gaits and how to cue a horse. Suzie and Carter had also been on horseback. Now both of them sat on the top rail and watched Wayne. Their horses stood outside the arena, tied to the fence, half dozing.

Shelly hoped the teenagers would prove to be of help once they'd learned the basics. And she crossed her fingers there would be no more accidents.

She returned to her computer and logged onto the Internet, then looked up reports from the war zone. She wanted to better understand the horrors he'd faced. And find out if there was anything people at home could do to help those returning.

At noon everyone but Adam trooped in for lunch.

"Where's Adam?" Shelly asked.

"Still out in the hay field," Pete told her. "He wants one of us to bring him a horse around four."

"He needs lunch," she said.

"Figured the man knew what he was doing. You want us to ride out and take him lunch? I planned to take these young'uns out this afternoon. Wayne'll be ready for the open range by then. Boy's learning fast."

"If he asked for the horse at four he probably took food and water for lunch."

Shelly asked the teenagers how they were doing, and was flooded with a rush of enthusiastic signing.

They would be dog-tired at the end of the day, Shelly knew. But the kind of tiredness that came from solid accomplishment.

Wayne complained he didn't have a proper hat. He was wearing a ball cap.

When Shelly interpreted, Pete said he'd seen one in the barn that Wayne could use until he got his own.

"We'll have to go to town, Wayne can get a hat there," Carter said. *"He could use some boots, too."*

"He'll have to make do for a day or two. Then we'll go," she returned.

Wayne grinned in delight.

As soon as they finished eating, the three teens dashed from the house.

"I wish I had some of that energy," Pete said. "Nice lunch, Shelly. Appreciate it. I landed on my feet with this job."

"I think I got the better end of the deal," she said. "You didn't know you'd be teaching a bunch of kids, did you?"

"No, but it makes a man feel good, passing on things he's learned. They're so eager. Guess I better get back out there before they lose some of that enthusiasm."

"I doubt that'll happen any time soon. It's a special opportunity for them. You aren't having any trouble communicating?"

"Naw. That Carter knows right much what to do and he's telling them. I usually just point to a trouble spot, he can recognize what's wrong. Makes those hands fly and the problem's corrected. A couple of times I took a page from Adam's book and drew a diagram in the dirt. Works perfectly."

"Don't let them do more than they are ready for—no matter how much they push," she said.

"Adam would have my head. He wants to vet them before moving to the next step. They'll be working on cleaning tack this afternoon—and the stalls. Not that there's much to do with the horses in the corral, but they can learn. We'll have a ride later when we take Adam his horse."

"Let me know when you go, I'd like a ride myself."

Pete touched the brim of his hat and headed out. Shelly quickly cleaned the kitchen and started dinner. If she got it all cooked, she could warm it up when they returned from the ride and not be rushed when she got back.

It was a beautiful afternoon. A few clouds hovered over the distant peaks, but nothing that looked like rain. She was pleased to have her horse saddled when she went to join the others. Pete had had Wayne and Suzie saddle it for the practice. Pete held the reins of Adam's horse as they rode out. The three teenagers led the way, Carter proudly displaying his knowledge of the ranch. Hank ran happily beside him.

Shelly fell in beside Pete. She kept alert, not fully trusting the twelve-hundred-pound animal she was riding. She'd let down her guard before with dire consequences. She didn't want to do that again.

She heard the engine long before she saw the machine. Cresting a slight rise, they all stopped and looked at the field stretching out before them. The baler was about a third of the way down the field. Every few moments a rectangular bale of hay fell out of the back. There were rows of bales ready to get onto a wagon and back to the barn.

"That'll be our task for the next few days," Pete said. "Hauling all that hay back to the barn. Plenty of feed for the winter months. Good thing these kids have energy, they'll need it. Bucking hay is hard work."

"Especially in this heat."

"Won't work midday. Too hot then. Early morning and late afternoon are the best times. We can stack them in the barn during the midday hours—cooler there. Once it gets too hot, we'll all be glad to rest."

The machine slowed and stopped, the engine idling. Adam climbed down from the cab and motioned for them to come closer.

The horses plodded down the slight incline and over to the baler. The horse Suzie rode eyed the machine warily. The others didn't seem bothered by the noise. Shelly was on alert.

When they reached Adam, he came to Shelly.

"Ask if Carter wants to learn how to drive this thing," he said. "We can do a couple of sweeps before heading back."

"He doesn't drive," she said automatically, eyeing the large farm equipment with some trepidation.

"He's old enough to learn," Adam said, looking at Carter.

"It's too dangerous."

"Shelly, what's he going to run into? Some uncut hay? The thing's too wide to ever tip over, even if we had hilly terrain. He just has to point it where he wants to go and run the gears to engage the baling mechanism. If he's going to be a cowhand, he needs to expand his skills."

"He's not," she said.

"For this summer he is. Tonight you can get permission from Paul Simmons and Wayne's family. The others can take turns tomorrow. Ask if they want to."

She gave him an exasperated look.

"Of course they'd want to. Are you kidding?"

"Then what's the problem? I'm not going to let them get hurt. You want a turn first?"

"I have no desire to learn to drive that thing."

She knew Adam wouldn't deliberately let them get hurt. It was just the machine looked so lethal and her brother was still a kid. Only–he was growing up fast this summer. And she couldn't hold him back.

"Okay, I'll tell Carter."

She signed to her brother. His face lit up and he slid off his horse almost before she'd finished. Handing Suzie the reins, he hurried to the cab, glancing over his shoulder to look at Adam as if to say let's go.

"*I want a turn,*" Wayne signed.

"*Me, too,*" Suzie said. "*I know how, I've done the baler at my granddad's ranch.*"

"*I'll check with your parents tonight. If it is okay with both of them then tomorrow you can have turns,*" Shelly signed.

She trusted Adam knew what he was doing.

For a moment, she went still.

She did trust Adam.

He was nothing like Thomas. His word was rock solid. And he knew how to manage the teenagers—letting them learn and push limits, but keeping them safe.

Pete signaled and they turned the horses and rode away from the machine. In only moments the sound of the engine changed and it began to crawl forward. A few moments later a bale of hay tumbled out the back and plopped on the ground.

"They'll be a while. Let's get the others riding. I want Wayne to get practice. Suzie is already good," Pete said, nudging his horse. He continued to lead Adam's horse; Suzie had Carter's.

Shelly almost suggested he tie them to one of the bales of hay, then realized exactly how much the horses would love that.

Wayne had been awestruck by the cattle they'd seen and was anxious to look at the main herd. Suzie fell in with Shelly studying everything Pete did with close attention.

Another hero in the making, Shelly thought, smiling.

24

An hour later they returned to the hay field. The machine had been turned off and Adam and Carter were standing around a bale of hay, Adam pantomiming. Shelly was relieved to find everything as it should be. If she had been able to afford the insurance, Carter could have started learning to drive a car after his birthday. But that was one expense she couldn't swing.

Oh, dear, what about insurance on the ranch? She'd have to check on that before she let those kids operate any machinery.

Adam nodded and clapped Carter on the shoulder. The teenager smiled broadly.

When everyone had mounted and started for the house, Adam fell in beside Shelly, slowing down until they dropped behind the others.

"Carter did fine with the machine. I won't let him drive it without supervision, but next year, he'll be ready to do it on his own."

"I hope it doesn't take until next year to sell this place," she murmured.

"What are you going to do if he wants to work the ranch?" Adam asked.

"He's sixteen. This is a novelty for him. He loves computers. Once the adventure wears off, he'll be glad to go back to his city life."

"He will or you will?"

"What do you mean?" Shelly asked.

"He loves this. He's eager to learn everything. He's glad his friends have come to spend time here, but even if they weren't here, he'd want to learn everything. It may be a passing fancy. But what if it's his niche in life?"

"It's not."

"What if it is?" he persisted.

"I don't know. He has to finish high school and then go to college before he starts a career. It's too early to tell."

"Maybe. But he's asked me to get him some information from the University of Wyoming on Ag courses. He questions me all the time about things, beyond what a casual curiosity warrants."

Shelly didn't want to hear that her brother wanted to be a rancher.

"Don't encourage him," she said.

"I'm not encouraging him. But I will answer a direct question when asked."

"And how do you do that? You don't sign."

"He talks. And usually forms the questions as yes or no so I only have to nod."

Adam was thoughtful a moment, then said, "He could come by it honestly, the desire to work the land."

"We don't know if Sam or that other cowboy is his father."

"I didn't mean that, I meant Mitch. Your mother is

descended from a long line of people who owned this ranch. Only one family's owned it since the country was settled. Might be Carter's heritage."

She thought about the journal she was reading, a few pages each night. The life her great grandmother Elizabeth described was hard. Despite the hardships, Elizabeth had loved the ranch. She had grown up on another ranch and moved to the Triple L when she'd married. That was the life she'd known. Carter had known army bases and urban living. This was just a phase he was going through. Didn't all boys want to grow up to be cowboys at some point in their lives?

Yet she hadn't been happy in the Bay Area once Thomas's perfidy had been uncovered. This last year especially had been hard and lonely. Here she was learning new skills, discovering things about herself, like the fact she could be alone and not necessarily lonely.

And she had the chance to be with her brother. That would end when they returned to California. He had to board at the school since she couldn't afford a larger place to share with him or to have him commute back and forth.

As they rode behind the others, Shelly studied the teenagers. This was a great environment for them. No drugs. No gangs. No traffic accidents. The list of advantages grew as she considered life in California.

If, and it was a big if, Carter really wanted to ranch, why not?

She couldn't impose her goals on him. He soon would be old enough to decide for himself. The fact he'd asked Adam to get him information about the university showed he was thinking about college. Just not the way she'd expected.

It hurt a bit that he'd asked Adam. Did Carter believe she wouldn't help him find out about the programs at the University of Wyoming?

She thought to herself that having Adam as a hero wasn't a bad thing for her brother. So what was the problem? Didn't she feel being a cowboy was worthy of Carter?

It wasn't that, she suddenly realized. It was a fear of being left out.

That evening Shelly called Paul Simmons. He'd have the answer to her insurance question. After several minutes of conversation, she was relieved to learn his company handled the insurance for the ranch and would cover any costs if injuries occurred.

"Not that I expect any," she said. She didn't want him to worry about his daughter.

"Nor I, but there are no guarantees in life and it's always best to be prepared. At least you know you're covered if something happens."

The next morning Adam hitched the wagon to an old tractor and made preparations to get to the field to start gathering the bales of hay. Pete would drive the tractor with one teen while two loaded the wagon with the bales already made. They'd rotate, one driving the baler, the other two loading. He was pushing to have everything finished by the end of the week.

"I can come help—maybe drive the baler myself," Shelly said as she watched Adam work.

"You stay away from anything that will set back your wrist healing," he said.

"But you need help," she said.

He looked at her over the tractor.

"We'll manage fine with the kids helping to load the bales on the wagon."

He looked at the western sky.

"Weather's supposed to be good for the next week. We should get everything under cover by then."

"I wish I could help," she said.

"Bring lunch around noon," he said. "Can you find us?"

She nodded. If she could have changed any one thing this summer, it would have been to be more vigilant when riding Bonny Boy so she wouldn't have fallen. Now she just had to wait out her recovery.

"That so feels like woman's work," she grumbled.

"You are a woman."

The way he said it had her looking at him again. For a moment the others seemed to fade away and it was only Adam and her, separated by a tractor. These last few days had been hard. She couldn't help remembering his kiss and wish for more. What had scared him away?

Or hadn't he enjoyed it as much as she had?

No, he hadn't faked anything. She yearned for the closeness she'd felt for a few hours.

But ever since Adam was all business.

He sent the others ahead and stayed back to saddle her horse. He instructed that no one was to touch the machine until he got there.

"Normally I wouldn't have Bonny Boy standing so long with the saddle on, but there's no way you can cinch it up tight enough. You can mount using the block over there, right?"

"Yes. I'll bring lunch, not to worry."

"I will worry. What if he shies again and you fall? Or if you get lost and wander around all afternoon in the hot sun? This is not the place for you."

"Give me a little credit. I'll manage. Women have for eons. And I can find you by listening for the baler. It makes such a racket I could hear it from forever. I'll just head for the noise."

He nodded, double checking the horse.

"Go on," she urged him. "I bet the horses outdistance the tractor anyway and they got a head start."

"A man can only take so much temptation," he said, leaning down to kiss her.

Shelly scarcely knew what was happening before the kiss was over. He'd ignored her for days, then kissed her?

"I was not tempting you," she said.

She pulled his head down for a longer kiss.

"Just your breathing tempts me," he said, gently putting her aside a moment later. "Sam's coming over tonight for the barbecue. Do you know how to start up the grill?"

She shrugged. "I can figure it out. I'll take care of the home front, you take care of those kids."

Adam nodded and started out.

Shelly heard the noise the tractor made when it started up. It rivaled the baler. Didn't farm equipment have mufflers? It was a wonder they weren't all deaf.

He pulled the large flatbed trailer behind him, soon moving out of sight.

She watched wistfully, wishing she were going with him, or that he had stayed. Or that she had a clue about what he thought of the two of them.

Not that there was necessarily the two of them. But could there be?

Shelly prepared lunch early to allow time to ride out to the hay field. She managed to get on her horse and followed the tracks the tractor had left that morning. The noise of the machine made a perfect guide. It was hot, not a cloud in the sky. She hoped everyone was taking care not to get overheated or sunburned.

When Adam spotted her, he stopped the baler. The quiet alerted Pete, who glanced over and saw her as well. With a big grin, he cut the motor on the tractor. Carter looked up. He was on the wagon, stacking bales of hay. Wayne was on the ground, lifting them to the wagon.

Adam waited for Suzie to climb down from the baler before hopping down himself. He'd been watching for Shelly. He was getting too involved with these kids, but couldn't seem to stop things from spinning out of control.

The way they had the other night when he'd kissed Shelly.

He wanted to be with her. She filled most of his waking thoughts, and a few sleeping ones as well.

He'd tried pulling back, treating her like a business professional, nothing more. But it didn't stop the longing. He watched her as she drew closer. She rode competently and was trying to do her share even with an injured wrist. For a fleeting second, he wondered if they could make something work.

But her fall proved how dangerous life could be. There were no land mines or assault weapons on a ranch, but cantankerous cattle, heavy machinery and unpredictable horses could wreak almost as much havoc.

He turned away. He couldn't bear the thought of Shelly ending up bleeding to death on some rocky outcrop.

She rode over to the tractor and let Carter help her dismount. Once Shelly spread out the blanket she'd brought, Carter and Wayne flopped flat out, pulled their hats over their faces and closed their eyes. Adam waited for Suzie to sit, then sank down near the edge.

"Tough morning?" Shelly asked Pete.

She flicked a glance toward Adam. He didn't blame her for being peeved. But he wasn't going to lead her on. They had no future together.

"Don't think these young bucks knew how much work haying can be. But they're doing fine. Might quit a bit early today and go swimming."

"Where?" Shelly's tone brightened.

Adam thought it was a great idea. The kids deserved a treat after working steadily all morning. That section of Wildcat Creek that ran through a portion of the ranch would be perfect. And he'd love to see Shelly in a swimsuit.

"The river," he said.

"Can we swim in it? I thought it was for cattle to drink."

Pete chuckled.

Adam looked away to smile. Sometimes she said the funniest things.

"Yeah, but we can still swim in it. They aren't that picky. The water's shallow enough to warm up so it's enjoyable. Doesn't move fast this time of year. So we'll put in another hour or so after lunch, then head for the stretch that cuts across your property."

"Sounds wonderful. You all must be hot as blazes working out in this sun. I didn't realize until I was riding how hot is it."

Adam nudged Carter's foot with his own. "Shelly, ask them if they're ready to stop?"

She quickly signed the question.

Carter sat up like a shot, shaking his head. *This is fun. Tiring, but look how much we've done.*

He shook Wayne, who opened his eyes.

Want to quit?

No way, I want to eat and drink a gallon of water and then get going. I bet we fill that wagon today.

I don't want to, either, Suzie added. *I'm just getting the hang of the baler.*

Adam watched as Shelly took in their reactions. She shrugged and nodded.

These kids weren't afraid of hard work. And their sense of accomplishment grew with each task they mastered. He wouldn't let them work too hard. Pete's idea of a swim was a good one. They'd have to quit early enough to get back to the house by the time Sam arrived.

When Shelly handed out the sandwiches, her fingers brushed Adam's. Deliberately? Her eyes held his for a couple of seconds when he met her gaze. A man could only take so much. He moved into the shade of the wagon and began to eat. Putting distance between them didn't lessen his desire, but it was prudent.

He glanced around at the contingency on the blanket.

Cutting hay this year was different from previous years. It felt like a family operation more than a business. Last summer Mitch had hired a half dozen men to bring in the hay, some with little or no ranching experience. Since he'd primarily wanted labor to move the hay, experience hadn't been required.

This year, however, the process felt different. These kids were soaking up every new experience like a sponge. And even though Carter and Wayne had known each other for years, Suzie fit right in. The three of them worked well together and seemed to enjoy each other's company.

They reminded him of Brian and himself when they were kids. Different setting, but the same kind of camaraderie.

He looked away. He hadn't thought about Brian in a couple of days. No nightmares recently, either. Mitch said he'd get over the worst of it one day. He never wanted to forget his friend, but he wouldn't mind the crushing sense of loss to fade.

Sometimes he wondered what Brian would have thought of the changes Adam made in his life. He wasn't going to be some hotshot businessman living in a penthouse near Central Park. Wasn't going to be a doctor or mechanic. Of all the jobs they'd discussed growing up, being a cowboy had never been one of them.

Now he was working a spread as a manager. Only because he knew a bit more than the new owners. What would Mitch think of this arrangement? He missed the old man. One day, he'd miss Brian like that, a poignant ache of what might have been if a land mine hadn't ended his life too soon.

As lunch progressed, Adam began to grow uneasy. He

was fitting in too well. He had made a pact with himself not to let emotions enter into day-to-day life. He didn't want to become attached.

But it was already too late. He cared what happened to Shelly and her brother. He enjoyed teaching Suzie how to run the baler and instructing Wayne in riding. This was a summer like no other.

It would end soon.

He'd do best to remember that.

Rising, he tossed his napkin in the bag Shelly had brought for trash and started for the baler.

"Time to work already?" Pete asked, surprised.

"I'm getting back to work. Lots to do."

Adam refused to look at anyone. He had let down his guard, but that didn't mean he would let himself get in too deep.

25

Shelly called Sam Hardman to postpone their planned barbecue until after the hay cutting was finished.

Since they were all focused on getting the hay in before the weather turned, the next day was a repeat of the first. The cowboys and teens headed out while Shelly worked around the house until it was time to take their lunch. After they shared the meal together she returned home, gathered bathing suits and towels and rode back out for fun at the river.

Shelly was having as much fun as the teenagers—and Pete. The only one who didn't join in was Adam. He'd reverted to the same taciturn man he'd been when they'd first arrived. He claimed there was too much to do to go swimming, but if Pete could spare some time, surely he could

Shelly also saw the light on in the barn late that night. Pete said Adam was keeping up with everything but pushing himself too hard. Something had to give soon or he'd burn out.

A few days later Sam called to see how things were going

"We're trying to get our hay in before the next rain, which is forecast in another couple of days, so Adam is running flat out."

"Need some help?" he asked.

"I don't know. Adam's working with the kids and Pete. They're bringing in hay every day. It looks as if most of it has been baled, but loading it goes slowly."

"I have two men I could spare for a couple of days. Nothing around here is critical right now."

"I'd have to ask Adam."

"Tell you what, I'll call him tonight, make the offer. I'll tell him I'm getting impatient to join you for that proposed barbecue. I'm looking forward to seeing Maureen's kids again."

Once again Shelly wondered if Sam was Carter's father. How would she ever find out?

"That'd be great. I'd love to count on Saturday, but according to Adam, ranching doesn't stop for the weekend. So I'm not too sure about that."

"I'll find out when I offer the men's help. How are you doing otherwise?"

"Fine."

"And that brother of yours? How are he and his friends getting on?"

"They love it. Who would have thought teenagers would take to hard, hot work so much?"

They chatted for a little longer.

When Shelly hung up, she sat back in the office chair and gazed out the window. She knew her great grandmother Elizabeth had favored the view from the kitchen—of the trees near the spring. Shelly liked this one, however. In the distance, the smudgy horizon of the mountains against the blue sky still gave her a thrill. The green grass was high, offering lush forage for the cattle.

She thought about Adam. They'd managed to stay out of each other's way without causing comments from the others. However, tonight she had business to discuss. She'd received all the statements from the bank, and even with watching every dime and getting virtually free help from Wayne and Suzie, they would run out of funds before long.

Adam had to advise her on how to get an influx of cash.

Shelly waited until after dinner to seek Adam out. The boys were in the bunkhouse with Pete. Suzie had asked for computer time to e-mail her parents. She was excited about all that was going on and wanted to share her experiences with them. They'd taken some pictures earlier and she wanted to send them as well so her parents would see her actually working on the ranch.

Shelly went to the barn. From what Pete had said, she was pretty sure she'd find Adam there.

As she walked inside, she looked with satisfaction at the hay that rose high against the back wall. More than half had been brought in. When finished, the stacked bales would occupy a major portion of the barn. The stalls were on the side by the corral. In winter, Adam had said, the horses spent time outside, but he usually brought them in at night. The temperatures dropped in winter months and the barn afforded shelter.

He was sitting on a bench, working on something leather with a tool.

She knew he'd heard her. He kept working.

"Hi," she said.

He looked up. "Need something?"

She shrugged and straddled the bench, looking at the leather strap he was working on.

"I need to talk to you about money."

That caught his attention. With six million and change coming in, what did she need? She hadn't gone through Mitch's money yet. He'd seen what she'd bought.

"What about it?"

"There's not a lot of it."

"There has to be. This is a profitable ranch."

"Mitch didn't have any insurance. That last illness cost a bundle. We're cash poor, according to the lawyer. If we can hold off until the fall, and the price of beef remains where it is now, then we should be okay. But I need something between now and then—that is, if you and Pete want to get paid and we all want to eat."

It shouldn't have surprised him, but it did. Mitch had never said a word.

"How much are we talking about?"

"I'm not sure. I've been going over his books for the last few years, trying to see what is seasonal so I know what to expect. Taxes are taken care of until later in the year. The monthly expenses seem to be fairly steady, but there are a couple of expenses I'm not sure about. The biggest infusion of cash each year is in the fall."

"When he sold the steers."

"So if we sell some now, will that tide us over?" she asked.

"Could. It'll mean less in the fall. You'd have to look into it."

"You have to. I don't know even what questions to ask."

He was silent for a moment.

"Sam called earlier," Adam said at last. "He's sending some men over to help tomorrow. With that help, we should finish getting the hay in sooner than expected. Once we see how much we have, you could sell off what you don't anticipate needing."

He could talk to Sam about the best plan. The older man knew better than he did all the ins and outs of keeping a ranch afloat. He'd been at it his whole life.

"Will that be enough?" she asked.

"Heck, Shelly, I don't know. This is one reason I didn't want the job. I'm not experienced enough in ranching to have a ready answer."

"Then ask Sam. You two talk the same language."

He nodded, resuming the work on the strap. He was making a new one for one of the saddles. This kind of work he liked.

After a minute he looked up. She hadn't left.

"Mitch had some investments that paid quarterly. The attorney is looking to see if he can sell some shares for ready cash. It would be better for a prospective buyer to think this is a profitable ranch."

"It is a profitable ranch. Something else?" he asked.

"No. I'll just visit for a little while. The boys are watching TV. Suzie's on the computer. I don't know where Pete is."

"He likes to listen to country music. Works out fine with the TV muted for closed-captioning and his music blaring. Everyone's happy. Unless I want it quiet. This is the best place for that."

"Or the house. Come up there if you want quiet."

"I don't think that's a good idea."

"Why not?"

How did he tell her he wanted things to go back to the

way they'd been before she'd arrived? She'd be hurt and he didn't want that.

"It just isn't," he said.

She didn't respond. A few minutes later she got up and left without saying another word.

Adam waited until he could hear her steps in the yard before looking up.

He could still smell the lingering trace of her scent, the strawberry shampoo she used, the sweetness that was Shelly herself. Blast it all, he wished she'd never come to the ranch to disturb his peace. He'd had everything the way he wanted. Now he was yearning for things that could never be.

His world was crashing in on him. Those teenagers looked up to him as if he were the only cowboy on the planet. Even Pete deferred to him in most matters, and the man had decades more experience.

But it was Shelly who bothered him most.

The more he saw her, the more she came to mean to him. Then one day she'd leave. And he'd be alone again. Better to build walls now to hold off any future heartache.

Still, he wished he'd handled things better. He hadn't wanted to hurt her and he was afraid he had.

By Saturday afternoon all the bales the barn could hold had been stacked inside. They had a second stack on the field that was covered with tarps. Those bales could be sold. The equipment had been parked in the large shed behind the barn and the haying was finished with the first cut.

Carter and his friends had done a good job. Wayne

improved in his riding daily. Carter was getting as proficient as Suzie.

Sam arrived around four. Pete had the grill going and Shelly had the steaks thawed. She and Suzie had made a huge chocolate cake for dessert and she'd asked Sam to bring some ice cream from town. The men who'd helped with the haying had also been invited to stay.

Shelly watched the preparations, thinking about the parties she had put on for Thomas. They'd been lavish, with a caterer supplying the food and drinks, florists decorating their home. She'd often had a new gown to wear.

Now she was in jeans, boots and still had a cast on her arm. The food was home cooked, though plentiful. And somehow, it seemed as if everyone was having a great time. Never mind that there weren't couples—she and Suzie were the only females in the group. But the respect the men had for each other shone through.

Shelly especially enjoyed the stories they told. Each man was, of course, the hero of his own tall tale. Some were hilarious. Her hands were flying as she interpreted each one for the kids.

Once or twice, she caught sight of Adam on the perimeter. He had a beer and seemed to join in, but she could tell he had to make an effort. If he had his way, he'd be back in the barn working. Or riding off into the distance.

Sam came to sit beside her after the meal was finished. The cake had been a big hit.

"Nice of you to include my men," he said, sitting on the bench she'd pushed away from the picnic table.

"They were super helpful. Did Adam talk to you?"

"About finances?"

She nodded, looking across the yard to where Adam was talking with Sam's cowboys.

"Yes, he did. We discussed options. You'll have to make the final call. I think you can get some quick cash now selling a portion of your hay and more in the early fall when you'll have the second cutting. It's a good ranch. Your family chose well when they picked this spot."

"I found a journal from an ancestor. Elizabeth Lancaster. She loved it here. I'm beginning to see the appeal. It's far from what I'm used to, but it's growing on me. I better get back to San Francisco before I turn into a cowgirl."

She spoke the words lightly, but in the back of her mind the prospect of staying was beginning to take root.

"Would that be so bad?" Sam asked.

"Carter keeps talking like he wants to continue ranching. Do you think he'll change his mind when the novelty wears off?"

"Might. Might not. From what I see, he's not afraid of hard work. And if he's still talking about ranching after cutting hay, he's seen some of the worst of it. Of course, he might change his mind after a winter here. Nothing like San Francisco—or what your mother told me about that place. She liked it best of all the locations your father was stationed."

"Did you and she talk a lot?" Shelly asked carefully.

She kept her gaze on the far horizon, wondering more about her mother that summer than she ever had before.

"Your mother came to visit because your father wanted a divorce. She was anxious to talk about what she'd done wrong or what she might do to change his mind. By the end of the

234 | Barbara McMahon

summer she had about accepted things. Then he called up and asked her to come back, said he'd changed his mind."

Shelly swung her gaze back, staring at him in disbelief.

"They separated?"

"You were too young to know what was going on. She was a wonderful woman and she didn't deserve the heartache your father put her through. He thought he'd found another woman and wanted out of his marriage. Never did learn what happened, but when he called, your mother went back. I never heard from her again."

Shelly was shocked by the revelation. She searched her memory for any indication that it was true. What had happened? Who would know at this late date?

Her father was dead. As far as she knew, her father had met Marjorie after her mother had died. The woman probably knew less about his background than Shelly.

"Was she close to anyone while she was here?" Shelly asked.

"Your uncle—he was crazy about your mother. Never had any kids of his own. He thought she was special. And you, too."

"And the cowboy in the pictures?"

"They went dancing a few times." Sam glanced at Carter. "Your father was a fool to want to leave your mother. Guess he recognized it before it was too late."

"I don't think she was happy. I never knew why. Maybe she could never get beyond that betrayal."

Sam looked at her.

"I'm sorry to hear that. She was a special woman. You favor her. Guess Carter favors your father."

"Not so much."

Shelly was dying to ask this man if he'd had an affair with her mother, but she couldn't. What if he had?

It wasn't any of her business—unless he was the father of her brother. If he was, would he acknowledge Carter? Want to establish any kind of family tie? Or would he repudiate him?

She'd do nothing to hurt her brother.

Rising, she began to gather the plates and utensils from the table.

"I better get this all cleared off before it's too dark to see."

Was there another way to find out the truth? Someone had to know.

"Let me help," Sam said, joining her.

Shelly smiled and nodded, her mind churning with ideas to find out the truth.

"I appreciate your sending the cowboys to help out. Adam said we wouldn't have gotten all the hay under cover this quickly without them. Another storm is coming in, I hear."

"This hot weather has to break sometime. Glad they could help."

She could think of several former friends who had not rallied to help when her ex-husband's crime had been uncovered, and at least one who had gone out of her way to hurt Shelly. Sam was almost a stranger and jumped right in to offer help. She really appreciated it.

"I think you made a wise decision in giving Adam the manager's position," Sam said a little later when all the dishes had been cleared. He leaned against the counter, watching as Shelly squirted liquid soap into the rising water in the sink.

"Here, let me do that," he said when he saw how awkwardly she was managing. "You fed us, least I can do."

"I don't mind."

He gently moved her aside and rolled up his sleeves. Shelly grinned at the sight. Sam was a special kind of man.

"Adam said he had all the kids take turns operating the machinery, under supervision, of course," Sam commented. "They're having the time of their life."

"Carter just turned sixteen, so he could have a driver's license in California, but living at the school he doesn't really need one. And auto insurance is so expensive."

Shelly stacked the rinsed dishes on the rack. She'd let them air dry and put them away later.

Sam paused a moment in his dish washing.

"Just turned sixteen?" he repeated.

She nodded. "Early May. He was thrilled Adam let him drive in the field. Maybe if he learns to maneuver that heavy equipment, driving a car will seem like a piece of cake."

Sam didn't say anything but continued to wash.

Shelly glanced at him, but his expression gave no indication of what he was thinking.

"I wondered where you had gone, Sam," Adam said a minute later, entering the kitchen through the back door. "Your men are heading back. That storm looks like it's heading this way faster than originally predicted."

"Almost finished here. Got a couple of things to check with you before I go."

"I can finish," Shelly said. "Thank you for your help."

Sam nodded, rinsing his hands and drying them. He replaced his hat and headed for the door.

"Mighty fine meal, Shelly. Thanks for inviting my men as well."

26

She finished cleaning the kitchen and headed for the office, reining in her curiosity. She booted up the computer to check her e-mail, then hesitated a moment before reaching for the phone. She had to look up the number. It was still early evening in California.

"Hello?"

The cool, cultured voice grated on Shelly's nerves. She remembered the warmth of her mother's.

"Hi Marjorie, it's Shelly. How are you?"

"I'm in perfect health. Where are you?"

"I'm in Wyoming."

"Still at that ranch?"

"We're staying the summer. It's a nice break for Carter."

"And you as well, I dare say. Why are you calling?"

No family feelings there, Shelly thought.

"I wanted to ask you something about my father."

"What?"

Shelly heard the wariness in Marjorie's tone.

"I just learned he and my mother separated for a time before Carter was born."

"That was before I met him, Shelly."

"I know. But you were his wife. He must have confided some things to you about his past."

"What goes on between a man and his wife is private."

"Did he ever say anything about my mother being involved with another man?"

"You mean Carter's father? If he'd had any suspicions before her death, don't you think he would have ended that marriage in an instant?"

"Sounds to me like he tried to end it that summer we spent in Wyoming."

"What is it you want, Shelly?"

She took a risk.

"There's a man here who might be Carter's father. I want to know if it's possible."

The line hummed in the silence that followed. Shelly was almost afraid Marjorie had hung up when she finally spoke again.

"Your father said something once and only once. Something about raising some damn cowboy's son. You know your father didn't have to keep supporting Carter. He wasn't his child."

"He didn't know that for the first six years of his life. Hadn't he bonded with Carter at all in that time? How could he have raised Carter for six years and then want nothing to do with him?"

"Your father was a difficult man sometimes, as I'm sure you realize. I can't help you further. Look for some cowboy who lives there."

Shelly thanked Marjorie and hung up. That had not been helpful.

She heard the distant rumble of thunder. It had grown dark while she'd been talking. Going to the window, she felt the stirring of fresh air. The storm would bring cooler temperatures. She was glad the hay was safely stored.

Carter came into the office a few minutes later.

"Nice barbecue," he signed. *"I like Sam and his cowboys."*

"Me, too," Shelly replied. *"You and Wayne and Suzie are working well together. I'm proud of you all."*

Carter sat in the chair across from the desk. *"I want to talk to you about an idea I have. What do you say to turning this ranch into a working one and offer summer vacations to deaf teenagers? Like Wayne. He's learned fast and loves horses. And there aren't a lot of places that offer vacations to deaf kids. I've checked. There are only a couple that offer ranch experience. It's just an idea at this point. What do you think?"*

Shelly looked at him in surprise.

Her immediate reaction was to say no. She knew next to nothing about running a ranch, period, much less taking on the responsibilities of a bunch of teenagers.

Carter continued with ideas for camping out and fishing expeditions. He suggested having different sessions for early summer, midsummer and late summer, to coincide with school vacations. Shelly knew how to sign. He bet Adam could learn quickly. And Pete.

She didn't want to squelch his enthusiasm right away, but the undertaking would be huge.

"Let me think about it," she signed.

"Truly, or are you just stalling?" he asked.

She wouldn't admit to stalling.

"I'll think about it. Talk to some people, like Paul Simmons. Maybe Adam. It would sure impact his job."

She had a mental picture of how he'd react. It had been

hard enough talking him into having Wayne and Suzie—and he'd already known Suzie.

"They are sure to go for it! Maybe we would end up hiring some deaf cowboys, too," Carter returned with a wide smile on his face.

"We couldn't get it going this summer, no matter what," she cautioned. *"And by next summer, the place might sell."*

"That's just it. Don't sell the ranch. I want to live here. I don't want to go back to California."

"Your school is in California."

"You could home school me. Maybe Suzie could stay and be home schooled with me."

Shelly shook her head.

"You are getting too far ahead of yourself. We are not ranchers."

"We come from ranchers. We could learn. Please, think about it. Please."

Shelly remained seated in the office after Carter left.

She was stunned at his idea to stay and run a camp for deaf kids. What about school? She wasn't a teacher. And the prospect of all the money the ranch would bring when it sold was hard to give up. They'd never have to worry about anything.

Except what to do for the rest of their lives.

But to establish a camp for deaf kids based on a few weeks of living here?

Maybe she should offer to let him stay for a year, see how he liked being home schooled and isolated from other kids his age, then discuss a camp.

She went up to her room to get ready for bed, arguments against his plan forming. Hoping to become sleepy, she took the journal and began reading. Because of the small writing, she took a long time to make her way through each page. Usually she managed two or three each night before falling asleep. Tonight the words began to blur before she finished the second page. Clicking off her light, she settled down to sleep.

Thunder woke her some time later. She sat up, startled. The curtains at the windows billowed out. She heard the sound of rain on the roof, smelled the scent in the breeze.

The sky lit up and thunder cracked again.

This time she got up to close the window so rain couldn't blow in. There was a light on in the barn. Were the kids still up?

Throwing on a robe, she slipped on her sandals and went to check on Suzie. The girl was fast asleep. Thunder wouldn't bother her.

Shelly went downstairs and peered out again. It was raining. The barn was lit up. Either someone was working late, or the light had been left on. Not a problem either way, she thought. But something prompted her to look again.

Maybe she'd dash across the yard and check.

She found an old slicker that had belonged to Mitch. Flinging it around her shoulders, she went outside. Her feet were muddy and wet within five steps. The wind whipped the coat open and the rain soaked the bottom of her nightgown.

By the time she reached the barn, she regretted her hasty decision.

It was warmer inside. The sweet smell of fresh hay filled the air. Glancing around, Shelly didn't see anyone. She went to the tack room and peered in. No one.

About to reach for the light switch, she heard a noise.

Instantly on the alert, she looked into the back part of the barn.

"Who's there?"

"Get down," Adam called.

She looked around, then walked toward him. He was kneeling behind two stacked bales of hay. Thunder rolled. He cringed and ducked. "Get the hell down before you get your head blown off," he yelled.

She ducked instinctively and looked around again. Was someone else in the barn?

"Adam?" she asked, inching closer. "Adam are you all right?"

He looked at her. Suddenly the tension left him and he uttered an expletive, rolling over to sit on the packed ground, leaning against the hay. He rubbed his eyes with the heels of his hands.

"Not again," he said in disgust.

Shelly dropped the raincoat and went to sit on the edge of the bale, watching him warily.

"What happened?"

He closed his eyes. For a long moment he said nothing, then spoke.

"Flashback. Thunder sounds like gunfire and if I'm not ready for it, I think I'm back in Afghanistan with all the horrors that place held."

"Does it happen often?" she asked. How horrible to have to relieve even a second of war.

"Whenever it happens, it's too much. But no, not often. Less frequently since you've been here. The thunder is the trigger."

He glanced at her. "What are you doing out in the rain?"

"I came to see why the light was on. Were you working?"

"Yeah. Couldn't sleep."

"Everyone else can sleep through this."

"Pete's probably awake, but he has better sense than to get up and go wandering out in the rain," Adam said rubbing his hands against his eyes again.

"As long as I don't get struck by lightning, I like it. It smells fresh and clean and the air's much cooler."

Another bright flash came from outside, followed a couple of seconds later by thunder.

She looked at him.

"I'm not going to freak on you," he said, rising to his feet. "I'm here and grounded. Besides, the storm's moving away."

"I called my stepmother tonight," she said.

He looked at her, confused.

"Why?"

"To see if she knew anything about my parents."

Shelly told Adam what she'd learned from Sam.

"Leave it alone, Shelly. If your mother had wanted the man to know, she would have sent word. Carter believes your father is his. What does it hurt to leave it that way?"

"Most of the time I think that. But then I think, what if he has a great father somewhere who doesn't know? Carter would benefit by having a father in his life, don't you think?"

"What if it's that cowboy and he turns out to be a drunken fool who doesn't earn enough to keep himself together?" Adam countered.

"Then it would be better not to know," she agreed.

Rising, she picked up the slicker and flung it over her

shoulders. Her robe was not warm enough now that the air had cooled.

"Carter suggested we keep the ranch, operate it as a cattle ranch and offer deaf kids a chance to come and work," she said.

"You told him no, I hope," Adam said.

He walked to the tack room and switched off the light. Heading for the door, he turned to look at Shelly.

"You did say no."

She followed more slowly.

"I haven't yet. Of course we can't do it. Can we?"

"No."

"Why not?"

Adam stared at her.

"Why not? Because it's a dumb idea, that's why not. Ranching is hard work, not some camp activity for kids."

"We're talking teenagers, not young kids. They could work. Wayne and Suzie are working."

"I don't believe what I'm hearing. It's not a good idea."

"I want to hear concrete reasons why not."

"You don't have the proper staff or training. You don't have room. You don't have the skill. You don't have the insurance. You don't know anything about teenagers."

"I was one once," she said mildly.

Adam was getting annoyed. Was she truly considering the idea?

"You need people who can communicate with the kids."

"You manage."

"Only because we're not doing that much and I can write down most of what I have to say."

"You could learn ASL," she said.

Adam stared at her. Then he frowned.

"If you have any other deaf kids come out, I'm leaving. I'm not going to take the risk."

"Adam, we'd make sure we're as safe as we can get. If we wanted to live risk free, we'd never get out of bed in the morning. And we wouldn't have pillows in case we might suffocate or blankets to get tangled in. We'd sleep on the floor, but wait, then we'd all have to live in the Sunbelt so we wouldn't freeze without covers."

"You're being ridiculous. I'm trying to have a rational conversation."

She reached out and caught his arm, her fingers pressing tightly.

"I am, too. Sort of. Think about the opportunity for kids who are often denied the same experiences as hearing kids. How many kids might learn to love it and want to work in ranching? How many lives could you touch by doing this?"

Adam couldn't believe the woman who had arrived ready to sell in a second would pass up six million dollars to put in years of hard work to give some strangers a few weeks on a ranch.

"I'm not buying it, Shelly. What about the money?"

"What money?"

"The money you stand to get once the ranch sells."

"What if it doesn't sell? Or not for ten years? Maybe this is an alternative."

One he couldn't condone. He wanted to get to his room and shut the door—on her and her wild ideas.

Every time he began to get comfortable, Shelly changed

246 | BARBARA MCMAHON

the rules. Why couldn't she understand he didn't want to be involved?

"You really want this?" he asked.

Shelly's grip on his arm eased. He wished he could see her in the darkness. Dumb move turning off the light.

"Carter wants it," she said. "I told him I'd look into it."

"Tell him it's not feasible."

She was quiet for a moment, as if gathering her thoughts. He was not going to be talked into staying if this was the new plan.

"There are nine years between Carter and me, almost ten. We weren't close as kids because of that age difference. Now we have a chance to build something together. Something he feels strongly about. Maybe we can't make it work, maybe he'll change his mind in another month. But I think I owe it to both of us to at least look into it."

He started to say something, but she held her finger up.

"My initial reaction was like yours—impossible. But the more I've thought about it, maybe it might work. Not to make a lot of money. I'm hoping the ranch will come back into the black and be self-sustaining. Then we could offer kids a chance to come at little or no cost. We'd teach them teamwork and riding—skills they wouldn't have an opportunity to learn elsewhere. Who knows? As Carter said, we may make some cowboys out of them. Haven't you ever wanted to be in on the ground floor of something really great?"

"And you think this would be?"

"We'd be doing a good thing for kids each summer. And the rest of the year the ranch would be just us."

"Just us," he repeated.

Us. There was no us. He couldn't take that risk.

"I'd want you to stay, Adam. I really would."

He heard the words, but superimposed on them were the echoes of words he and Brian had shared growing up. It'll be us against the world. We'll make it so big the neighborhood won't know what hit it. You and me are a team. It was to be Adam and Brian all the way.

Only a land mine had ended that. Ended Adam's faith in the future.

"Think on it, Adam. Maybe tomorrow you and Pete and I can brainstorm questions we'd need addressed before continuing. It's only a thought right now. But the more I consider the idea, the more I see possibilities. We have the ranch anyway, which can provide us a living. If it works out, great, if not, at least we tried."

"In the six weeks you've been here you've gone from wanting to sell the place instantly to wanting to live here and work it?" he asked.

She couldn't have changed her mind that fast. What was she up to?

"There's still a lot to decide. And the way everyone talks about the winters, maybe I'll reserve a final decision for a few months. But I've been reading a journal from one of my ancestors, telling about the hardships they endured and how much they loved this land. I've never had a place to call home for more than two or three years. We moved so often with my dad. Then Thomas and I moved three times in the five years we were married. Carter doesn't have a home either. This could be it for both of us."

"Or a disaster in the making. Think of all that could go wrong."

"Think of all that could go right. Maybe I want to take a chance. I did what I thought was right all my life. I ended up married to a crook and then got stiffed by a woman who should have been my friend. I'm young, healthy and have had this ranch given to me. Maybe it was meant for a better purpose than just lining my pockets with a bunch of money."

"You still need money to run it, until you get it in the black again," Adam warned.

Why was he fighting so hard against the idea? Could he at least give it some thought? If only to point out the pitfalls.

It was apprehension, plain and simple. He couldn't deal with kids coming to the ranch. His time here would be limited if they turned the place into some camp.

He should have left weeks ago. Maybe now was the time to make the break. Pete could run things until she got more help. And Shelly was smart. She could learn the important business aspects of the ranch quickly. Sam would help her. Or one of her other neighbors.

"Please, Adam, just think on it overnight," she said.

27

He could think of other things he'd rather do overnight. Being alone with her for starters.

"I'll think about it," he said reluctantly.

Time enough in the morning to decide when to leave.

"Want to come in for some hot chocolate?" she invited. "I'm too cold to go back to bed right away."

A prudent man would say no. But if he were leaving soon, what could a cup of hot chocolate hurt?

"Sure."

Shelly put the slicker over her head and ran for the house. Adam ran beside her, his hat keeping the worst of the rain off his face. The rest of him would dry.

Once in the kitchen, Shelly switched on the light over the stove. It provided plenty of illumination for making hot chocolate, yet gave the room a cozy warmth with shadows that fit the rainy night.

Adam put his hat on one of the chairs.

"Need any help?" he asked.

"No. I have some of that cake left. Want a piece?"

"Yes. That was a hit at dinner."

"Everyone likes chocolate cake, I guess," she said. "You could get that while I fix the drinks."

In a short time they sat at the table eating cake and drinking the hot beverages. Adam didn't talk about her plan for the ranch. He didn't want to talk much at all. The quiet suited him.

She seemed equally content to be silent.

A few moments later, he began to wonder what she was thinking about. Did she dwell in the past, or was she looking toward some nebulous future? Sometimes just being in the present was enough. It was what he did best these days.

Shelly licked the last of the frosting from her fork and pointed it at him. "Did you ever think how long sweets have been part of our lives?"

"Never thought about it."

"Me either, until right now. In the journal I'm reading, they made popcorn balls, peanut brittle, candy apples, had taffy pulls and made pies and cakes. I've never been to a taffy pull."

Adam frowned. "Did you ever want to go to one?"

"Actually, I don't think I've ever heard of a real one. I've read about them in books. Might be fun. I know Carter likes caramel apples. I bet he'd like candy ones as well. Anyway, we could do things like that if we had a camp—show what a ranch was like a hundred years ago."

He leaned back in his chair and looked at her. With the soft kitchen lighting, she seemed even younger than she was. Her robe covered her nightgown completely. Was it sheer and lacy or plain cotton?

He finished his chocolate. He knew he had to get going. It was after midnight and he was starting to have thoughts about his boss that had no place in his life. He'd made his choice, now he had to stick to it.

"Adam, please consider it. Whatever we decide, I want you to be a part of the ranch."

"That may not be possible," he said, startled she'd picked up on his thoughts.

"If you could do anything you wanted, what would that be?" she asked.

"Bring Brian back," he said without hesitation.

"Oh, if you could change the course of your life, then I wouldn't have my mother die. Wouldn't have married Thomas. Would have finished college. But I'm talking about right now. What would you do?"

"Kiss you."

Shelly felt the heat flood through her. She stared at him.

"We tried that and you ignored me for days."

"So I'm stupid. I'm just talking about a kiss."

She swallowed. Her mind went blank. She wouldn't mind being kissed by him again. She'd loved it before. But would he then grow all distant and ignore her again? She enjoyed their time together; she didn't like being ignored.

He rose and reached for his hat.

"Forget it, Shelly. Thanks for the chocolate."

It was decision time. Yes or no?

She surged to her feet and crossed the short distance.

"Okay," she said, looking up at him.

He stared at her for a long moment, then dropped the hat on the floor to reach for her, drawing her into his arms, snug against his chest. He was so slow she grew impatient but at last he lowered his head until his lips touched hers.

For a moment she thought that light touch was going to

be all. Then he deepened the kiss.

It was magical. She closed her eyes and kissed him back. Forgotten was Thomas's betrayal, the problems with finances and raising a teenager. Tonight was for her alone. A passionate kiss that reaffirmed her femininity. An embrace that set her body on fire and had her yearning for more.

Adam slowly ended the kiss, moving to trail his lips across her jaw, down her throat to that soft pulse point. Her good hand touched his hair, his cheek, his neck. She wished she had both hands available to learn every inch of him, to feel what her eyes could see.

He rested his forehead on hers and gazed into her eyes.

"I have to go."

She reached up to kiss him again. The soft token flared into another passionate embrace. Endless moments ticked by.

He ended the kiss too soon for her. He stooped to reach for his hat and turned to leave, all in one fluid motion.

Shelly was half tempted to step out into the backyard and let the rain cool her heated skin. She felt less like sleeping now than she had when she'd come in for hot chocolate.

"Good night," she said as he headed back to the bunkhouse.

The next morning dawned clear. The air was cooler but promised to heat up by midday. Shelly heard the horses whinnying in the corral and Pete calling out something. She dressed quickly and hurried to the kitchen to get breakfast going.

She barely had the bacon cooked and the pancake batter

made before they started trooping in. Suzie came in first. A minute later Pete came, heading right for the large coffeepot.

"Nice day," he said. "Might get us some swimming in later if we do all the chores first."

Shelly nodded, signing his comment to Suzie. Her face lit up.

Wayne and Carter clumped in. Shelly looked beyond them, expecting to see Adam, but he wasn't there.

"Adam not eating?" she asked Pete.

"Haven't seen him today. Truck's gone."

Shelly felt her breath catch. She was not going to panic. He'd left once before without telling anyone. He probably had run into town to pick something up for—for what? All the machinery was working as far as she knew.

"Tell these kids we want to do saddle checks today," Pete said. "Make sure that leather is getting good care. A saddle is a cowboy's best friend. A good one, that is."

Shelly conveyed the information.

Then Carter asked her about the camp.

Wayne and Suzie immediately wanted to know what he was talking about, and before long all three were making suggestions to Shelly on how to run it and how they could help.

"I bet my father would have some good ideas, too," Suzie signed. *"He'd volunteer to help. I've often heard him say he'd do that at the school if it were closer. Maybe some of the teachers from the school would want to come for a vacation as well."*

Shelly nodded. That was a thought. Maybe it wouldn't be as hard to staff as she'd thought. Still, there was so much to think about.

Signing as she spoke, she looked at Pete.

"I asked Adam to see if you and he could talk with me this morning about the idea Carter has for a summer camp for deaf teens. Letting them actually work on the ranch. You and Adam would have a better idea of what they could do—based on these kids."

She smiled at the three teens.

Where was Adam? Shelly wondered. Why hadn't he told anyone where he was going?

Pete asked Shelly to sign instructions to the kids on how to clean their saddles using saddle soap. Then he told them to work on all the saddles in the tack room and he'd check on them when he finished talking with Shelly.

Pete poured another cup of coffee when the teenagers quickly headed out.

"Want to talk about that camp idea now?" he asked.

"Yes, but let's move to the office," Shelly suggested. "No dirty dishes there."

Soon they sat facing each other. Shelly outlined Carter's idea, adding her own growing conviction it could possibly work. They could try it one summer to see what happened.

"I thought this place was up for sale," Pete said.

"It is, but no one has expressed any interest. The real estate agent said it could take years to sell. I'm growing to love it here. This house, old as it is, beats a tiny apartment with a washing machine down the block. I don't know if I can home school Carter, but it's something else I can look into. And if so, all the better. He'll have time to see if he really loves ranching or if it's a passing fad."

"You can't have kids run your ranch," Pete said. "They don't know enough. By the time they learn, they'll leave."

"I would have regular cowboys as well. But I'd really want the campers to have tasks to do, so they are learning, not just playing."

It was late morning by the time they finished discussing all the pros and cons they could think of.

Shelly was going to get in touch with other camps for the deaf and see what aspects she hadn't thought about. Then she wanted to talk to Wayne's parents and Suzie's, to get their initial reaction. There was a lot to do before finally deciding to give it a try, but at least she was exploring the possibility.

She wished Adam had been part of the discussion. Even knowing he didn't approve, he would have solid insight into the plan. Where was he?

The sound of a vehicle in the driveway came through the open window.

Shelly went to look out. Disappointment flooded her when she saw it wasn't Adam's. Then she smiled. Looked like Jenny and Val had stopped by.

"I'll head on out to the barn. Check on the kids," Pete said, stepping around her.

He touched the brim of his hat when Jenny came around the front of her Jeep.

"Hi Jenny. I'm glad to see you."

Shelly smiled a warm greeting to her new friend.

"Likewise. How are you getting on?"

Shelly raised the cast.

"I hope I get this off soon. But I'm managing fine."

"Is Adam around?"

"Not at the moment," she said.

"Someone sent him a package. I said I'd bring it by. I brought the mail, too."

She opened the passenger door and took out a large rectangular box with envelopes and newspapers balanced on top.

"I told Margaret at the post office I was coming this way. This way it'll save you a trip."

Shelly took the box and thanked her. "Can you stay for a cup of coffee?

"I'd love some."

They sat at the table in the kitchen and Shelly brought Jenny up to date with what she and Carter had learned this summer.

"Glad you're settling in. Next week a couple of us are meeting in town for dinner and a girls night out. We might go to the country-western bar on the edge of town for some dancing. Want to come with us?"

Shelly didn't have to think about it, "I'd love to. I'm getting used to the ranch, but some girl time would be highly welcomed."

"So come by my place on Thursday around five and I'll drive us in. You should be home by eleven. We don't keep really late hours. Two of the women are married to cowboys, and one works at the bank. My friends since high school."

"I look forward to it.

When Jenny left, Shelly sorted through the mail. She couldn't help wondering who had sent Adam a package. The return address was New York. Was it something from his grandmother? No name, just the street address. Brooklyn sounded right. Maybe she'd ask when she handed him the package.

28

By mid afternoon, Shelly was pleased with the accomplishments of the day. Dinner was baking. She'd made a pineapple upside-down cake for dessert and had scheduled an appointment with the doctor to remove her cast next week. By her Thursday dinner, she'd be cast free.

She had written a draft proposal for operating the ranch as a working deaf camp during the summer months. Paul Simmons had been very helpful with insurance information and enthusiastic about the idea. He'd said he'd contact some of the people he knew at the school Suzie attended to get more information.

Shelly had also checked with the lawyer. Nathan had been cautious about the undertaking but agreed to look into it. He'd even made a sensible suggestion that she wanted to take up with Adam when she saw him.

When she'd tested the waters with Sam Hardman, the man had quickly offered any help she needed. He'd suggested she consider getting some chickens for eggs and maybe a hog or two to slaughter each fall for pork. There was beef aplenty.

Late afternoon she heard Adam's truck. She went out to the porch, but he entered the bunkhouse without a glance her way. Later she heard him leave on horseback.

She could hardly contain her enthusiasm when the others arrived from the range. She took a glass of tea and sat out on the porch while they brushed the horses and fed them. Sipping from the frosted glass, she watched Adam. He had an air of authority the others lacked. Wayne and Carter imitated him in their mannerisms. She smiled. They'd do well to emulate him.

Finally the men headed for the bunkhouse to clean up and Suzie walked briskly toward the house. She smiled when she saw Shelly and began telling her about their day.

When Suzie went inside to wash up, Shelly wanted to run across to see Adam. Ask him where he'd been. Tell him about the various conversations she'd had during the day about a camp. But she had dinner preparations to finish. She'd catch him later.

It was almost eight by the time she finished cleaning the kitchen. She'd be glad to get rid of the cast to speed washing-up time.

When she went outside, she wasn't surprised to see the three teenagers near the corral. It was as if they couldn't bear to be far from the horses no matter what. They looked as if they were swinging ropes, trying to lasso a barrel. Hank lay in the soft dirt near the corral fence and watched.

Pete sat in the shade of the barn watching them. She didn't see Adam.

"What are they doing?" she asked when she got closer.

"Adam wants them to learn roping. They've been practicing."

He laughed when Suzie threw the rope and let go. The entire thing sailed over the barrel, missing it completely. The others laughed at her. She frowned and went to retrieve the rope.

"They're no good, but if they practice, they'll get it," he said.

"Where's Adam?"

"In the bunkhouse, I believe."

She turned and headed for the building.

"Adam?"

She no longer knocked, but entered the common room without fanfare.

The package that had arrived earlier was sitting on the table against the wall—still unopened. She'd given it to him at dinner, but he'd merely glanced at the return address and tucked it beneath his chair.

"Adam?" she called louder.

She heard footsteps coming from the back and quickly moved away from the box.

He entered from the hall.

"I was hoping to talk to you," she said.

"About?"

Honestly, the man drove her crazy. Last night he'd kissed her as if she were the last woman on earth. Today he looked at her as if she were a stranger.

"About the ranch, what else?"

She sat on the leather sofa and Adam went to one of the large chairs flanking it. "What about the ranch?" he said, stretching his legs out in front of him.

She glanced at the box. "Is it your birthday?"

"No."

So much for satisfying her curiosity.

"I spoke with a lot of people today about our idea of a camp. And the local school board about home schooling. It really might be possible."

She knew it was possible, but after all the setbacks of recent years, she was almost afraid to believe it would work.

"I still have lots more to do before giving a definite go or no go. We'd need to fix up this bunkhouse to be able to house more men to work the ranch. And then we'd have to build another building or two to house the students and counselors. Or maybe we only offer camp for boys initially. See how it works. The thing is, I think it could. With a lot of work on my part. Some on Carter's. Most of it depends on you."

"I don't—"

"Wait and hear me out, please."

She leaned forward in her determination to make him share her vision.

"I'll need the money the ranch earns. We would charge the teens a nominal fee. So I'd need money for more horses, for food, transportation to and from town. There are a list of things I came up with and I'm sure as we go, even more will be identified. I've studied the records of the last five years— all my uncle had on his computer. This is normally a very profitable ranch. With proper care, it will be again."

"You may want to hire a more knowledgeable manager," he said.

"I may want to offer you a partnership of sorts."

"What?"

"That's what Nathan suggested, that I offer you a portion of the ranch for you to stay. How about two hundred and fifty acres with another two hundred and fifty every five years until you have fifteen hundred acres total? And a percentage of any profit we show. You could start your own herd, run the cattle with mine, and get any proceeds from that. We'd be partners. What do you think?"

Adam stared at her, dumbfounded. She was willing to offer a piece of the land that had been in her family for generations, just for him to stay and run the ranch while she tried some dumb-fool idea of a camp for deaf kids?

"You could get an expert manager for a small percentage of the profits," he said. "You don't have to give up your land."

"I was planning to sell it until today. I think Carter and I can make a nice living on four thousand acres. And I want you as manager. I would like you to stay."

"Why?"

"Because I don't want you to leave."

He looked at the pretty brunette watching him so earnestly. He wanted to pull her into his arms and kiss her like crazy. But he couldn't stay and become partners. The thought made him feel sick.

"I can't do it," he said.

"Why?"

She looked deflated. Slowly she leaned back on the sofa, the bright sparkle of excitement extinguished.

"We've been through this before, Shelly. I'm not one for putting down roots, for becoming involved with others. There's a lot of country to see."

"Baloney. You're just blowing smoke. I think you're feeling guilty."

"About what?"

That caught his attention.

Of course he was guilty. He hadn't been able to save his friend. What kind of man moved on and became a partner in a ranch when the partner he was supposed to have had lay in a grave in Brooklyn?

"I know what it's like. Truly, I do, because of Thomas. I was so angry at him for being a crook. Then I thought everyone was judging me like I was him. I felt guilty for just being in San Francisco, for trying to make a living for myself. I almost felt as if I should somehow make restitution for what he did. You feel guilty because Brian died and you didn't."

"He died because I couldn't save him."

"You're not God."

"I'm a trained medic. I should have been able to save all of them!"

He almost shouted the words. The anguish wouldn't let up.

"All of them?" she said softly.

He closed his eyes, rubbing the heels of his hands against them. Wishing he could erase the images that would never fade.

"That's right—the little girls who will never grow up. The old woman who died with such a stunned expression on her face. The other men in my platoon that I couldn't save. They're all gone. Why was I left?"

"Maybe to make something special of your life as a tribute to them," she suggested.

He dropped his hands and looked at her.

"That's what I feel when I think of this project for Carter. Thomas stole money from a lot of people—most of whom couldn't afford to lose that money. I can't pay them back. But I can pass on some kindness, something no one else will offer these kids. Maybe that's what I'm supposed to do."

"I'm not a rancher."

"You look like one to me. You weren't a medic before

you were trained. You know, even doctors lose patients—in fancy hospitals with a billion dollar's worth of equipment around them. Could such a setting have saved Brian?"

Slowly Adam shook his head.

"Nothing on earth could have saved my friend."

"Then why do you think you should have?"

"It was my job."

"Your job was to do your best to patch up wounded soldiers and ship them back to medical facilities. You did your best. I can't imagine you doing anything less. Just as you do on this ranch. I don't want you to leave. Please, Adam, stay and help me and Carter give this a chance to work."

Pete came in, then stopped in the doorway and stared at them.

"Is this a private conversation?" he asked.

"Maybe you can convince Adam to stay. I've offered him a partnership. I want him to run the ranch while Carter and I focus on a camp. He says he can't."

"Now why in the world would you even think that, son?" Pete asked, stomping over to sit in the chair opposite Adam. "This is a good setup. I'm thankful I found work here. Not a lot of places take an old cowboy."

Shelly smiled.

"I don't think of you as old, Pete."

"Nice words, missy." He looked at Adam. "I've been working ranches since I was sixteen. Never heard of a cowboy being offered a partnership before."

"It's a bribe so I'll stay," Adam said, getting up and pacing toward the package.

He glared at it and turned to walk back.

"Could be," Shelly admitted. "But I want you to stay. Whatever it takes."

"I'll screw up," he said.

She shrugged.

"You still know more than I do. We can probably rebound from any problems."

"Sounds like a plan to me," Pete said.

Adam paced back toward the wall, turned and walked to the center of the room again. He stopped in front of Shelly.

"And if there are thunderstorms, what then?"

"We'll deal with it."

"What's with thunderstorms?" Pete asked.

Adam stared at her, suddenly longing to agree. To know where he'd be in another year or two or ten. To know he was accepted just as he was, failures and all. Wayne and Suzie would be leaving soon, but Carter and Shelly would stay. And Pete. Could he stay here and remain apart emotionally? Not risk making friends to lose them if the camp didn't work out or if Shelly got an offer for the ranch one day?

The camp could fail, the ranch sell, and Shelly and her brother would take off for California in a New York minute. Better if he left now. Cut the ties before they bound too tightly. Leave before he was left.

"No."

He turned, went down the hall to his room and closed the door.

Shelly stared after him in dismay. She'd offered the most she had and he'd turned her down. She couldn't believe it. Had he not understood?

Or was it she who didn't understand? He'd told her over

and over that he wasn't comfortable becoming involved. Just because they'd shared a few kisses, just because she may be starting to have feelings for him, jumbled as they were, didn't mean he'd changed.

She'd guessed wrong about Thomas. Looked as if she'd guessed wrong again. This time the hurt went even deeper.

How could she be so misguided about men?

"Well, I tried," she said, wishing for more than she was going to get.

She bid Pete good-night and went back to the house.

Her excitement about the camp faded with Adam's unswerving refusal to participate. She was walking a fine line and knew she needed a lot of luck to make the project work. She and Carter could end up hating Wyoming by the end of the winter. Or they could plant deep roots like Mitch and those who had gone before and never want to leave.

She went inside feeling drained. Walking up to her room, she grabbed the journal, then lay on her bed to read. But the words blurred and all she could hear was Adam's refusal.

29

Shelly had a pile of scrambled eggs on the platter with sausage links surrounding the mound and hot toast ready for buttering when Wayne and Carter showed up the next morning. Suzie had been up for a while, helping her with breakfast.

"Tomorrow, you two can come in and help fix breakfast," Shelly signed. *"I'm not the ranch cook."*

"You do it so well," Carter returned, grinning. He ducked when she threw a pot holder at him.

Pete came to the door.

"Shelly, I need to see you a minute."

"Sure, what's up?" she asked, going to the back door and stepping outside.

The sun was already climbing. It would be another hot day.

"Adam's not around. Truck's missing. I checked his room. He packed up everything. I think he's gone for good."

It took a moment for the statement to sink in.

"As in gone?" she asked, stunned. Had he really carried through and taken off for parts unknown?

"Lock, stock and barrel," Pete said.

"I'd like to smack him. How dare he do this to me just because I offered him a partnership."

Anger flared. She'd been on an emotional roller coaster with the man, but this was the last straw. She was furious.

"Oddest thing I ever heard of," Pete said.

"He claims he has too much baggage, well so do I. So does everyone. We could have made it work. I thought the land would swing the deal. What an idiot."

"Adam?"

"Me, to think a few kisses meant a relationship. Why can't I learn? Men are the most fathomless creatures in the world. I can't believe I fell for another one who had no intention of sticking around. I should become a nun!"

She turned and stomped inside. She was so angry.

She was also incredibly hurt. She'd wanted Adam to stay. Not only because she needed him to run the ranch, but because she'd truly believed they had something special between them.

She was falling in love with the man, irritating attitude and all.

He'd left. As if she meant nothing.

For a moment, the hurt pierced.

Three pairs of eyes looked at her when she returned. Carter asked what was wrong. So much for trying to hide her feelings. Before she could control herself, she burst into tears. Her brother jumped up and came to wrap her in his arms. A moment later she felt Suzie hug her, then Wayne. They didn't know what was wrong, but they were there for her.

Which Adam should have been.

Finally she drew a shaky breath and nodded against her brother's shoulder. He slowly released her. All three watched with concern.

"Adam's gone," she signed.

She still couldn't believe it. Shelly thought things were finally going right for a change. There'd been special kisses. And she liked working together to keep the ranch afloat while she and Carter learned what was needed.

She'd offered Adam a part of all she had. And he'd not only said no, he'd left.

Carter asked why. Wayne and Suzie asked a dozen questions. Shelly had no answers. She would never tell them Adam hadn't wanted them there in the first place. They thought highly of the man. She wouldn't destroy that image.

"Time to eat—Pete will be in charge for now," she signed.

The eggs were cool, so she dumped them back in the pan for a quick reheating. The sausages went into the oven. Silence reigned behind her. She blinked back tears. Time for crying later, when she was alone. Now she had to rally for these three young adults and find some way to get beyond the fear that threatened to choke her.

How could she manage without him?

When breakfast was finished, Pete sent the kids out to get the horses ready for the day.

"You okay?" he asked Shelly when they were alone.

"I will be," she said, gathering the plates.

"That man has rocks in his head," Pete muttered on his way out.

"I agree."

She bit her lip to stem the flow of more tears. What did it take to get through to her that men could not be trusted? Why not just rip out her heart and stomp on it and be done with it.

At least she hadn't married the guy.

Tears threatened again. She'd refused to dream about such a thing, but secretly, deep inside, she had thought they might build a life together. It was that possibility that had got her past the notion that she had to live in California. Even beyond the idea that six million dollars would buy happiness.

People brought happiness, not money.

But apparently not all people.

She washed the dishes quickly and then headed for the office. She refused to stop just because Adam had cut and run. She'd explore the camp idea, find a dozen cowboys to work the ranch, and spend her life doing exactly what she wanted!

First thing, she called Sam.

"I need a favor," she began. "If you can spare a man, can I borrow a cowboy for a few weeks, until I can find one to hire?"

"What brought that on?" Sam asked.

"Adam left."

"What? When?"

"He was gone this morning."

She would not break down again. But the ache in her chest didn't go away.

"Why?"

"Because I offered him a partnership," she said carefully.

"What am I missing?" Sam asked after a moment of silence.

"He never wanted to stay. He told me that a hundred times. I just never took him seriously."

"I'll come over and you can tell me the whole story," he said.

"Fine, but think about lending me a cowboy."

It was after eleven when Shelly heard the truck in the drive. She got up from the desk. Her enthusiasm for the camp had waned as the morning progressed. It wasn't looking as easy as it had yesterday. There were so many things to consider. And her heart just wasn't in it.

She went out onto the porch and stopped dead. It was Adam's truck. He halted near the steps and just sat there, looking at her through the windshield. She debated going back inside the house, but her feet seemed rooted to the porch.

Impasse. Neither moved.

Time ticked by.

Shelly grew angrier the longer she stared at him. Finally she'd had enough and turned, entered the house and slammed the door behind her.

A moment later she heard him on the porch, crossing to open the door.

"What do you want?" she asked when he came in.

"To apologize. I should have told you I was leaving."

"I believe you did tell me many times," she said.

Every fiber of her being wanted to launch herself into his arms, hold him so tightly he'd never leave again. But she didn't move a muscle.

"I talked about it but didn't know how serious I was after that first day. Last night was just too much. Brian's dead. I don't deserve to be part owner of a ranch."

"Brian has nothing to do with us. Why did you return?"

"Sam told me something that made me come back."

"Good grief, you came back because a neighbor told you to?"

"No. Come in here and sit a minute and let me explain."

He walked into the living room and sat on the sofa. She watched warily for a moment, then went to perch on the edge of a chair.

"I'm pretty sure, and Sam's pretty sure, he's Carter's father. He fell in love with your mother and she fell in love with him. Yet, apparently no one around here knew about Carter until you showed up. If your mother ever told Mitch, he never said anything to Sam. I never heard your uncle mention Carter either, though he did talk about you once in a while. Sam said they fell in love that summer. They became lovers, then your father called and wanted her back. She felt the ties she had with Robert Palmer were important—more important than breaking up her family and putting her little girl through such turmoil. She left and never returned."

"Sam told you this when?" she asked.

What did this have to do with his leaving?

Had her mother really sacrificed her own happiness for her daughter's sake?

"When he found me at Rosie's. I didn't know where to go. I didn't want to stay here, but there's no other place I want to be."

Shelly frowned. "That makes no sense."

"I stopped for gas, filled up the truck and then went for coffee. I sat there wondering where I was heading. Sam found me and told me I was a damn fool. He'd let the woman he loved go without a fight and still misses her to this day. If he's Carter's father, then he's missed knowing his son all these years. Do you know what he said—I would never forget you. I would never get over you. I would regret leaving to my dying day."

Shelly stared at him.

"He also told me I was an idiot," Adam said. "If he could do one thing differently in his entire life, it would be to go after your mother."

"I can't take your coming on to me, then growing cold, then coming back," she said. "I've done a really stupid thing and fallen for you. You tear pieces of my heart up each time you turn from me."

Shelly couldn't believe she was telling him. When would he begin ignoring her again?

30

"Then it's about equal. I love you, Shelly. I can't even tell you how much. And it scares me to death. What if something happens to you like it did to Brian? I don't think I could live through something like that again. I think of you when I'm working, when I'm trying to sleep, when you're in the room with me, and when we're apart. You've changed my life. And I'm scared spitless about it."

Shelly tried to understand what he was saying.

"We're not in a war zone," she said slowly.

"Ranching is dangerous. Look what happened earlier this summer. What if you'd hit your head on a jagged rock and died?"

"Uncle Mitch was in his nineties when he died. If he'd been a stockbroker, would he have lived that long?" she asked.

He stared at her.

She began to smile, her heart thumping so hard she could hardly hear over the blood rushing in her veins.

"Tell me again," she said.

"I love you."

He spoke slowly, deliberately.

"I'm a mess, have flashbacks, am wary of getting too close to anyone, haven't even seen my own grandmother in longer than I want to think about. But as God is my witness, I love you. And I think Sam's right—I always will."

Shelly launched herself off the chair and straight into Adam's arms.

"I love you, too, cowboy. Let's live dangerously and take a chance together."

"Marriage, babies and the whole nine yards?" he asked, his arms enfolding her.

"Yes. You can teach me everything you know about ranching and we can pass on the land to our kids when we're old and gray."

His mouth covered hers in an explosive kiss. Hungry for her, he deepened the kiss until Shelly's head spun.

"Carter may have something to say about that," Adam said some time later.

"He'll want you to learn sign so you two can talk more. Do you think Sam really is his father?" she asked, content to snuggle in his arms on the sofa.

"Sam thinks so. We could ask for DNA testing. The question is, how do you think Carter will react?"

"I think he'll be okay—eventually. It will be a shock, though. Maybe that's the reason he took to ranching so fast—like father like son."

"We wouldn't have to do anything right away. Let them get to know each other better," Adam suggested.

A thought struck her.

"Oh no, what are we going to tell them all? They think you left."

"I did. We'll tell the truth. I was a fool to leave, but fortunately came to my senses before I got too far."

He nuzzled her jaw.

"Maybe my grandmother just might come out for the wedding."

He pulled back a little and gazed into her eyes. "You are going to marry me, right?"

"You bet, cowboy," she said with a happy smile. "Would your grandmother consider moving here with us?"

"I can ask. I'd really like that."

"Carter's going to be over the moon. He's wanted to stay here since the day we arrived. Guess he'll get his wish."

"We can make a good life here, Shelly."

"Anywhere you are will be a good life for me."

She had no qualms despite her earlier vow not to have anything to do with men. Adam was nothing like her ex.

They'd put down roots, raise a family and maybe even explore the idea of a camp for deaf kids.

"Was your grandmother the one who sent the package?" she asked a short time later.

He shook his head. Slowly he sat up, pulling her with him.

"The box was from Brian's mother. I haven't opened it."

"Why not?"

"What could she send me?"

"Get it and find out."

He went out to the truck and returned in a moment with the box in hand.

Sitting back beside Shelly, he used his pocketknife to slit the tape and then took the top from the box, revealing a photo album.

There was a letter. Adam opened it and slanted it so Shelly could read along.

Dearest Adam,

When you get this, I'll be gone. Cancer. Brian always said those cigarettes would get me. I'm sorry I didn't get to see you again, Adam. You and Brian were both special boys to me. You were my second son. I never got to thank you for being with Brian in Afghanistan. It meant a lot to me to know he didn't die alone. I know it was hard on you, son, it was hard on us all. Impossible to believe some days. You may never be able to come back, but we in the neighborhood remember you, Adam. And miss you.

But think back to the happy days you two spent. Remember playing in the spray from the fire hydrants? How about stick hockey? You two were always running in the middle of the street. It was a miracle you didn't get hit by some truck.

I'm sending you my album. No one else will want it when I'm gone. I've spent the last few weeks going over it, writing down what I remember by the pictures. See what memories it brings back for you, Adam. Happy ones, I hope.

I loved you as if you were my own.

Ellie

"Oh, Adam, I'm so sorry," Shelly said gently.

"I should have gone back," he said, staring at the letter.

"She understood," Shelly said, squeezing his hand. "It's a wonderful letter."

He didn't need another layer of guilt. It sounded as if Ellie understood why he couldn't go home.

Shelly opened the album and gazed at a picture of two little boys. One she clearly recognized as Adam. The other had to be Brian.

Adam would come to terms with his past. And now,

together, they had a bright future ahead of them. Time enough for her to learn how to be a rancher. Times to explore the idea of a summer camp for deaf kids. Time enough for her brother to decide if ranching was for him.

And time enough to build their own family, to continue the tradition on the old family ranch.

A few minutes later the teenagers barreled into the kitchen. Shelly heard them getting cold drinks out of the refrigerator.

"Come on, cowboy, let's share our news," Shelly said with a smile and a quick kiss.

The three teens were ecstatic with the news–Carter most of all.

Pete had a big grin on his face and congratulated them.

"*So we get to stay here forever?*" Carter signed with a broad smile on his face.

"*Yes,*" she replied.

"*Then we can have the deaf camp,*" he said.

"*One thing at a time. You and I need to make plans for the coming year, what to do about school, and we can look further into the idea of a camp.*"

She looked at Adam and took a deep breath.

"*After dinner you and I need to talk just the two of us,*" she said to Carter.

She'd tell him tonight her thoughts about his father. She wasn't sure how he'd take it, but it wasn't fair to keep the information from him. He'd be hurt if he found out later that she'd known all along and never told him.

He was growing up fast. These weeks on the Triple L clearly showed that. And just maybe, he'd love to know Sam was his father. Her own had never been the same once he learned Carter wasn't his.

She and Adam would be there for him either way.

She smiled at Adam and relished the smile he gave her. She never expected in a million years that her future now was tied to the land that had been in her family for generations. She gave a silent thank you to Uncle Mitch. Because of his legacy, her life was happy and full of love.

—The End—

If you liked **Shelly and the Cowboy,**
you'll love **Kristi's Cowboy Hero,**
book 3 in the Cowboys of Wildcat Creek series.

If you enjoyed **Shelly and the Cowboy,**
please consider leaving a review.

More books by Barbara McMahon

Cowboys of Wildcat Creek
Valentine's Cowboy Rescue
Shelly and the Cowboy
Kristi's Cowboy Hero
Holly's Reluctant Cowboy
A Cowboy for Eliza

Sweet Reunion Romance Collection
Unexpected Reunion
Unpredictable Reunion
Unanticipated Reunion

The Talmadge Sisters
Letters to Caroline
Michelle's Marriage Deal
Trusting Abby

The Harts of Texas Series
Rebel Heart
Tangled Hearts
Reckless Heart

Cowboy Heroes Series
Blue Bells on the Hill
Cowboy's Bride
One Stubborn Cowboy
Crazy About a Cowboy
Never Doubt a Cowboy
Cowboy Marshal
Summer Cowboy
Second Chance Cowboy
Movie Star Cowboy

Tropical Escape Series
Island Rendezvous
Come into the Sun
Island Paradise

Tropical Escape Series
Island Rendezvous
Come into the Sun
Island Paradise

Rocky Point Series
Rocky Point Legacy
Rocky Point Reunion
Rocky Point Promise
Rocky Point Hero
Rocky Point Inn
Rocky Point Dawn

The Ultimate Billionaires
The Cynical Sheikh
Falling for the Sheikh
A Sheikh of Her Own
The Unforgettable Sheikh

Sweet Romance Stand-alone Collection
Because of You
Cowboy Charade
I'll Take Forever
Jared's Promise
Mail Order Bride
Not Really Married
Sweet Meant To Be
The Cowboy Comes Home
The Paper Marriage
Trusting Jake
The Banished Bride

A Sweet Clean Christmas Romance Collection
The Christmas Cop
The Cowboy's Special Christmas
A Soldier's Christmas
A Teaspoon of Mistletoe
The Christmas Locket
A Key West Christmas

www.ingramcontent.com/pod-product-compliance
Lightning Source LLC
Chambersburg PA
CBHW060525260626
47161CB00003B/770